P9-BYA-662

TWICE UPON A TIME

Beauty *and the* Beast

The Only One Who Didn't Run Away

TWICE UPON A TIME

Beauty *and* *the* Beast

The Only One Who Didn't Run Away

WENDY MASS

SCHOLASTIC PRESS
New York

To all the readers who asked for more
Twice Upon a Time books. This one's for you.

Copyright © 2012 by Wendy Mass

All rights reserved. Published by Scholastic Press, an imprint of Scholastic Inc.,
Publishers since 1920. SCHOLASTIC, SCHOLASTIC PRESS, and associated logos are
trademarks and/or registered trademarks of Scholastic Inc.

No part of this publication may be reproduced, stored in a retrieval system, or
transmitted in any form or by any means, electronic, mechanical, photocopying,
recording, or otherwise, without written permission of the publisher. For
information regarding permission, write to Scholastic Inc., Attention:
Permissions Department, 557 Broadway, New York, NY 10012.

Library of Congress Cataloging-in-Publication Data available

ISBN 978-0-545-31018-5

10 9 8 7 6 5 4 3 2 1   12 13 14 15 16

Printed in the U.S.A.   23
First edition, June 2012

The text type was set in Minister.

CHAPTER ONE

~ Beauty ~

Today started poorly and got even worse. It is now night-fall, and I am certain even the village's dung heap cleaner would not want to change places with me. I should have known the winds of good tidings were not blowing my way the moment I laid eyes on the baker's new apprentice, a boy a few years my senior who I have never seen in the village before. Our kitchen maid usually does the errands, but she is visiting her family today, so I went to fetch our order of barley rolls.

I do not often venture out into town alone, for Papa worries and his worrying makes me nervous. But this morning I made sure to hold my head high and to look more confident than I felt. I ignored anyone who called out for me to buy whatever they were selling, and made sure to step carefully over the waste constantly being tossed out the windows to the street below. Part of me wanted to take off running in the fields behind the village church and forget the barley rolls. I never feel nervous when I run. But that would be unladylike. I have not been allowed to run freely for years now.

When I arrived at the bakery, the baker — a kind man who always smells like fresh bread — greeted me by name. One of three things happens when someone hears my name for the first time. The worst is when they laugh. The second worst is when they *start* to laugh but quickly turn it into a cough so as not to appear rude. Lastly, if they are a halfway decent sort, they will squint at my face as though searching for some prettiness that perhaps they missed initially. Upon finding none, they will then say something like, "Have you seen the new juggler performing in the town square? Such talent!"

No one, in all my twelve and three-quarter years, has ever said that the name *Beauty* suits me.

I blame my mother (may her soul rest in peaceful slumber amidst fields of wildflowers). She used her very last breath to bestow my name upon me. If I were the betting type, I would say she was more likely referring to the beauty shining forth from the gates of heaven — which were no doubt opening wide in welcome — than to the infant held up before her, red-faced and sporting a nose that leaned a bit too far to the left. My nose, thankfully, has righted itself as I have grown. Mostly.

When the baker said my name, his new apprentice turned to look. I figured he would choose the first option and laugh. He had the type of sharp chin and thin lips that indicate a certain meanness of spirit. But he did not laugh. Rather, he surprised me with a response I had not heard before. He tipped an imaginary hat at me and said, "Good day, Beauty, my name is Handsome!" And *then* he laughed. The baker gave him a sharp jab in the ribs and waved off my coin as he handed me my sack of rolls.

I cannot tell if my face flushed from the heat of the baker's huge oven, or the hurtful words. Likely both. I know the teasing should not bother me, for I have many good qualities. My sister, Clarissa, insists no one makes better ginger candies. And I can outrun a hare, not that there is much use for this skill unless one is chasing hares. (Which I am not allowed to do anymore after chasing away the Easter hare three years ago.) Plus, no one in our village reads as well as I, including the monks at the monastery, and they read all day long.

But the teasing bothers me nonetheless.

I wish my name had gone to Clarissa, nearly three years my senior, who truly *is* beautiful. You know the type — hair soft as the finest silk from across the sea, round blue eyes like robins' eggs, and a forehead so high she has been mistaken for royalty. She is also sweet and gentle and does not furrow her brow by thinking of serious things. All of the boys in town want her hand in marriage, but she turns them down. Though she cares deeply about maintaining (or bettering) her social standing as the daughter of a successful merchant, Clarissa is holding out for love.

Where she is a romantic, I am a realist. Romantic love is something found only in the books Papa sells to the lords and ladies of the kingdom for a tidy profit. I should know, for I have read many of them. My head is full of stories from the books Papa buys and sells without ever opening the cover himself. Clarissa's head is full of purple silk gowns and dances and handsome troubadours playing the lute. One day soon, Papa shall tire of Clarissa's silliness and will marry her off to whomever he deems her best match. Although the thought of marriage currently makes me shudder, neither my sister nor I shall marry for love. It is simply not the way of things.

Clarissa insists I should not look at life so bleakly, for it makes me seem unpleasant and no one will want to be in my company. She says that if I took the time to comb my hair and powder my cheeks and stopped wearing Papa's old tunics and breeches, people might actually smile when they hear my name. She may be right, but I do not intend to find out.

Much to my surprise, being insulted by the apprentice turned out to be the high point of my day. For sometime between this afternoon when my sister lit the hearth to stave off the first autumn chill, and sunset when I returned home from my errands, our house burned to the ground.

CHAPTER TWO

↞ Beast ↠

Darkness. Cold. Silence, but for the fearful panting in my ear. The breath warming my ear is not mine. My own mouth is closed tight against the cold air and the tiny winged bugs that surround us. My vision is clear, though, impeded only by the thickness of the forest.

"Jump!" the voice screams. So I spring up, easily clearing the top of a ditch. We run deeper into the forest, thick trees ominous and unyielding, the ground hard and unforgiving on my bare feet. I do not know why my feet are bare. My mother, the queen, would never allow me to step foot outside the castle without boots on, even when the sun is high and hot in the sky. Yet I clearly feel the dirt and rocks and twigs beneath me.

"Duck!" the voice yells. I try to twist my head to see to whom the voice belongs. But it is dark, so dark.

"DUCK!"

I have waited too long to obey. The top of my head crashes into the branch above, but it does not hurt. It never hurts. But after the crash, the voice shouting in my ear is silenced. It is at this point I always wake up, my nightclothes stuck to me with sweat. My first thought is always to look around for the person who shouted to me in the dream. But I am always alone. I've had this dream every week since I turned thirteen a few months back, but this is the first time I have had it while out of my bed.

I hear my brother calling my name, but do not reply to Alexander's shouts. I shake off the cobwebs of the dream, surprised that I actually fell asleep while hiding atop the castle's tallest tower. I turn my attention to the stars above. In my dream I cannot see them. My tutor, Master Cedrick, says that there is a star in the heavens for every person who walks the ground below. Mother says my tutor has peculiar ideas. I think that's why I like him, for I, too, have been called odd.

If I were a normal prince, I would be inside with the rest of the royal family escorting our remaining guests across the dance floor. Instead, I am sitting with my back against the hard stone wall, trying to pretend my nightmare does not bother me. All I wanted to do tonight was to play my bagpipes and admire the bright stars of the Summer Triangle, which shall soon be disappearing from view as the summer turns to fall. Was that so much to ask?

The door to the balcony creaks open behind me. I know without turning that it is Alexander, the heir to our father's throne and a much better prince than I. A much better *everything*, actually. But I don't mind. If only one of us should have the ability to speak five languages, it should be the one who will one day have a kingdom to rule. If only one is able to discuss the great works of philosophy and mathematics with the finest minds in the land, while also being charming, witty, handsome, and an excellent rider of horses, it should be Alexander.

And tall, did I mention tall? At fourteen, he is easily a head and a half taller, although I am only a year his junior.

"Riley, Riley, Riley," he says, sitting down next to me and

pulling his knees to his chest. "I have given you as long as I could. I even pretended to check the dungeons, and you know how I feel about them. You must return to the party immediately. Mother is beginning to turn various shades of purple."

"Must I truly? I have already stepped on the toes of two princesses, a duchess, and a lady-in-waiting who I am pretty sure snuck into the castle when the royal guards' backs were turned."

Alexander leans over and straightens the silver chain that links the tips of my velvet cape. "There are worse things in the world than dancing with beautiful girls, little brother. You make it sound more unpleasant than cleaning the dung heaps. Now come. Duty calls."

I do not know why everyone always assumes the worst job is cleaning the latrines. It is smelly, without a doubt. But sometimes, amidst the waste, a pearl will turn up, lost from some woman's necklace, or coins from a nobleman's pocket. Or so I am told, since Mother keeps me far from the laborers.

I blow one last forlorn note on my bagpipes and follow Alexander back into the small room inside the tower. I rest the bagpipes against the wall before heading down the winding staircase. If I brought them with me, Mother would no doubt make me play them for the gathered guests. Being the center of attention gives me hives, and I do not want to end this already disagreeable evening with a visit from the castle doctor. The man is all too attached to his leeches.

CHAPTER THREE

∽ Beauty ∾

Although neighbors had rushed to douse the flames with barrels of water, only a handful of our belongings survived the fire: my mother's old locket (although the rose petal inside is now a pile of cinders); our iron bathtub; one chest of Papa's books, which had been with him at the time of the fire; a basket of clothes that my sister grabbed when she ran from the burning house; and a few jars of jellies and pickled pig's feet from what used to be the pantry.

All of the books, all of the paintings, all of the furniture, all of it is gone. Clarissa has taken the loss of our belongings very hard, and is barely speaking. Even though I lost my collection of found objects — arguably my most valued possessions next to my mother's locket — the fact that we all escaped from bodily harm has kept me from wallowing too deep in self-pity.

Three days have passed and we can no longer accept the charity of our neighbors. They were kind enough to give us beds to sleep on, and bread and cheese to eat although we've been without an appetite. Papa has sold off the few books that had been stored in the chest and bought us the most basic belongings. We are moving to a tiny cottage on the western edge of the village. I will have to find employment while Papa works hard to build up his business again.

Without our maids, Clarissa will be charged with making sure our home is in order, as before.

Well, perhaps *better* than before, what with burning it down and all.

I have gone to the church to contemplate our new life and to seek comfort. Soon I will not have the luxury of stealing away to think, and Papa is too upset to worry that I am off alone. He (and I) will have to get used to it, since there are no more maids to accompany me.

I have positioned myself in the last pew, right beside my favorite stained-glass window. I close my eyes and allow my face to be bathed in warm blue-green light.

"I thought I would find you here," Clarissa whispers, sitting down next to me. Her voice is small and sad, but at least she is talking again.

I turn to look at her. Her skirt is wrinkled, her boots unlaced and scuffed. Her usually shiny hair is dull and pulled back in a messy braid. Without her face powder, she is blotchy and pink. This is not good. Only one of us is allowed not to care about our appearance, and that person has to be me.

"Clarissa," I say, lifting her hand into mine. Her nails are bitten to the quick. "I have good news!"

"Will it bring back our home? The many possessions Papa worked so hard to get for us? Return us to our rightful status in society?"

"Well, no," I admit. "But you can stop blaming yourself for the fire. It was not your fault. It turns out a pigeon had gotten caught in the chimney and blocked the path of the smoke. You could not have known."

That gets her attention. For the first time in days, her eyes widen with interest. "Truly?" she asks. "How do you know?"

"The carpenter went over to see what materials he could salvage for us," I tell her, which is the truth. "And he found the bird." (Not true.) "Wedged in tight, poor thing." (Also not true.)

Clarissa exhales deeply. "That is good to hear. Well, not for the bird, of course."

I look around the church, glad that we are alone. It is not like this is my first falsehood, but surely my first inside a church. Perhaps in light of all we have been through, the parish priest will let this one pass.

"It is time," she says. "We must make our way to the new house."

I nod, aware that when I stand up, I will be leaving my comfortable, familiar life behind, and walking into the unknown. I do not want to let on how scared I am. I have to be the brave one. Both for her and for Papa. He tries hard to raise two daughters on his own, but I know it is not always easy.

By the time we step out onto the road, a new determination has settled upon Clarissa's face. She is standing taller. When a fancy woman in a lace dress sniffs in disapproval at our appearance, Clarissa even tosses her braid in defiance. Once the woman turns into the shoemaker's shop, however, Clarissa's shoulders slump again. "Our new home has no well," she laments. "Papa's back is so bad he cannot possibly lug water from the stream all the way to the edge of the village. How will we bathe?"

I reach out for her hand, feeling, not for the first time, as though I am the older sister. "I shall fetch our bathwater."

We enter the crowded marketplace, lively with peddlers hawking everything from hair ribbons and rabbit pelts to carrot soup and chamber pots. If this were a normal day,

Clarissa would already be haggling for the best prices, her arms laden with objects she simply *must* have. But this is not a normal day.

"And what of food?" Clarissa asks as we pass a vegetable stand, the sacks of corn, peas, and beans from the summer harvest piled as high as my head. "Papa puts on a brave face, but he is worried, I can tell. We have no money and no land to farm."

I swallow my own fears. "I shall find work," I assure her. "Our bellies will not be empty."

After a long pause, Clarissa says, "Do not take this the wrong way, dear sister, but there are only two things you could be — a maid, or a lady-in-waiting. And you have the skills for neither."

Normally, I would pinch her for a comment like that, but I restrain myself due to her still-fragile state. That, and the fact that she speaks the truth. I have watched our various maids perform all the household chores but was never encouraged to learn them myself. And although Clarissa was the unofficial "lady of the house," she certainly did not dirty her hands preparing roast duck or beating our woolen tunics with a broom. Neither of us can weave cloth or spin wool into yarn or even mend the holes in Papa's socks. We cannot make candles or butter or cheese or ale. We have never gathered eggs, and have not picked our own berries or nuts since we were little children playing in the fields.

We stop to watch a group of boys play leapfrog on the riverbank. They leap over one another's backs and then run to the end of the line as fast as they can. They have given me an idea. "I know! I can earn money by running!"

"How?" Clarissa asks. "By challenging the squires to a footrace and charging them a shilling when you win?"

"Do you think I could earn that much? I am certain I would win!"

I have missed the sound of Clarissa's laughter, but she indulges me now. "Beauty! No squire would risk his knighthood by being outrun by a girl."

She speaks the truth. We start walking again, and I continue to ponder how else to take advantage of my speed. "I have it! I can be a messenger! Papa's friends are always muttering about how slow the messengers are, and how by the time they receive word on anything, months have passed. I would make an excellent messenger." I can already imagine myself running like the wind to some distant land, an important document rolled up and tucked inside my belt loop. I would run so fast that I would leave all my fears behind in the dust. And no one would be able to fault me for wearing pants. A messenger could not be expected to run in a skirt across roads of dirt and rock.

"A messenger needs a horse," Clarissa points out. "You, however, do not have a horse. Besides, the roads are much too dangerous for a young girl to travel on her own. You are the one always scolding Papa for riding after dark, or staying at an inn without a guard. You must keep thinking."

I sigh. I may jest that Clarissa's head is full of more air than a pig-bladder balloon, but she knows a lot about the ways of the world. Plus, I have a feeling my fears would follow me no matter how fast I ran.

We continue to follow the stream until we reach the mill. A line of farmers and peasants stands with arms full of bundled stalks of rye, wheat, or malt, waiting for their turn to have their crops ground at the millstone. I watch as the power from the stream turns the huge waterwheel, which then turns the millstones in a graceful partnership. An argument has broken out amongst the group, with angry voices and flailing arms. This is a common occurrence at the mill, since the miller is known throughout the village as a cheat.

A man in a gray traveling cloak has stepped between the miller and the farmer. From what I can tell, the farmer is accusing the miller of not handing over the full allotment of flour due to him, and the stranger is telling the miller something in a low voice. A few rotations of the waterwheel later, the miller ducks behind the giant millstone and returns, grumbling, with another sack of flour for the farmer.

"Who is that?" I ask Clarissa, pointing to the stranger in the cloak.

"I have heard Papa and his friends speak of him," she replies. "He can tell if someone is lying, and then he convinces that person to own up. He must get a lot of business at the mill."

As we watch, the farmer doles out three handfuls of his flour to the stranger before picking up the handles of his wheelbarrow and heading off. The stranger adds his small sack of flour to a growing pile at his feet, and leans back against the fence, no doubt waiting for another fight to break out. "I can do that job!" I exclaim.

"*You?*"

"Certainly! I always know when people are fibbing." I do not tell her that since I have some practice with lying, I am an excellent candidate to catch someone else doing it.

Clarissa throws her head back and laughs. "Beauty, you *never* know when I am fibbing."

"Yes, I do. Like the other day, when you told me I had a turnip in my hair, I knew you were only jesting."

She laughs again. "No. A turnip really *had* taken up residence in those curly locks of yours."

"What?" I reach back to feel the top of my hair. I do not feel any vegetables.

"It fell out the next day as you ran to greet Papa when he came home from his latest trip. Truly, sister. You need to comb your hair more often. If you like, I can comb it before bed as I do my own."

I sniff. "No, thank you. I am quite capable of combing my own hair."

"Then why not do it?"

I shrug. "I simply forget."

She rolls her eyes. We pick up our pace as the sun sinks lower in the sky. The road soon veers away from the stream and toward the forest, thick with trees and the sounds of unfamiliar wildlife. I get a chill, although it is a warm day. By the time we reach the wooden cottage with the thatched roof and the tiny windows, we have walked an hour and not seen a single person.

"This is it," Clarissa says, stopping on the overgrown brick path that leads to the front door. "Right where Papa said it would be."

"Do you have the key?" I ask. A glance at the rusted old door handle tells me we will not be needing one. "Never mind." I step forward to reach for it. But before I can grab the handle, the door swings open to reveal the most beautiful woman I have ever seen. Long black hair straight as a sheet on the dry line, eyes the color of the green sea glass I once found along the riverbed, skin like the finest caramel. And I am not prone to sentiment.

Clarissa and I stumble back in surprise. Papa said nothing about a beautiful woman coming with the house. To my further surprise, Clarissa reaches out to touch the woman's arm. "Mother?"

CHAPTER FOUR

↢ Beast ↣

Upon the queen's orders, the entrance to the tower room has been nailed shut until further notice. My bagpipes are locked inside, along with my astrolabe (which I use to chart the planets) and my collection of dried plums that look like various members of the royal court. I would be quite irked at this, were I not focused so keenly on a more pressing problem. Instead of transcribing the five rules of knightly behavior as instructed by Master Cedrick, I have used my last piece of vellum to come up with five compelling reasons why the royal caravan should leave me behind when they set out for the Harvest Ball tomorrow at a kingdom so distant we shall be forced to spend the night.

1. My feet remain quite swollen from the dance last night and will not fit in my dress shoes. I shall be forced to wear my slippers, and everyone will whisper about the queen who let her son wear slippers to a ball.
2. While admittedly unlikely, what if all the girls take one look at me and are so overcome by my dashing good looks that they no longer want to dance with Alexander? I should not want to damage his self-esteem in any way. He may give off an air of confidence (some may even say *over*confidence), but inside he is quite fragile.

3. I have an exam next week on the proper way to storm a castle. If I am forced to go to the ball, I may turn on my family and storm THIS castle while you are all dancing without a care in the world.
4. I do not travel well in the back of the royal coach on bumpy roads. The journey to the Harvest Ball is nearly a full day. I shall complain bitterly the entire journey.
5. My experiments are at a very sensitive stage. If I leave, weeks of work shall be for naught. Plus, I ask for very little.

I wait until the stewards have whisked away our plates from supper before reciting my list. Mother listens, her hands folded in her lap in that queenly way of hers that is supposed to indicate a gentle, patient nature but fools no one. When I have finished, Alexander sprays the table with the mouthful of cider he had been about to swallow. "I am not fragile. Neither inside, nor out!"

"Not so, son," Father says, leaning back in his seat. "You helped me care for that wounded falcon, and when it did not survive, you wept."

"I was three years old!" Alexander cries.

"Nevertheless," Father says, calmly picking gristle from his teeth with the tip of his knife. "Your brother has a point."

Alexander lays his head upon the table in frustration.

"Thank you for your support, Father," I tell him. "I can always count on you to be the voice of reason in this family."

Alexander begins dramatically banging his head against the solid oak table. He would never say it aloud, but I know he does not approve of Father's non-kingly gentle nature. Or his fondness for good-natured trickery. Or his inability to sit still during a meeting with his lords and barons for more than a moment without glancing longingly toward an open window.

Sure, Father sits on the largest throne in the castle and wields the largest scepter. And whenever he gives an order in his deep, measured voice, all his subjects scurry to obey. And, of course, it is his family's crest that our knights display proudly on their shields. But everyone knows Mother is the true ruler of our kingdom. And that is the way they both prefer it.

"Alexander!" Mother raps him atop his head with the closest object within her reach (a wooden spoon). "Stop that banging before you break your forehead, or our table, or both." To me, she says, "You are going to the Harvest Ball, and that is my final word."

"But, Mother, what of my reasons? Are they not most worthy?"

She sighs deeply, a noise I am all too familiar with. She taps my list, now wet from Alexander's cider. "First, instruct Godfrey to soak your feet in honey and primrose oil and they will heal overnight." She glances down at my list again. "Second, while both my sons are equally deserving of attention, neither your brother's reputation, nor his ego, will be at risk should you dance with girls. Third, your exam can wait. Knowing your tutor, he is likely off wandering the fields, deep in thought about why the sky is blue, and will not even notice your absence. In addition, you have never showed the slightest inclination toward the knighthood, so I do not think we need fear you storming our own castle. Fourth, you can chew ginger root if your stomach ails you on the journey. And last, if you do not ask for much, how is it that we had to build an extra room upstairs for your laboratory, filled, at last glance, with a dozen bottles and beakers and beeswax candles, pots and bowls and all manner of jars and tools and flasks, which, as far as I can tell, have been useless but for bleeding dry our kingdom's funds?"

"And the smells," Alexander adds, rubbing his forehead where a small bump has indeed formed. "Sometimes I am not sure which emits an odor more foul — the butcher shop in town, or Riley's laboratory."

Father begins to laugh, but ceases when I glare across the table at him.

Other than when I am looking up at the heavens, I am happiest in my laboratory, grinding minerals, mixing potions, and aiming to understand how air, fire, water, and earth can create all that we see around us. Even Master Cedrick does not understand as well as I the nature of plants and base metals, and it is he who introduced me to the misunderstood art of alchemy in the first place. I am aware Mother only allows my experiments to carry on because it keeps me busy. The second son of a king has very few responsibilities, and a bored prince is a troublesome prince. Or so the saying goes. When I am grown-up, my hobby will no longer be tolerated.

"Forgive me, son," Father says, holding up his goblet of wine and turning it back and forth in his large hand. "If you turned this into gold for me, I should laugh no more."

At that, everyone (except me) begins to laugh. Even the kitchen girls sweeping the remnants of our roast quail from the floor are tittering. No matter how many times I insist that my goal is not that of the ordinary alchemist, my family insists on taunting me. They do not understand that my aim is much grander, much nobler, than turning lead (or wine, or anything else) into gold. I intend to find the secret to ever-lasting life.

My chair scrapes against the stone floor as I push it back and get to my feet. "Laugh now, beloved family. For when I am celebrated throughout the seven kingdoms for my great discoveries, you shall laugh no more."

Alexander raises his mug to me. "I shall look forward to that day, dear brother."

I turn on my heel and stomp upstairs. Even though my shoes have little effect on the hard stone stairs, the act of stomping makes me feel better. My chamberlain Godfrey is waiting inside my chambers, pouring honey into a large bowl of smelly oils and ground-up tea leaves. A trunk is laid out upon the bed, my traveling clothes and boots beside it. Godfrey does not waste any time. He is completely blind in one eye and mostly blind in the other, but he makes up for his lack of sight with an unearthly sense of hearing. He can hear the seamstress drop a pin from down the hall, and the fluttering of the falcons' wings all the way from the mews on the other side of the castle. Hearing my mother's words through the thick stone floor taxes him not at all.

I slip off my shoes with a grimace (for my feet well and truly ache) and point to the bowl. "That looks like my old chamber pot."

Godfrey nods. "I assure you, young prince, it has been well washed."

"There is nothing else we could use for this task?"

Godfrey shakes his head.

I try not to focus on the bowl's previous life as I slip my feet into the murky water. Godfrey adds more honey and I have to admit, the feel of it sliding between my toes is not entirely unpleasant.

"As you recall," he says as he sprinkles a few more tea leaves on top, "the Harvest Ball is where your parents met for the first time."

I groan. "How could I forget? I hear the story all the time. Father was hiding under the table with the gilded goose, and when he jumped out with it everyone shrieked except for Mother."

"It was love at first sight," Godfrey says with a sigh. He dabs at his eyes and I roll mine. Honestly, it is easy to see why Father is so sensitive. Godfrey was *his* chamberlain for nearly twenty-five years, more like a second father than a servant. His kind and gentle manner clearly rubbed off on Father.

I lift my feet from the sludge. "The last thing I am interested in is falling in love." I shudder involuntarily. "I would rather drink the contents of this bowl."

Godfrey pats my feet dry with the towel. "That will not be necessary. One day you shall change your mind about love."

"Do not hold your breath, my faithful and trusted companion."

Once I have been dried and dressed in my nightclothes, I send Godfrey to his chamber for the evening and retreat to my lab. Master Cedrick had taught me that to practice the ancient art of alchemy, one must be clear of mind and spirit. Dances and love fade from my mind as I take in the shelves of beakers and bottles, the small furnace that I am only allowed to use under supervision because of one tiny incident involving some scorched nose hairs (Father's, not mine), and the notebooks where I carefully record the results of my experiments. In the corner of the room lies the pallet of hay where I sometimes rest if the night grows long. I am pleased to see that next to the pallet is a large box of mineral samples that I ordered from the apothecary shop. One of the new pages must have brought the crate up while my family and I were dining. I have not gotten to know the pages by name yet, and in truth, I probably will not. Although usually of noble descent, they are taught to bow their heads when addressing us. How am I supposed to tell them apart by the tops of their heads?

Most nights, my first task would be to stand before the room's one small window to measure the movement of the planets. But since my trusty astrolabe remains locked in the tower, I turn to the new box instead. I am convinced the secret to everlasting life is to be found somewhere in the combination of ingredients that I already possess, along with something I have yet to obtain. This confidence is due to the fact that I have successfully kept a small river worm alive for a month longer than its natural life expectancy. I figure a little dash of this, a dropperful of that, and the next worm may live to see a hundred. The key is figuring out what the *this* and the *that* actually are.

I reach for one of my sturdiest long-necked spoons and use it to pry open the wooden slats on top of the crate. I expect to find ingredients ranging from copper and zinc to gobo root and crushed dung beetles. Instead, only three small glass bottles lay nestled in a bed of dried hay. Each dark green bottle is labeled in a fine handwriting, although in a language with which I am not familiar. I could ask Alexander, but I am still annoyed at him.

I sift through the box to make sure nothing is hidden below, then sit back and tuck my slippered feet beneath me to ponder. My first inclination is to pack the crate back up and return it right away. For whoever got my order must be feeling the same disappointment.

But then I glance over at the tray full of worms that sits atop my workbench (some alive, some not so much) and a thought occurs to me. My longest-living worm was the result of an unexpected happenstance. I had thought I was mixing crushed milkweed into the elixir. It turned out I had labeled the bottles incorrectly and had added milk thistle instead. Had I actually used milkweed, the worm would not have lived to see another sunrise. Perhaps some power greater than myself has guided the hand of fate and allowed this package to come my way. Might these ingredients be exactly what I have been looking for?

I lift out the bottles, careful to hold them upright so nothing seeps from the wooden stoppers, and set them gently upon the workbench. I pull my best iron pot from the cabinet, determined not to squander what fate has delivered by using inferior equipment.

With the help of a pair of wooden tongs, I pull out the stopper of the first bottle to reveal a gray powder ground more finely than any I have seen before. The other two are the same, only one is white as snow, one a coal black. I am accustomed to spending hours chopping and grinding my ingredients before they are fine enough to blend into an elixir or a paste. But now my job has been done for me!

I grab my measuring cup from its hook on the wall, only to find that I had forgotten to clean it after my last experiment. Master Cedrick has told me time and again that if the equipment is tainted with other ingredients, you can never be certain of your formula. I would wash it now, but I am banned from cleaning my tools within the castle walls merely because one time Mother got a rash after I rinsed out a bowl of crushed ivy in her bathtub. How was I to know she would be so sensitive to the three-leafed plant?

It is too dark to clean it in the moat, so I resign myself to making a smaller mixture using a spoon instead. I carefully top off each spoonful and mix the three ingredients into the pot. I then add a few drops of water and some grape-seed oil to thicken, then pluck a worm from the tray. After five minutes of squirming around in the watery paste, it stops moving. Hmm. That is not good. Perhaps the mixture is too strong. Heating it would lessen its strength, but I am not supposed to use the furnace without Godfrey overseeing it. It is much too late to bother him, though, and after all, he cannot truly oversee much in his condition.

As I debate the question, I stir the mixture a bit. It is such a small amount that it will heat through in only a moment. I am fairly confident that my tiny rule-breaking will simply escape Mother's notice.

Before I change my mind, I blow on the smoldering embers, secure the lid on the pot, and close the furnace door. Since a watched pot never boils, I pick up my latest notebook and record the details of the experiment while I wait. I then return to the recently deceased worm on my workbench in the hopes that it has somehow revived itself.

I am about to poke the worm with my finger when BOOM!

The furnace explodes with the loudest noise ever to ring through the castle, shattering most of the glass in the room and forming a furnace-shaped hole clear through the wall.

Now THAT Mother's going to notice.

CHAPTER FIVE

∽ Beauty ∾

The beautiful woman laughs sadly and says, "I am sorry, dear, I am not your mother."

I stare at her, wishing I had known what my mother looked like. But if Papa had a portrait of her, he had never hung it up. And now, of course, it would have been destroyed in the fire.

"I . . . I am sorry," Clarissa says, her brows furrowed with confusion. "At first you looked just like her. But now, I mean, it must have been a trick of the light." She releases the woman's arm and steps back onto the overgrown path. "Again, I am sorry."

"It is I who should apologize," the woman says. "I hope you do not mind that I took shade in your home. I am looking for someone and thought he might have come this way. Come in, come in. This is your house after all."

She steps aside and holds open the door. Clarissa goes in first, and I follow. The woman stays at our side, for which I am glad. I had not looked forward to entering the strange new place without Papa.

I am very pleased to see that the front room of the house is actually quite lovely. Not nearly as grand as our old house, but the furniture is sturdy and colorful, and the yellow rug is thick. The room gets a lot of light, and we can cover the bare walls with crafts.

I had almost forgotten the woman's presence until she says, "Would you girls have happened to see a man in a long silver cloak today? Very tall? I am looking for him."

"We have indeed seen such a man," Clarissa says, clearly happy to be able to help this nice woman. "He was solving disputes up at the mill."

The woman smiles. Two rows of perfect white teeth. I have never seen such teeth. "Thank you," she says. "I shall set out, then."

"But it is growing quite dark," Clarissa says. "And the mill is a good hour's walk from here. 'Tis not safe for a woman alone. You should stay the night. Papa will be home soon, and he would not mind."

She shakes her head. Her hair ripples like blackbirds in flight. Perhaps my sister is correct. I *should* indeed comb my hair more often. "I shall be fine," the woman insists, still smiling. "Thank you for your kindness."

"But we did nothing," I say, thinking we should have at least offered her tea. Not that we *have* tea.

"You did a lot," she says, turning away. "Now I must —"

She stops mid-sentence as Papa steps through the door, his face streaked with the grime of a busy day spent delivering his last few sales. He lugs his empty chest behind him. He sees the woman and freezes in his spot, dropping the chest halfway through the doorway. "Who are *you*?"

The woman pushes her hair slowly away from her face. "I am nobody of consequence. Your daughters were kind enough to point me toward the mill. I shall be going now."

Papa makes no move to dislodge the chest, so the woman is forced to climb over it. "Papa," Clarissa hisses, "you are being rude!"

But Papa does not reply. When the woman has both feet

on the brick path, Papa yanks the chest out of the way and closes the door so quickly you would think the grim reaper himself was standing outside.

"Papa!" Clarissa says again. "What has gotten into you? I am certain that beautiful woman meant us no harm."

"Beautiful?" Papa repeats, sounding astonished. "She was hideous!"

"Hideous? But she —" The words get stuck in my throat. I am too busy noticing that the room is not at all as lovely as I first thought. The furniture is nothing more than discarded pillows on the floor, mold streaking their edges. The walls have holes clear through to the forest. No amount of charcoal drawings or watercolor paintings can hide those. Was the light indeed playing tricks on us as Clarissa suggested? The shadows hiding the holes and adding a rug where there is now only bare stone? "Clarissa," I say shakily, "did the room look different a moment ago?"

She does not reply. She simply takes my hand, her face as pale as when we watched our house burn.

"Now, girls," Papa says, "I know this house is not too pretty, but soon enough I'll be on my feet again and we can move back to town, into a proper home again."

"When, Papa?" Clarissa asks, tearing her eyes away from the largest of the holes. I can see the weeds through it.

He pats our heads. "Any day now I should get word about a trunk full of books that will fill our pockets with coins once again. The ship was delayed in a storm, but the latest report is that the waters have cleared."

"And until then?" she asks.

"Until then, I shall knock on the door of everyone who still owes me money. That will be enough for the bare necessities. And, Beauty — I found you a job already!"

"You did?" I ask, trying — but no doubt failing — to sound enthusiastic. I had hoped to be able to choose my own job. I suppose that was naive of me. I know how things work.

"Well, most places had little interest in taking on a girl apprentice, but the butcher said that in return for your assistance, he will allow you to take home a chunk of meat at the end of the day. Is not that wonderful?"

"Yes, Papa," I say, knowing it is what he needs to hear.

"That's the spirit!" he says, clapping me on the back a little too hard. I think sometimes he forgets I am not a son. If I *were* a son, I would be allowed to make more of my own choices. I wonder if I cut my hair . . . hmm, no. I am fairly certain no one would believe in a boy named Beauty.

That night I toss and turn in my small bed. The smell of lavender and tansy rises up from the straw mattress. It shall keep the fleas away, but it is causing my head to ache (although hunger may also be to blame, because all we had for dinner was cheese so hard that Papa had to hack at it with a hammer).

Clarissa's bed is within an arm's reach of mine, and I hear her tossing, too. Part of me is glad to share a room with her in this unfamiliar place, but I miss what little privacy I used to have. At home, when everyone else slumbered, I could sift through whatever treasures I had found that day. The brass button in the gutter behind the marketplace, the sea glass washed up on the riverbank, the perfectly round beechnut stuck under a tree root. Then I would make up a story about how the object wound up there. The pirate on the high seas who broke a bottle overboard, only for it to wash up as sea glass dozens of years later. Or the little girl whose button popped off her coat after she ate too much plum pudding. Perhaps it does not matter. My whole collection is gone now, and with it the leisure time to collect it in the first place.

An animal howls. The wind howls along with him. I shiver and hope that the thin pieces of wood that Papa used to mend the open holes will hold against both animal and wind.

I sit up. "Clarissa, do you slumber?"

"No," she says, with no sign of sleep in her voice. "Is something the matter?"

I pause. "Will you comb my hair?"

CHAPTER SIX

← Beast →

"Some people will do *anything* to get out of going to a ball," Alexander says. "But was it truly necessary to blow up the castle?"

He and I stand beside the large pile of stones, shivering as we stare out at the moonlit night. Even with the flurry of activity swirling around me, I cannot help but admire how well I can see the moon and stars now that half the wall is missing.

Nearly all of the residents of the castle had rushed upon the lab, most in pajamas, some with weapons, ready to respond to whatever threat they came upon. I had to insist over and over that we had not been attacked. Upon seeing the damage, and hearing my rushed explanation of my experiment-gone-horribly-wrong, Father had wanted to call the castle doctor who lives on the outskirts of the castle grounds. Instead, Mother inspected me from head to toe and declared me all in one piece. She then left to instruct the stonemasons to rebuild the wall upon first light.

"I did not do this on purpose," I tell Alexander as the maids begin to sweep up the mess. I wince at the loss of so many precious ingredients — jars of herbs and minerals and potions that took me years to collect.

"Nobody faults you," Alexander assures me. "But I would not be surprised if Mother turns your laboratory into another sewing room."

I sigh. "No doubt you are correct."

Alexander pats my shoulder and I feel my body begin to shake a little less. The crisp autumn air is not the only thing causing my limbs to quiver. Had I not walked away from the furnace when I did, there would also be a Riley-shaped hole in the wall. I shudder again as I think of what could have happened had I used cupfuls of those ingredients rather than spoonfuls.

"What material did you use to ignite such a powerful flame?"

"I do not know," I admit. "The labels were in a language I could not recognize. There is no need to point out the error in my judgment. I am well aware."

"Do you still have the bottles? Perhaps I can read them."

I look around at the rubble and broken glass. "They were likely destroyed, but I shall endeavor to find what I can."

I pick my way through the mess, glad for the thickness of my slippers. I try not to look too closely at what I am stepping around, lest I weep at the loss. Thankfully, the precious books Master Cedrick loaned to me were on the highest shelf against the farthest wall, where they remained safe. The crate that the mystery ingredients came in was totally destroyed, and the hay burnt to a crisp. But to my surprise, the three bottles remain intact, lying in a pile on the ground beside the workbench. I lift them up, certain that the labels must have been burnt off, but they are as crisp as when I saw them last. I make my way back to Alexander and hold them up to him.

He peers close, then shakes his head. "I am sorry, but that is not any script I have seen before. How did you come to be in possession of them?"

I begin to tell him about the error with my order, when Father returns from examining the damage outside the castle. I slip the bottles into the pockets Godfrey had sewn into my pajamas and wait for the lecture I am certain is about to come.

"Young Riley," Father begins, placing his hand firmly on my shoulder. "So curious about life, so inventive and creative. Your mother and I have decided that after all you have experienced this night, you shall remain home to rest under Godfrey's watch while we travel to the ball."

My eyes widen in surprise. "Truly, Father?" Not that staying home from the ball was worth blowing up my lab for, but I cannot help be pleased at the turn of events.

"No, Riley," he replies. "*Not* truly. In fact, you should be prepared not only to attend the Harvest Ball but the winter, spring, and summer balls as well."

"Good trick, Father," Alexander (the traitor!) says.

I wrangle myself out from under Father's grip to glare at my brother, who had been so supportive only a moment prior. "Why is it that the only time you think Father's jokes are funny is when they are at my expense?"

Without giving him a chance to answer, I turn my back on the ruins of my once-favorite place and hurry from the room. Immortality shall not come tonight.

CHAPTER SEVEN

～ Beauty ～

Clarissa manages to scrape together a breakfast of sorts. She had picked berries from the bushes out back before Papa or I awoke (getting scratches on her arms in the process), and gave us each a chunk of bread from the loaf the baker had kindly given to Papa after the fire but which is now harder than a rock. We tell her how delicious it is. She forces a smile and says, "It was no trouble." We are all lying.

Papa and I walk into town together as the sun begins its climb. We are both wearing our finest clothes. In his case, that means his *only* clothes, which he has worn for five days straight now. I am stuck in one of Clarissa's dresses and I am certain I look ridiculous. Why did she have to grab a basket of *her* clothes and no one else's? Why I need to wear a dress with white lace around the edges to stand amongst animal parts and all manner of grime, I do not know. But I am always the dutiful daughter, and I did not want to argue with Papa. He has been through so much.

By noon I have been fired. Apparently it is "bad form" to pet and nuzzle the pig before slaughter. It is even worse to let him out the back door and yell, "Run, be free!" But I could not help it! I kept thinking that perhaps, somewhere out in the woods, that pig had a mother who was looking for him.

So now I find myself sitting on a tree stump at the edge of the marketplace, wondering how I shall break the news to Papa that we will be having hard cheese again for dinner. No one tried to sell me anything as I crossed the square. Clearly they can see I am no longer carrying a pocket of coins.

A group of girls walks right by me with nary a glance. Their parents traveled in the same social circles that Papa used to, which I suppose means they used to be my friends. They do not ask what new downturn has led me to this spot. Nor why my ill-fitting dress is dirty with the splatterings of those animals I could not save. Until we are back in the village in a proper home, I am not a suitable companion for them. I do not take it personally. Again, it is the way of things.

I debate walking through the marketplace to see what lost objects I can find, but I fear that now people will mistake me for a thief if they find me searching the ground and dropping items into my pocket.

Someone sits down on the next tree stump over and begins taking food out of a sack. I glance over and then quickly away. It is the last person I want to see right now.

"Sorry about the other day," the baker's apprentice says, biting into an apple. He chews fast and swallows hard. "Mama says I am cursed with the worst social skills in all the northern kingdoms."

I do not reply, hoping he will go away if ignored. Instead, he chomps faster. My stomach rumbles with hunger. I hope he does not notice. My own social skills may be somewhat lacking (since I usually hid behind Clarissa at every social event Papa dragged us along to), but even *I* know it is not polite to talk with your mouth full of food.

"I laugh when I have the nerves," he explains, spitting out tiny drops of apple between each word. He truly *does* have the worst social skills. I wish he would stop talking to me. But on he goes.

"I get the nerves when I have to tell people my name," he continues. "The baker thought I was called Thomas till you came in and I let the cat out of the bag. Not a real cat, of course, for a cat in a bakery would be bad for business."

Since my subtle ignoring is clearly *too* subtle, I turn to look directly at him. "You are making no sense."

He tips an imaginary hat at me, just as he did when first we met. "Handsome's the name, miss. Although I know I am far from it."

I blink. "Sorry?"

"Me, too. But what can I do?"

"What? No, I meant I do not understand. You are telling me your name truly *is* Handsome? You were not insulting me the day I came in for rolls?"

"I was not."

I shake my head, trying to clear it. "That is truly something."

"Never met anyone with a name like mine before," he says.

"Nor I."

" 'Tis a burden."

"Indeed."

Silence. I think we have run out of topics to discuss.

He reaches into his sack. "Barley roll?"

I hesitate, unsure if I should be taking food from a stranger, but then my stomach asserts itself and rumbles again. I take the roll, still warm from the baker's oven.

"If you do not mind me asking," he says, "how is it that

you are sitting here alone, midday, with what looks like, um, animal parts splattered across your dress?"

When I do not reply right away (for I am enjoying my roll too much), he quickly says, "Do forgive my forwardness. I warned you I am socially lacking."

I shake my head, and swallow my last bite. "No, it's all right. I have just been fired from a job with the butcher."

"Why? Did you let the animals go free?" He chuckles at his joke.

"Yes."

He chokes on his last bite of apple and spits it out. "Truly? You did that?"

I nod.

"The butcher must have been quite irked."

I nod again. "Quite."

Handsome grins. His lips do not appear nearly as thin, nor his chin as sharp, as when I thought him insulting me. In fact, his face is quite pleasant. He may not exactly live up to his name, but at least he is talking to me, unlike everyone else who looks the other way.

"So you are in need of a new job, then?" he asks, tossing the apple core into the clump of bushes behind us. It is instantly set upon by two squirrels and a mouse.

"I suppose I am."

"The fuller is without an assistant," he says, standing. "I heard him complaining just this morn that he needed someone to work the cloth once it comes from the loom. He has piles of it and the weavers are getting tired of waiting for him to prepare it."

I have never had a need to visit the fuller, but I have seen him at work. A happy man, stomping in his huge bucket late into the eve, marching like it matters not that he never goes anywhere. "I can stomp," I tell Handsome. "I have a lot of experience stomping away in a huff."

"Indeed," he agrees. "You did that quite well when first we met." To my surprise, he sticks out his hand. "Friends?"

Again, I hesitate. That word has never meant much to me. I always knew the only real friends I had were Clarissa and Papa. But he still has his hand out. And he's clearly not the type to turn his back on a friend if she has a little animal gore on her skirt. I am not certain I have what it takes to be a friend, but I shake his hand and he grins. "All right, then, friend. I shall introduce you to the fuller, if you like."

Before I know it, I am stomping with my bare feet on a warm, squishy, very smelly mound of wool that will one day be woven into someone's cloak or blanket. As payment, the fuller could only offer me two farthings a day, which would not even buy the barley roll Handsome gave me at lunch. But I am allowed to keep the scraps of wool that rip off from the larger pieces, which I figure we can use to make new clothes, or even to feed the fire, if necessary.

As I march in what looks like clay but smells much worse, holding my skirts at the knees so I do not trip, I find I am quite pleased with myself. Not even a week has passed since we lost all of our worldly goods, and here I am, gainfully employed, and not too proud to accept scraps of wool in order to contribute to the care of my family.

"Let me see your work," the fuller says with his usual easy smile. This is the first time he has checked on me since I began working the wool. In fact, he has been napping under a tree for most of the afternoon. Perhaps that is why the weavers are complaining.

I step out of the bucket, nearly tripping over the edge in the process. My legs are wobbly from the steady marching, and I have to grab hold of the side to steady myself.

The fuller peers into the bucket and shakes his head. "Your wool is almost dry. Have you not been adding urine to the clay? If you do not keep the wool moist, the fibers will not tangle properly. The weavers will not be able to make cloth out of it."

I tilt my head at him. "Are you telling me I have been stomping in urine all afternoon?"

"Of course! Although you need much more, as I have pointed out."

"I need more urine?" I repeat, having trouble grasping this turn of events.

He nods. "If you go over to the alehouse, you can collect quite a bit from the trench out back."

I stare at him to see if he is perhaps joking with me. "So you are saying that you want me to go to the alehouse, bring back a trench full of urine, pour it into my bucket, and stomp on it?"

"That is right, young miss."

It would not be entirely accurate to say I have been fired from two jobs in one day. This one I quit all on my own.

CHAPTER EIGHT

← Beast →

I awake to a persistent knocking on my door.

"Come in, Godfrey," I reply, rubbing my eyes. I did not sleep well after the laboratory incident and am anxious to inspect the damage in the light of day. I climb out of bed and wait by the dresser for Godfrey to bring my washing bowl. To my surprise, a young page enters instead, pulling a cart piled high with clothes and boxes. I cannot imagine why.

Although attired in the fine clothes that all our castle pages are given, he looks out of place in them. He bows low and says, "Good morn, Prince Riley. I am Fredrick, but my friends call me Freddy." He instantly reddens. "I . . . I mean, not to presume that you are my friend, I mean, of course, as a prince, you wouldn't be expected to . . . oh, I am nervous. Forgive me!" He hangs his head, peeking up through the floppy hair that falls over half his face.

Unsure what to do, I lean over and pat him on the shoulder. "Er, there, there, Freddy. You need not be nervous. I would be happy to be your friend. Truly. I do not have many of my own."

The boy looks up at me with wide brown eyes. "I am sorry, Prince. It is just that I have never been assigned to anyone of your greatness before. I want to do a good job."

I try not to laugh when he is being so earnest. "You have not been at the castle long. My brother is the one worthy of such praise, not I."

He peers into my face. "Are you not the great alchemist?"

I stand straighter. "Is that what you heard?"

He nods. "Your mother's lady-in-waiting said that you spend all your time playing in your laboratory trying to turn lead into gold."

"I am not trying to turn lead into gold!" I cry, louder than I had intended. I lower my voice. "Nor am I merely playing, like a child."

Freddy shakes his head. "Oh, I know that, Prince. I believe trying to understand the true nature of the world is the highest of goals."

No one has ever said anything like that to me before, other than Master Cedrick, and even he never put it quite that way. I peer at Freddy more closely. Most pages are from noble families, sent away to learn the skills of the knighthood while serving the masters of the house. I have always felt a bit sorry for them. I would not want to be sent away from my family at such a young age. Perhaps Freddy fears a bad report being sent back to his own father. "How old are you, Freddy?"

"I am ten years of age, sire."

"And how long have you been here?"

"Coming on three weeks."

"Does your family live nearby?"

He lowers his eyes to the floor. "I am an orphan, Prince. My mother passed on when I was a babe, and my father a few years ago. He was a knight in the service of the good King Rubin."

We are silent for a moment. "I am truly sorry, Freddy."

"Thank you, Prince. Since his death, I have been passed between distant relatives, and now your parents have brought me here, to train for the knighthood. They have been kind to me. I want to make them proud."

"I am sure you will make an excellent knight one day."

He looks down and replies so softly I almost miss his words. "I do not wish to be a knight."

I have never met a page who did not dream of being a knight. Of fighting in battle, of being admired for bravery and skill, honored for his good deeds and his noble virtues. "Why not?" I ask.

Freddy begins to pace my room. "Do you know how many ways a knight can perish?" he asks.

I shake my head.

His pacing continues as the words rush from his mouth. "He could die in battle, pierced by a lance, clubbed over the head, or suffocated beneath his horse. Or if he does not die immediately from his wounds, the wounds could become infected with all manner of disease, or he could bleed to death. He could fall into a pit hidden by rushes and leaves, and break his neck. He could overheat in his armor on a hot August day, or freeze in winter while hidden in the woods against some unseen enemy. Or he could be captured by opposing forces and left to starve in a dungeon somewhere."

"Well!" I exclaim when fairly sure he has finished his list. "That is certainly something!" I dare not ask which of those fates befell his father.

Freddy sits down on the edge of the bed and his voice falls again to a whisper. "Father was the greatest knight our kingdom had seen in two hundred years. He never lost a fight, and always stood up against injustice wherever he saw it. If a man like that could be taken in the prime of his life, what chance do *I* have?"

Fortunately, he does not leave me room to answer.

"I like to stare at the moon at night," he says, his voice rising. "My real dream is to study the stars. I know it is absurd to think such a thing possible. I cannot change the path destiny has set for me."

My heart quickens with his words. I sit beside him. "I love the stars, too. I have never met anyone other than my tutor who shared this interest. You should pursue your dream."

He beams at me. "Truly? You believe I could do it?"

I begin to nod, and then stop myself. If I'm being honest, one's social position in our society does not change much. As an orphan at the mercy of other people's kindnesses, his situation is even more dire than most. I do not want to give him false hope. "One can never tell what the future may hold," I say carefully. "Tomorrow our lives could change forever."

He smiles, but his eyes dim. "My tomorrows are likely to resemble my yesterdays. But I shall remain hopeful."

"That is the spirit, young Freddy! Now I must go check on my laboratory. You may have heard a large bang last night." I turn away to find my slippers.

Freddy clears his throat. "Prince Riley? I am afraid your mother has other plans for you." He walks over to the cart he had left by the door. "I have been sent up here to fit you in your attire for the ball. Since I spent my growing years at King Rubin's castle, where the Harvest Ball is held each year, your mother thought I would be more familiar with how your outfit works than your usual chamberlain. Then, if adjustments need to be made, there is still time for the seamstress to work on it."

I stare at him, uncomprehending. "How my outfit works? But my clothes are already packed."

"This particular outfit was, um, made special for you. You have an important role in the festivities."

I narrow my eyes. "What kind of special role?"

He blushes. "Um, it's not really for me to say."

I sigh. This just keeps getting better and better. I don't want to get him in trouble by sending him away, so I say, "All right. But can you please hurry?"

"I will try," he says, "but there is quite a lot to put on."

He did not lie. It takes a very, very long time for him to get me dressed. Besides the layer of stockings and undergarments, shirt, vest, breeches, dress coat, and boots, he spends what feels like ages affixing things to the back of my outfit with pins and hooks. Medals? Coats of arms? I do not know. I have been instructed to stand very still so I do not get stuck. A hat of some sort is placed upon my head, more objects pinned upon it. The outfit is growing quite heavy at this point. I do not know how I shall be expected to move on the dance floor.

Finally, FINALLY, Freddy announces that we are done and turns me around to face the mirror inside my wardrobe door. I step forward and stare at my reflection. It takes a moment to process what I am seeing.

Then I run screaming from the room to find Mother. This is made infinitely more difficult than normal because I am covered, from head to toe, in FOOD.

CHAPTER NINE

∽ Beauty ⌒

"It would appear you left out some details of my job with the fuller."

Handsome grins as he reaches into the baker's oven with wooden tongs as long as his arms. "So you discovered what softens the wool, eh?"

"Indeed."

He pulls out a piping-hot loaf and rests it on a flat stone to cool. Then he slips the tongs into his apron pocket and says, "I did not figure you for the squeamish type."

"I am not usually squeamish," I insist. "I do not care if my clothes are neat and pressed. I like the feel of mud between my toes, and I can even pick up a spider with my bare hands. But everyone has their line in the sand."

"True," he agrees. "I, for one, refuse to trim the baker's nose hairs when they get too long. Even when he offers me an extra shilling for the trouble."

I laugh, not thinking I would be capable of such a thing after a day like this. "You jest."

" 'Tis the truth," he says, pulling off his apron and rolling it into a ball. "The man's nose hairs would reach his chin if he did not tend them."

"Where *is* the baker?" I ask. "I did not expect to find you alone."

"Aw, you made a special trip all the way here simply for *me*?"

"Do not be too flattered. The fuller is but four stalls down."

"I know," he says, grinning that easy grin of his. "I was only teasing. The baker has gone for the day. I am closing the shop. If you want, I shall walk you home afterward."

I am about to say, *Thank you, but I am perfectly capable of getting myself home*, when I remember that home is actually nearly an hour's walk from where we stand. That is a long way to go with only my thoughts for company. Plus, there may be some leftover bread to be had. "I live quite far," I warn him. "My family has fallen upon hard times of late."

He nods. "I know. I have heard people talking."

I raise my brows. "You have? Who?"

"Just some customers," he says, and busies himself wiping up flour from the floors. The cracks in the dark wood are thick with it. He would have to wipe for ten years to actually clean it all.

After he sweeps the ashes out of the oven and soaks them down, he tosses a few rolls into a sack along with the loaf I had seen him take out earlier. "I need to make a quick stop on the way, if you do not mind."

I shake my head. "We should probably stop at the butcher shop, too. In case my father came by there to walk me home."

We begin the two-block walk, the sack swinging on his shoulder. I can smell the fresh bread, and once again my stomach growls. Without me having to say anything, he reaches in and pulls off a chunk of the new loaf. It is delicious. The best I have ever tasted, which I do not think is due purely to hunger.

My feet slow as we approach the butcher shop. "Perhaps this is a bad idea. He might still be angry with me."

"I am sure he has forgotten all about it," Handsome says. "We better check if your father awaits inside."

I nod and follow him up the lane. I am truly hoping Papa is not there, for I am not anxious to tell him that I lost two jobs today. The butcher comes around the back of the shop, dangling a (bloody) cleaver at his side. He stops when he sees me. "You!" he cries, raising the cleaver into the air. "You lost my best pig! Your father shall pay for that!"

Handsome grabs my arm and we run in and out of alleys until we can no longer hear the butcher yelling. Even though I was just threatened with a cleaver, it feels good to run. It would be easier if I weren't wearing this stupid dress.

We cross into the center of the market, and Handsome slows to a halt. "All right," he says, panting. "Perhaps his memory of you lingers still."

"It would appear so."

"You should probably steer clear of him for a while."

I nod in agreement. "That seems wise. Do you think he meant it about making my father pay for the pig?"

"Probably. I would tell you otherwise to make you feel better, but I try not to fib."

We make our way across the square, checking behind us every few steps to make sure no irate butchers are following us. We soon find our path blocked by a large crowd gathered outside the apothecary shop. As we get closer, we can hear shouting. I peek over shoulders until I see the apothecary, Master Werlin, kneeling on the ground outside his shop. A man sits beside him, babbling nonsensically, alternately fainting and sitting back up again.

"Joan!" Master Werlin shouts into the store. His assistant

comes running out, clutching at her skirts, her face blotchy with tears.

"How much did you give him?" he demands.

"J . . . just a pinch, sir, in a cup of tea. I swear it."

"Burdock root does not cause this reaction," he yells. "Are you certain that is what you gave him?"

She runs back into the store. The crowd holds its collective breath as Master Werlin pulls on his hair. I have visited the apothecary shop upon occasion, and found him to be a brilliant though quite unpleasant man. He has always been able to cure Papa's aches and pains (and the occasional boil on his rear) with swiftness and discretion. He must not be easy to work for, though, for I have never seen the same assistant twice.

The woman called Joan returns with a bundle of roots in a large glass jar. She holds them out. He snatches one and holds it up to the rapidly fading sunlight. Then he drops it back into the jar as though it burned him. "This is nightshade! The man came in for an itchy scalp and you poisoned him!"

She peers at it, frowning. "But it looks just the same. . . ." she says, her words trailing off. Even from my position I can see the words *Atropa belladonna, Nightshade, Dangerous* printed clearly on the label.

"Can you not read, woman?" he bellows, grabbing the jar from her hands.

I can tell the answer by the reddening of her cheeks.

The apothecary reaches down and helps the poisoned man to his feet. "Come inside and rest," he says. "I have called for the doctor. Now that we know the cause, we shall fix it." Without even looking at Joan, he says, "You are fired." He flips the *OPEN* sign over to *CLOSED*, and the door bangs shut behind him.

Joan bursts into tears, pushes her way through the crowd, and runs down the street wailing.

"I trust you took your own firing with a tad more dignity?" Handsome whispers.

"Which one?" I joke.

The crowd begins to break up. I turn to go, too. "Wait," Handsome says, pulling me toward the entrance to the store. "The apothecary needs an assistant now."

Before I can respond, I find myself pushed inside the door. The man sits on a wooden stool while Master Werlin spoons what looks like honey or molasses into his mouth. Judging by the large pan set on the floor at the man's feet, the apothecary must be trying to get him to vomit. I try to turn back around, but Handsome holds me firmly in place. I clear my throat.

Master Werlin looks up at us, then scowls. "You are not the doctor. What do you want?" Up close, I can see the worry sketched onto his forehead.

"If you are looking for an assistant," I say, trying to keep my voice steady, "I would like to apply for the job."

The poisoned man gags and makes a retching sound. We all jump back in case the retching leads to worse. I glare at Handsome, but he motions me to keep talking. "Um, I can read quite well, and I am reliable and trustworthy."

Master Werlin spoons more of the syrupy mixture into the man's mouth, then turns back to me. "You are the book merchant's daughter, correct? What do they call you?"

Handsome nudges me from behind. "My name is Beauty," I force myself to say as I step forward.

Master Werlin raises a brow, then coughs. I figure I have gotten off easy.

Then the poisoned man vomits all over my shoes.

CHAPTER TEN

⤙ Beast ⤚

I can hear Alexander and Father coming up the stairs so I duck into the first door I come to — the castle library — and hold my breath. I have no intention of being seen with assorted squash, corn, yams, potatoes, nuts, and berries hanging off my back and down my sides. I would never, ever, hear the end of it. Why would Mother wish me to wear this? Clearly I am being punished. Was it because I blew up the lab?

Alexander says something and Father laughs. It sounds like they are right outside the door! Why will they not move on? Why choose this spot to have a conversation? As quietly as possible, I slide the lock closed.

Since I'm stuck in here, I might as well pick out a book. Father collects rare, old books, and has many that are unequaled in their beauty, even in kingdoms far larger and richer than our own. More arrive each month, too. I walk slowly around the room, careful to avoid the one window. I don't want a gardener snipping the hedges to spot me.

"It's really not that bad," a voice behind me says. I am so startled that I grab on to a random book, yank it out, and hold it over my head like a club. I whirl around to find myself facing Freddy. I look from him to the still-locked door, and back again. "How did you do that?"

"Do what?" Freddy replies.

"Enter the room without coming in the door. And how did you find me?"

Ignoring the first question, he holds up a small ear of corn. "I found this in the hallway. I know you do not want to go, but it is tradition for a visiting prince to have the honor of dressing as the ceremonial symbol of the harvest."

"I cannot wear this," I argue, lowering the book that I had still been holding over my head.

"Now that we know it fits, you do not have to wear it on the ride, but they will expect you to put it on when you arrive at the ball. We must get back to your room now, for the royal caravan is to set out very soon."

I shake my head. "I cannot possibly go. I happen to be right in the middle of this excellent book, and I make it a habit never to put down a book mid-chapter." I wave the book in the air for effect.

Freddy leans forward to examine the cover of the book in my hand. He chuckles. "I have no doubt that *Fairies, Goblins, and Witches of the Western Kingdoms* is proving excellent reading material considering there ARE no fairies, goblins, or witches in the western — or any other — kingdoms, but I must insist you allow me to escort you back to your room to change or else you shall certainly be late."

I redden in response to the book title. As a man of science, it is embarrassing to be caught reading such things. Or even fibbing about reading them.

He continues in response to my silence. "I beg pardon for being blunt, but what other option do you have? Hiding away in here while your father sends his best knights to find you?"

I set the book down on a small round table and attempt to fold my arms across my chest in defiance. This would work better if a butternut squash and an ear of corn were not in the way. So I stick out my chin instead, and ask, "Since when did you get so bossy?"

He laughs. "Since your mother told me that if I do not get you into the royal coach on time, she will put me on dung chute duty and make me sing for my supper."

I shrug. "Idle threats."

"Perhaps," he says. "But I would rather not chance it. I sing quite off-key."

I do not budge.

"Come now, Prince Riley. This is just for one night. A great alchemist can handle anything that comes his way. Now hold your head high and be the best symbol of the harvest King Rubin's guests have ever seen!"

"You will make a better knight than you think," I grumble. "You are very persuasive."

"Thank you," he says, relaxing his shoulders a bit. "Now let us go quickly."

I wait until he gives me the "all clear" in the hallway before following him out. It is only once I am back in my regular traveling clothes and Freddy has left me at the coach that I realize he never told me how he entered the library.

CHAPTER ELEVEN

∽ Beauty ∾

"I am concerned that you find my ongoing misfortunes so entertaining."

Handsome is doing a poor job of stifling his laughter as he watches me scrub my shoes in the apothecary's sink. I try my best not to disturb the plants soaking there. "I am sorry," he says, gulping some air. "I told you I laugh when I get the nerves."

I point my shoe at him. "You do not seem nervous. Only full of mirth."

" 'Tis better than what *that* poor sap is full of," Handsome says, gesturing to the corner of the shop. The village doctor and the apothecary are in the process of carrying the poisoned man out, where a carriage awaits to take him home.

For the first time, I allow myself to feel a powerful wave of loss for my previous life. If this were a normal day, I would be able to walk three blocks to my home, where fresh water would quickly be heated for my bath. My clothes and shoes would be properly washed clean of the guts of animal and man. Of course, if this were a normal day, I would not HAVE the guts of animal and man on my clothes and shoes. I scrub harder.

The apothecary storms back inside, grumbling about how much money the carriage ride will cost him. He stops when he sees us, as though he had forgotten our presence.

"You still want that job?" he asks wearily. "It is demanding work with no room for error."

I nod.

"You can read?"

I nod again.

"You can grind seeds, shred roots, mix lotions, boil teas?"

"I can."

"And you will promise not to attempt to diagnose any illness in my absence? You can see how well that worked out the last time."

"I will not," I promise.

"Fine. We shall try it for a week. Now go. I have a splitting headache." He heads over to one of the many rows of small wooden drawers lining the wall and pulls one out labeled *Willow Bark*.

I push my wet shoes back on my feet and turn to go.

"Wait," Handsome says to the apothecary. "You did not tell us Beauty's wages."

"A pound a week," he says without turning around.

Handsome and I stare at each other, wide-eyed. We hurry out before the apothecary changes his mind.

"Life is looking up for you!" Handsome says as we head down the street toward the south end of town.

I allow myself a small smile. "Now we shall see if I truly can grind, shred, mix, and boil."

"Something tells me you are a fast learner."

I glance up at the sky. If we do not move quickly, Handsome will be walking back from my house in the dark. Even for a boy his age, nearly sixteen I figure, it is not safe. "We best hurry."

"I just need to drop off this bread at the monastery, and we shall be on our way."

The square is bustling with people leaving their jobs or buying food at the marketplace. Three shillings a day is more than enough to buy my family a proper meal. I believe I have a skip in my step. Clarissa would be pleased.

The monastery is attached to the village church by a long hallway. They are only a block away, and we arrive without any more distractions.

"I would invite you inside," Handsome says, pulling open the heavy door, "but the monks are very private. I can go only to the kitchen and no further."

Father used to drop books off here for the monks' library, but we were never allowed inside. Judging from what the monks have purchased from him over the years, I imagine the library is quite grand. It's probably best that I stay outside anyway. I worry my fib to Clarissa about the cause of the fire still hangs in the air above the last pew of the church, trapped there in the shaft of light. I do not want to go inside to find out.

He returns only a moment later, stuffing the now-empty sack into his pocket. Before he reaches me, a little girl runs out from the back of the monastery. She looks to be no older than nine or ten, with hair so yellow it is nearly white. She reminds me of a drawing I saw once of a fairy girl. Not that fairies truly exist, of course. At least, not anymore. Still, I catch myself looking to see if the tips of her ears are pointed. They are not.

"Wait, Handsome!" she calls out.

He stops and turns to her. "Hello, Veronica." He bends down to her level. "What can I do for you this fine evening?"

"Did you find it?" she whispers.

He shakes his head. "Not today, but I shall keep looking."

"Do you promise?" she asks.

He holds up his palm. "I promise."

I wonder what the girl has lost. I have developed quite an eye for finding things. Perhaps I have seen it while combing the ground for my assorted treasures. But before I can ask, Veronica points a finger in my direction and asks, "Who is *she*?"

Handsome straightens up. "This is my new friend."

She looks at me with suspicion. I give her a small wave. I do not have much experience around children. The direct way they stare you in the eye unnerves me.

"Her name is Beauty," Handsome says. Then to me he says, "And this is Veronica."

The girl looks from me to him and back. "Her name is Beauty? You jest!"

I stand up. "Let us go," I snap. "I do not need to be insulted any more today."

The little girl stands her ground. "I only meant that it is funny that you two have the same kind of name." She squints up at us. "Are you related? Cousins, perhaps?"

We both shake our heads. "I am from a village a few hours east," Handsome explains. "My mother gave me my name when she thought I would not live. But I surprised everyone with my ability to cling to life, and now I am stuck with it."

They turn to me for my explanation of my naming. I shrug. "Perhaps my mother was blind when she named me." It seems easier to joke than to tell them the sad truth.

Neither of them smiles, though. The girl does not meet my eyes. "I shall see you tomorrow," she says to Handsome, and turns back into the building.

"I was only joking," I say as we begin walking again. "Did I offend her somehow?"

"Her grandfather was blinded in a woodcutting accident. That is why she lives with the monks. He cannot take care of her any longer."

"Oh." We walk in silence toward the river. "She asked if you found something. What is it she misses?"

"A pink stone of some sort," he says as we turn to walk along the bank. "It used to be part of a necklace. I guess it's pretty important to her."

"I will keep my eyes open for it."

"That would be kind of you," he says.

We pass the mill and I glance behind me to see if the tall man in the gray cloak is still there. A few farmers wait in line by the millstone, but I do not see the man who could solve a dispute so easily. I have the vague sense that someone was looking for him, but I cannot put my finger on who it was.

We continue into the woods, where the air is noticeably cooler. Handsome asks about Papa's job, and I tell him about all the wonderful books I get to read and how each book has its own feel and its own smell. He does not even laugh at me for smelling books. When we are about halfway to my house, I work up the nerve to ask a personal question. "So why were you not expected to live?"

He is quiet for a moment, then replies, "I had a twin brother. We were born too soon. He did not make it. No one expected me to survive, but I was a hardy little runt."

"I am sorry," I tell him. "About your brother."

He nods. "I think of him sometimes. I wonder what he would have been like. He probably would have been smarter than I, and better fitting of my name!"

"You are plenty clever," I assure him.

He shakes his head. "I cannot read without mixing the letters up. I cannot do simple addition. It is a good thing

I love baking bread, for I need not do much of those things. I can memorize a recipe or simply make it up as I go along."

I do not reply right away. If I could not escape in a book, I do not know what I would do. Then I remember the delicious bread he gave me earlier. "Did you bake that last loaf?"

He nods.

"You are truly gifted, then!"

He beams. "The baker lets me experiment with the recipe when he is gone for the day."

"You should share it with him. I am certain he would want to make it."

"Perhaps I will," he replies. "Or perhaps I shall save it for my own bakery one day."

"It is nice that you have a dream," I say. "I have never thought much past the next day."

"Truly?" he asks.

I nod.

"You do not dream of marriage and children?"

I shake my head. "That is my sister's dream."

"Then what is yours?"

I shake my head. "My future will not be of my choosing, so I see no reason to think about it."

"I told you my story," he says. "Now how did you really get your name?"

I take a deep breath. I have never told anyone of this before, but I trust him. "My story is similar to yours. My mother named me as she passed out of our world and into the next. I never knew her."

"I am sorry," he says, putting his hand on my shoulder as we walk. It feels comforting.

We are still a good distance from the house when Papa and Clarissa appear before us.

"We were worried!" Papa says, hugging me tight. "I went to the butcher to fetch you, but he waved a cleaver at me. He yelled something about me owing him a pig, but I did not stick around to hear it. Perhaps he mistook me for someone else."

"Probably not," I tell him. "It is a long story."

"And who is this?" Clarissa asks, eyeing Handsome with suspicion.

"He is the baker's apprentice. And my new friend."

She tilts her head at me in a way that clearly says she does not believe me. I sigh. "Truly, Clarissa. I can make a friend on my own, you know."

"Since when?" she asks.

"That is enough, girls," Papa says. He puts out his hand. "I am Beauty's father. And you are?"

Handsome clears his throat. I know exactly how he feels. "My name is Handsome," he says, shaking Papa's hand. "And before you say anything, yes, it is truly my name, and yes, I realize it is not the most fitting."

Clarissa and Papa glance at me for confirmation. I nod at them. "'Tis true."

"How wonderful!" Clarissa says, her eyes shining like they used to before the fire dimmed them. She gives me a hug as tight as Papa's. "You have found your perfect match! Beauty and Handsome! I always thought I would be the first to find true love, but I am truly happy for you!"

I can feel the heat on my cheeks at her words. *Love?* We have just met! Love is the last thing on my mind.

Handsome laughs. "Beauty and I are a pair indeed. But not in the way you suggest."

Clarissa places her hands on her hips. "And why not, pray tell? Is it because of our circumstances? We will be back on our feet again, I promise you that."

He shakes his head. "No, it is not that at all."

"Is it because of her appearance? She can be quite pretty when she combs her hair and puts on some makeup. I tell her all the time to —"

"It is not that, either," he says.

I wish she would stop pressing him, but she does not. "Then why?" she asks again.

He takes a deep breath and says, "I cannot marry your sister because in a few months I shall marry another."

"Oh," Clarissa says, her bright face dimming. "Well. That is that, then."

After an awkward moment of silence, Papa claps his hands together and turns to me. "So! What did you bring us for dinner?"

CHAPTER TWELVE

⤝ Beast ⤞

Chewing on the ginger root is not helping, and it tastes like feet. The coach has just pulled over for the third time so that I could settle my queasy stomach. Each time, my family groans in annoyance. But they can't say I didn't warn them. When our coach stops, the entire royal caravan has to stop, too, so no doubt there is groaning up and down the line.

We are only going for two nights, and yet besides our luxurious carriage, we have four royal guards on horseback and three coaches filled with luggage, the customary gifts, and Mother's lady-in-waiting, a woman named Clea who has attended my mother for twenty years.

I climb back in the carriage and wrap my cloak tight around me. We pull back onto the road, and the rest of the caravan follows. The guards take up their places on all sides of our coach. I gaze out at them, envious of the fresh air on their faces, the freedom they enjoy from the confining carriage.

I cross my arms over my chest, trying to ignore the ever-present sway as the carriage picks up speed. "I do not understand why I couldn't have simply ridden along on horseback."

"Princes do not ride outside the carriage on long journeys," Mother replies, returning to her knitting. "It is dangerous if you veer from the road. Bandits and all sorts of ill-mannered thieves could be lurking in the woods."

"I would not veer into the woods," I mutter, pulling the thick curtain closed so I will not have to see the guards. I knew Mother would never let me ride outside. Even Alexander with his exceptional riding skills is stuck in here.

I could take up the argument over my outfit again, but Mother has already insisted it is an honor to have been chosen and I shall be expected to make the best of it.

Mercifully, I begin to feel groggy. The clomping of the horses' hooves on the hard dirt road becomes muffled, like someone has thrown a blanket over them. The next thing I know, I hear a lot of yelling outside and realize I am curled up on the seat like a babe.

I untangle myself and sit up. Are we being attacked? Across from me, Alexander is sitting upright, proud as a peacock. "What is afoot?" I ask. "What is all that noise?" Alexander does not reply, he only sits there, beaming. I look to my parents. They, too, have pleased expressions on their faces. Father has even put down his book of poetry. They do not appear to be frightened, so I relax a bit.

The yelling outside grows even louder. The curtains on both sides of the carriage remain drawn, though, so I cannot see. "Please, won't someone tell me what is happening?"

"Have a look," Alexander says. He pulls aside the curtain and the afternoon sun streams in. It takes a moment to figure out the scene before me. Then my eyes grow so wide I fear they may fall out of my head. Dozens, nay *hundreds*, of people line both sides of a long, narrow road. We are in the midst of a town I have never seen. The townspeople — many in fine clothes marking them noblemen and noblewomen — are not merely watching the procession, though. They are running after the caravan, cheering as they go. In fact, they are cheering the same words over and over. "All hail Prince Alexander! All hail the future king! Welcome! Welcome!" They obviously know who we are, and that we would be passing through their village.

Alexander pulls the curtain closed. I sit back in my seat, at a loss for words. The volume outside continues to increase, if such a thing is possible. Now I hear chants like "I will see you at the ball! Dance with me first!" and "No, me! I shall make the best wife of all!"

Mother reaches over and pats Alexander's knee. "And to think Riley was worried about you not having enough dance partners tonight."

Alexander winks at me and grins. But as the cheering gets more insistent, more frenzied, his grin fades. He presses his back deep into the seat and doesn't peek out of the curtain again until the noise fades and the carriage is once again on the open road. A light rain begins to fall, and the sound lulls me back to sleep. I awake to the carriage lurching, and my stomach along with it.

The rain has grown heavy. The dirt roads have turned to mud and the wheels keep sinking into it. The coachmen must stop to dig us out, only to have to stop again moments later. Finally, the horses give up even trying to make us move, no matter how hard the coachmen drive them. We have no choice but to wait out the rain. Maybe we shall miss the ball!

Mother takes out her knitting. Father begins to recite a poem about a wayward traveler who meets a robber on the road, only to discover he is his long-lost brother. It must be the worst poem ever written. And it rhymes. Alexander starts humming to drown out Father's words. Between the poetry and the humming, I am ready to stuff chunks of cheese in my ears. Just when I think I can take it no more, the sun breaks through and the rain slows, then halts completely.

"Thank goodness!" Mother says, tossing her knitting below the seat. "Silas, do feel free to end your poem now."

But there is no stopping Father once he begins to spin a tale. We must simply wait until the wayward traveler and his reunited brother make up for all the years they lost by moving to a farm and raising goats. Admittedly, I have not read much poetry, but if it is all like that one, I do not see the art form lasting much longer.

The coachman appears at the door to tell us that in order to dig out the wheels — which have sunk even deeper now — everyone must vacate the carriages to lighten the load. At this rate it would be faster to *walk* the rest of the way to King Rubin's castle. Not that I will suggest that.

Since there is nowhere to stand that isn't knee-deep in mud, the four guards hop off their horses and allow the four of us to climb on. It feels so much better up here than in the stuffy carriage. Alexander and I share a glance, and I know he is thinking the same thing.

"Mother, Father," he says, circling his horse around to face theirs. "Shall we ride ahead a bit? The caravan will catch up soon."

"Excellent idea," Father says, patting the mane on his large white stallion. "What say you, my darling queen?"

Mother looks uncertain for a moment, and then a tiny gleam enters her eye and she nods. As much as she tries to rein it in, Mother has a bit of an adventurous streak in her.

She alerts the guards that we will be going ahead. I can tell by the way the head guard, Parker, has crinkled up his face that he wants to tell my mother it is not a good idea for the royal family to ride alone in unfamiliar territory. I do not fault him for holding his tongue, though. It usually does no good to argue with Mother.

"Please, Your Majesty, do stay on the main road," he finally says, glancing ahead worriedly. "We shall meet you at the next pass."

She nods and turns her horse back around. Without hesitation, the three of us trot after her, sticking to the sides of the road where the puddles are not as deep. My mood lifts even higher. Out in the open like this, with the fresh breeze in my face, it is easy to forget my troubles.

I ride up alongside Alexander. "Brother, do you recall the last time we four traveled on horseback together with no guards?"

He shakes his head. "I believe I like it."

"I think they do, too," I say, pointing to our parents, who are riding close to each other, giggling like children.

We reach the next pass sooner than any of us wants to, and pull off to the side to await the caravan. I pat my horse's flanks and he breathes heavily. "I think my horse is thirsty," I tell the others. "I hear a stream."

"We must wait here," Mother replies.

So we wait. A few moments later, my horse begins to pant. "I truly think he needs to drink."

Mother glances at the horse and sighs. "Fine. Let us be quick."

We turn and enter the woods, with Alexander taking the lead. We stay close together. The sound of the stream gets louder and louder, yet I still do not see it.

Father glances anxiously at the road behind us, now all but gone from view.

We ride a few more moments as the rushing of the babbling water continues to intensify. Still, no stream appears. Just as I am about to suggest we turn back, we ride right into a small clearing. I can see the stream at the far side. It is surprisingly small for such a noisy thing. Other than that, it looks like any ordinary stream.

The beautiful yellow-haired girl standing beside it, however, with her hand resting on an enormous buffalo, is anything *but* ordinary.

CHAPTER THIRTEEN

～ Beauty ～

"You should fight for him," Clarissa insists as we climb into our beds. I am exhausted from the long, strange day and do not wish to discuss this topic any further.

"I asked you to leave it be," I tell her, pulling my blanket around me. Papa had recovered enough money to purchase a few more necessities. We now have blankets, chairs for the table, a few candles, and enough food to last three days. Four if we do not eat much.

"But —"

"Look," I tell her, sitting up. I can only see her outline in the bed since we are saving the candles for emergencies. "Handsome is my friend. My first friend in years. I am not interested in becoming his bride. I am happy for him if this marriage is what he wants."

"But perhaps you two met for a reason."

I groan. Clarissa and her romantic notions! "Perhaps we did," I reply. "But it is not to break up his engagement."

"Fine," she says, flipping over onto her belly. "I shan't mention it again."

I lie down. "Yes, you will."

"Probably," she admits.

Papa has hidden the clothes I was wearing the day of the fire. I cannot find them anywhere. I am afraid he has buried them near the outhouse in the backyard, where he knows I will not dig for them. I think Clarissa put him up to it. She says I am a woman now and must dress like it.

I do not see how I am a woman today when I was a girl yesterday, but I allow her to pick out another of her frilly dresses for me because I am fairly certain I would be fired if I turned up at the apothecary shop in only my undergarments. Clarissa offered to tuck the dress with pins, but I do not trust her with anything sharp too close to my body. Her mind tends to wander.

"This will be fun!" Clarissa says, bouncing along beside me as we make our way into town. "I was so bored all alone at the house." She refuses to call it *home*. It certainly does not feel like one.

I grip my lunch sack tighter. "Do not make me sorry I agreed to let you come to work with me."

"You did not agree. Papa gave you no choice."

"I hope the apothecary will not mind your presence."

"Me? Who would not want to have *me* around? I shall brighten up the place!"

I glance sideways. It is true, she will. She has chosen her fanciest dress, which would be much better suited for a castle ball than for sitting on a stool in the corner of the apothecary shop all day. I think all the talk of Handsome's engagement yesterday got Papa thinking that our only real chance of rising from the ashes is to marry one of us off. He was very quick to agree when Clarissa said she wanted to come with me today. The boys who had flocked around her this past year have quietly moved on. Whether they have found other girls, or whether they are no longer interested due to our fall from society, I know not.

"You promise you will not get in the way?"

"I promise. I shall be as quiet as a church mouse."

"I doubt that."

"Unless a handsome boy comes in. I do not mean your friend Handsome, of course."

"I figured."

We pass by the riverbank and I remember the talk Handsome and I had about our births. Now that I know he is engaged to be married, perhaps it is not right to spend time with him. I debate asking Clarissa her opinion, but I do not want to get her talking of boys again. She's likely not to stop.

Master Werlin does not even turn around when we enter the shop. He is busy hanging batches of herbs upside down from a string. The string reaches the length of the shop and hangs high above the long, marble counter where I have seen him grind his herbs and roll pastes or ointments. Cabinets as high as my shoulders line the wall behind the counter. Each one is made up of tiny wooden drawers with a knob on the end. Most of these are sticking halfway out, their colorful contents visible. A long shelf runs above the cabinets, full of all manner of tools, pots, different size scales, mortars and pestles, oils, and one particularly nasty jar full of black leeches twisting and turning lazily in murky water.

I shudder and clear my throat. Master Werlin turns around quickly, and I worry he will fall right off his stool. But he recovers himself and says, "Not a moment too soon. My last assistant put all the drawers back in the wrong place, and I cannot find a thing. I need you to sort it out. *A* starts in this corner, *Z* over by the sink. Can you do that?"

I nod.

"Good." He reaches up for another clump of herbs.

Clarissa nudges me. I reluctantly step forward. "If it pleases you, sir, may my sister, Clarissa, join me?" I feel foolish even asking, as though I am too young to do the job myself.

He sighs, gives Clarissa a cursory glance, and says, "Fine. But do not expect double the wages."

"No, sir," Clarissa says. "You shan't even know I'm here."

"I doubt that," he grumbles, reaching up for the string. I giggle. He knows her already.

I get to work pulling out the drawers and ordering them correctly. Each time I rest a drawer on the counter, Clarissa peers inside. "What is nutmeg for? What does mandrake do? Why would someone use sassafras root?" The apothecary gives her one-word answers until finally he says, "If you are so interested, you might as well make yourself useful. Go wash your hands in the sink." Clarissa heads over to the sink, which I know she had been eyeing earlier. Our old house had a sink with running water in it, but our new one does not. She allows the water to pour over her hands until the apothecary tells her that is quite enough. He then places a mortar down before her, pours little red seeds into it, and hands her a pestle. "Grind this to a fine powder."

"Yes, sir," Clarissa says, pushing up her dress sleeves. She begins to hum as she works, and within moments, the apothecary is humming along. When he catches himself, he mutters something about needing to pull some nettle roots from the garden and disappears out the back door.

After Clarissa has completed her task (and quite well), she sets out to wander the marketplace. She says she is just going to admire the wares, but I think she is trying to find any of her old friends. I know she misses her active social life. She is not gone more than a few moments when an elderly woman comes in and asks if her order is ready. She points to a box on one of the shelves, full of jars labeled with different people's names. The apothecary had not told me what to do in case this happens.

"I am sorry, but this is my first day. Let me go ask Master Werlin."

Before she can reply, I hurry out the back door. I find myself in a small garden, as colorful as the powders and seeds and oils and minerals inside. The garden is fenced in on two sides, and reaches all the way up to the back wall of the store on the other. Master Werlin is nowhere to be seen.

I duck back inside to ask the woman to come back later, but now she is gone, too. Six shillings rest on the counter, gleaming against the shiny surface. I guess she found what she needed. I hope she did not leave with anything else! I take one last look in the garden for the apothecary, then sweep the coins into the top drawer of the apothecary's desk.

Two more customers come in, one complaining of a bumpy red rash on his shoulder (which, of course, he had to show me, although I told him I can do nothing to help), and another whose grandmother's cream for "rosy cheeks" had run out and she needed more. I am able to convince them both to come back later, but they are not particularly happy about it.

I have made it all the way up to *Nutmeg* before the apothecary finally returns, through the front door. Unless they are stuffed in his pocket, he does not have any plants with him. I am about to tell him of the customers when two well-dressed men step in right behind him. All three seem quite anxious.

"Are you certain, Master Werlin?" the taller of the two men ask. "His wife reported that he was a customer of yours."

"Everyone in the village is a customer of mine," he replies as he pulls down one of the clumps of herbs, now dry, and lays it on the counter. "When did you say he was last seen?"

"Two days ago," the man replies, "at the mill. Some farmers reported seeing him there. They recalled his silver cloak."

I am wondering when someone will notice I am in the room, but no one takes the slightest interest.

"I have not seen him for at least a fortnight," Master Werlin says, pulling the stalks off the herbs and tossing them into a large yellow bowl. "He had a toothache, which I offered to pull. He declined. He paid me two pence for a handful of poppy seeds to chew on, and I have not seen him since. Do you suspect danger has befallen him? A bear in the woods, perhaps?"

I freeze at this. There are bears in the woods?

"Perhaps more sinister than a bear," the man replies.

The shorter man clears his throat and tilts his head in my direction. The others turn, finally noticing me. The shorter man says, "Let us continue this conversation outside."

As the front door whooshes closed behind them, I feel a shiver run down my back. Something about a man at the mill with a silver cloak sounds familiar. Someone else was looking for him? It is too hazy, like trying to remember a dream.

By the time Clarissa returns from her wanderings, I have already forgotten it.

CHAPTER FOURTEEN

⤝ Beast ⤞

"Hello, travelers," the girl says, her voice soft as a moth's wing, as sweet as honey cakes. I blink a few times to be sure I am not imagining her. I cannot tell her age, perhaps sixteen or so. Her dress is a deeper green than the grass, her smile warm and friendly. "Have you lost your way?" The buffalo stamps a front paw and huffs, his eyes wild. Careful to avoid his large horns, she pats him until he quiets.

We all shake our heads in response to her kind question. Mother turns her horse around and says, "Come, we must return to the road." But the rest of us do not move. Exasperated, she turns back to the girl. "We are not in the habit of talking to strangers in the woods. We will be on our way."

Again, she turns to go. The girl's long, yellow hair lifts and falls, scattering rainbows of color. I do not seem able to look away.

"Are *you* lost, young lady?" Father asks. "Can we assist you in any way?"

"Silas!" Mother says. "You've heard the warnings. We are not to talk to strangers in the woods!"

"But she is not a stranger, Mother," Alexander says, hopping off his horse. "She is —"

"A friend," the girl says, stroking the back of the buffalo. "A good friend."

"See, Mother?" Alexander says. "She is our friend. Our *best* friend."

Mother glares at him. He either does not notice, or pretends not to. "Good day to you, miss. I am Prince Alexander." He bows so low his hair grazes the ground. "We are heading to the Harvest Ball."

She tilts her head at him and smiles. "Welcome to my stream, Prince Alexander. It gets very lonely out here in the woods. Would you like to dance with me? To practice for the ball?"

He strides toward her, his hand outstretched.

"Alexander!" Mother scolds. "I told you not —"

The girl gracefully turns toward Mother, and her eyes flash. Mother swallows whatever she had been about to say. I have never seen *that* happen before. "With permission, Your Royal Highness, might I dance with your son?"

Mother pulls a little too tight on the reins, and her horse whines in complaint. Her head moves in a close approximation of a nod, however.

The girl steps toward Alexander, and they clasp hands. They begin to dance around the clearing. The girl's eyes never leave his. When they have twirled around the clearing twice, the girl brings the dance to an end right in front of me. I am still atop my horse, who has shown no interest in drinking from the stream after all. "What of your brother?" she asks Alexander. "Does he dance as well as you?"

Alexander laughs. "Not quite."

"'Tis true," I say, once I can find my voice. I have never given girls more than a passing thought before, but truly, she is astonishing to look at. Her rosy cheeks, her white, perfect teeth. I quickly scramble off my horse, not wanting to appear rude.

"Prince Riley may not dance well, nor will he win a beauty contest, but he has other excellent qualities," Alexander says.

"Thank you," I reply. "I think."

"No doubt he does," the girl says, her eyes twinkling at me. "But dancing, what greater joy is there?"

Off the top of my head I can think of twenty, but I hold my tongue.

"Would you like to be a better dancer?" she asks.

I shrug. "It does not really matter much to me."

"Would you like to be handsome? Like your brother?"

I shrug again. "That is not a big matter, either."

"Riley does not mind looking like a beast," Alexander explains. "He only combs his hair for church on Sundays!"

"I cannot change my looks," I explain. "And Alexander is vain enough for the both of us."

"Come now," she says, holding her hand out to me. "Let us talk while we dance."

And suddenly we are away and dancing. Surprisingly, I have no problem following the steps at all. Before I know it, we have made a full circle already.

"See?" she says, her eyes glistening bright. "You are a natural!"

Father, still atop his horse, claps.

"And you are certain you would not like to be handsome?"

I shake my head. I am glad that my face won't make girls scream for me in the streets. Alexander can have that particular blessing. I know he finds it difficult to believe, but I honestly do not care what stares back at me from the mirror. Especially since I almost never gaze into one.

"I told you," Alexander says, grinning. "He enjoys being beastly!"

She laughs in response, and we keep dancing. "Riley is not beastly," she says. "A real beast would have nails as sharp as an eagle's talons!"

"And tufts of fur all over his body!" Alexander calls out.

"And a nose the size of . . . well, the size of his nose now!" Father shouts.

We all laugh then, even Mother.

"Only pointed, like a hawk's!" Alexander adds.

Mother joins in. "With hair like a lion's mane!" she says. "So even if he combed it, it wouldn't matter!"

More laughter. It is at my expense, but I do not care. I am having too much fun. "As broad as two men, and as strong as an ox!"

"Is that all?" she teases as we begin our third time around the clearing.

"Well, I would not mind being taller," I admit. "That way I would be closer to the stars."

"As tall as a giraffe!" Alexander calls out. "Then you can pick our morning oranges straight from the branches!"

"Done," the girl says, her voice clear and strong. I assume she means we are done dancing, so I stop. But suddenly, I feel very strange. Heavy and hot. The ground seems to be farther away somehow. The girl's eyes are closed. Her lips are moving, but I hear no words coming from her mouth.

Then Mother's screams echo through the woods and do not stop until she falls from her horse.

CHAPTER FIFTEEN

∽ Beauty ᴄ

"You have done well," the apothecary tells me, peering over my shoulder. I am up to *R* — *Rose Hips* — and am getting quite an education in the tools of the apothecary trade. I had no idea so many different ingredients existed. This job is a hundredfold better than the butcher shop.

The hours pass quickly. I learn how to boil herbs into tea over the cauldron, to grind minerals like sulfur and lead into a fine powder, how to measure dry ingredients with the scale, and wet in glass beakers. Master Werlin teaches me how to make pills by pressing the paste into a long thin roll like a snake, then cutting the roll into even sections. He has just set aside a dozen or so sections to dry when the door bangs open.

"Please, Master Werlin," a little girl cries. "You must help us. It is Grandfather. He came to visit me at the monastery, but he is acting strangely. I am afraid he is ill!"

I recognize her right away. Handsome's friend, the girl with hair so light it is nearly the color of snow.

The apothecary reaches down under the sink and pulls out a black leather bag. "You, older sister," he says, pointing at Clarissa. "You'll hold down the shop. Beauty, come with me. This is part of your education."

"Are . . . are you certain?" I ask, looking from him to Clarissa.

"I shall be fine," Clarissa says, waving us out. "I have been listening to your lessons."

I find this hard to believe since she has spent most of the afternoon sampling different lotions for the face and oils for the hair. But I take off after Master Werlin nonetheless. Hopefully, when we return the shop will still be standing and there will be some face cream left over for the customers.

I follow the pair through the streets, past the cobbler, the spectacle-maker, the fishmonger. Past the group of singing schoolchildren marching across the square. I duck my head as we run by the butcher shop. We round the corner to the churchyard and run right into Handsome, who is panting hard. He flashes me a quick smile, then turns to Veronica. "I received your urgent message. What is the matter?"

Veronica grabs onto his sleeve and tugs him along. Handsome looks at me, but I shake my head, as confused as he is.

We reach the courtyard between the church and the monastery. I don't know what I expect to see — a crowd of monks surrounding an old man on the ground, perhaps. There *is* an old man, but he is sitting on one of the benches, bouncing the tip of his wooden cane on the ground and humming. He certainly looks healthy to me.

"Bartholomew!" Master Werlin says as we approach. "Are you ill?"

"I am fine," the old man replies, keeping his eyes closed. "Should I not be?"

Master Werlin turns to Veronica and narrows his eyes. "Your granddaughter led us to believe you were on your last breath."

"Veronica!" her grandfather scolds. "Why would you do that?"

She shrugs. "I needed to get everyone here quickly. You always tell me to use my wits."

He shakes his head at her disapprovingly, but does not look too angry. "Yes, you should use your smarts, but use them wisely, not to lie to friends. Especially not ones to whom you are about to ask a large favor."

Handsome clears his throat. "Um, can someone tell me what is happening? I have three loaves of rye in the oven that will soon turn to black bread."

"You must be Handsome," the man called Bartholomew says, lifting his face toward where Handsome stands. "And the girl, Beauty? Is she with you?"

"M-me?" I stammer in surprise. How does he know my name? He turns his head toward me. Even though I know he is blind, it is as though he can see right through me. Although the old man is not frightening, I still find myself shivering.

"Yes, Grandfather, she is here, too."

Master Werlin sits down beside his friend. "Bartholomew, what is going on?"

Bartholomew reaches into his cloak and pulls out the largest coin pouch I have ever seen. It bulges in all directions. Handsome's eyes widen, too, as do Master Werlin's. I am certain my expression is the same. Veronica's grandfather must be quite wealthy. Why is it she lives in the monastery, then? Surely he could afford maids to care for both of them at his own house.

"How old are you, Beauty?" he asks, drawing my attention away from the purse. I am glad he cannot see that I had been staring. And then I instantly feel shamed for thinking such a thing.

"Beauty?" he repeats. "Are you still here?"

I clear my throat. "I . . . I am nearly thirteen years, sir."

"Have you lived in the village long?"

"All my life, sir."

"Have you gone past its borders?"

"Um, yes, sir," I reply, surprised at the question. "My father is a traveling bookseller. My sister and I have gone with him on many short trips."

"Excellent, excellent. And do you find yourself a resourceful person?"

"Resourceful?" I repeat. "I . . . I am not certain. It is only of late that I have had to fend for myself. My family has . . . come on hard times."

Veronica tugs on her grandfather's arm and says, "She will do fine! Ask her."

"Sweetheart," he says, patting her on the head, "the young lady already *has* a job. I cannot simply steal her away."

"What is this talk of stealing my new assistant, Bartholomew?" Master Werlin asks. "I may finally have found someone competent. So far she has not burned half the store by leaving the dried herbs too close to the flame, turned anyone's hair orange by giving them the wrong oil, or nearly killed a man because he had dandruff. That already sets her well above all my other previous assistants. Plus, she can read, write, and is eager to learn."

I am touched that he thinks those things of me! And his last assistants must have all been quite horrible.

"What about you, Handsome?" Bartholomew says, turning away from me. "My granddaughter tells me you shall be married soon."

"Yes, sir," he replies. "A few months hence."

"Then I imagine you could use some extra money?"

He tilts his head and nods. Veronica jabs him in the side in a not-so-subtle reminder that her grandfather cannot see a nod. "I mean, yes, sir," Handsome says loudly. "I suppose that is true."

"And you plan to become a baker?"

He nods again, then quickly says yes.

"So you would call yourself responsible? Able to care for youngsters? To protect them from unforeseen harm?"

He raises his brows at Veronica but says, "Yes, sir. I have younger siblings back in my own village."

Bartholomew is about to ask another question when Master Werlin interrupts. "What is this about, old friend? I need to get back to the shop before I have another misfortune to add to the list."

Bartholomew takes a deep breath. "I have heard rumors of late, no doubt you have, too. Rumors of strange things going on in the seven kingdoms. People going missing. Others feeling like no time has passed only to find themselves in a place other than where they thought. The last time I heard such rumors is when my daughter Katerina — Veronica's mother — was lost to us. She had found a valuable object, a powerful object, and had gone to seek answers of its origins. She never returned."

A hush falls over the courtyard. Even the birds have stopped their song.

"What we would want from you both," Bartholomew says, his voice both firm and hopeful, "is for you to act as my granddaughter's guardians. She wishes to follow the trail begun long ago by her mother, to seek out the truth of what befell her. I knew one day she would take on this burden, and I had hoped it would be when she was older. Yet it is hard to deny that, with the rumors flying about, the time is right. It would not be proper to send her alone with a young man. Nor would it be safe to send two girls alone. That is why both of you are the logical choice as her companions on this quest."

Handsome and I exchange looks. He is clearly as surprised by all this as I am.

"Besides all of your expenses," Bartholomew continues, "I shall pay you triple your current weekly wages."

I gulp loudly. *Triple my wages!* That would be a lot of books for Papa!

"But I am merely an apprentice," Handsome says. "An education is my only salary."

Bartholomew smiles. "I shall offer you the same wages as Beauty. And I shall provide your employers with the salary of your temporary replacements."

Master Werlin's eyes widen.

"I trust you can find a replacement easily enough, Master Werlin?"

The apothecary glances at me. "I may have someone who could step in."

I hope he does not mean Clarissa. The longest she ever stays on one task is when she brushes her hair before bed.

"So you will do it?" Veronica asks, fixing her eyes on me and Handsome.

When neither of us answers right away, her grandfather tells us to take the night to think on it. Then he reaches out for Veronica's arm and she helps him to his feet. Before they head toward the path, Veronica turns and smiles broadly at us. She may be young, but she is smart. She knows the offer is too good to turn down.

The walk back through the village is a blur of sights and sounds and smells, but I notice none of them. All I can think about is the offer. For a girl who never thinks of her future, it is suddenly rushing upon me. We enter the shop (which I am relieved to see still stands) to find Clarissa dabbing on pomander from a small tin ball. Perfumes are her weakness. I should have known she would find the apothecary's stock. She places a dab on the underside of her wrist, and is reaching her finger in again when Master Werlin clears his throat. Clarissa jumps and drops the ball on the counter where it bounces once, rolls, and finally clinks up against the large jar of leeches and stops. I am certain Clarissa had a good reason for moving the jar from the shelf to the counter, but I am not sure I want to know what it is. She quickly tosses the ball back into the bin with the rest of them.

"That perfume is made from the shells of crushed beetles, you know," Master Werlin says.

Her blue eyes grow even larger and rounder than usual.

"I am jesting," he says. "We only use the crushed beetles in the lip coloring. That apple pomander is actually made from a substance found inside the buttocks of polecats."

With a shriek, Clarissa runs over to the sink and sticks both arms into a bowl of water. "Are you certain you want to take on Clarissa?" I ask the apothecary as we watch in amusement.

He shrugs. "I have had much worse assistants. She has a pleasant bearing, and seems harmless. You do not think she is likely to poison anyone, do you?"

"Well, not on purpose," I reply honestly.

"And truly, what have I to lose?" he adds. "Bartholomew would be paying her wages."

I watch as Clarissa reaches for the ball of soap, places it between her two wrists, and starts frantically moving it back and forth. "You are aware of what happened to our house?"

"I shall keep the flames low," he promises.

"All right," I say, turning back to watch my sister. "But perhaps you should not tell her that the pomander also contains whale intestines."

"Agreed."

And just like that, I have a new job. Again.

CHAPTER SIXTEEN

↞ Beast ↠

"What have you done to him?" Mother shouts, her fury overriding any pain she must feel from her fall.

The girl smiles sweetly and returns to petting her buffalo. The fact that she is petting a giant buffalo in the first place should have been a sign that something was not quite right. How did we all overlook such a thing?

"I have simply granted your requests," she says, her shining eyes dimming, like the setting sun on a cloudy day. "Is he not exactly like you specified? Are you not pleased?"

"Pleased?" Father roars. "He is a beast!"

Alexander, pale and shaken, steps forward. "Please, undo this horrible deed. We only joked of turning him into this . . . this creature."

She shakes her head. "I cannot do that."

"We will give you whatever you want," Mother begs. "Riches beyond measure. Just turn our son back."

She shakes her head. "There is one way only, and I would not count on it."

"Anything."

"A kiss," the girl says. "If a girl falls in love with him by the first bloom of spring, he shall become the prince again. If she discovers his identity before she loves him, the deal shall be broken."

"Look at him!" Alexander exclaims. "How is he supposed to find a girl to love him in only six months? Or ever?"

I clear my throat. The sound is much deeper than I expected, almost like a growl. "Is it truly that bad?"

Alexander nods. "Yes."

Mother begins to sob.

I glance down at my arms, which feel itchy. Gone are the sleeves of my traveling shirt. In its place are tufts of fur, in a seemingly random pattern up and down my arms and on the backs of my hands. My first reaction is to scratch and pull at the fur to see if it will come off. This proves a bad idea due to the thick, sharp, eagle-like nails that now draw blood. Mother's sobs have turned to wails.

I am torn. A huge part of me is horrified. I, Prince Riley, second in line to the throne, lover of the stars, dedicated alchemist, devoted son and brother, am now a beast. Half man, half animal. Or *animals*, as the case may be.

On the other hand, I am also living proof that one can manipulate the forces of nature. One can, in fact, change something into something else. For a scientist such as myself, evidence like this comes but once in a lifetime, if ever at all. So there is a bright side, however dim it may be. Plus, the Harvest Ball is clearly off.

Father marches over to the girl, draws himself up to his full height (which, I cannot help noticing, is now only as high as my chest), and grabs her by the shoulders. "I demand you undo this right now. This is an order from your king!"

"What care I for your demands?" she asks, shaking him off with nothing more than a twitch of her shoulder. As I watch in amazement, her once bright green dress fades to a dull brown. In a voice empty of emotion, she adds, "He now has only five months."

Wide-eyed, Father sputters, "But you cannot . . . this is simply unacceptable . . . you must . . ."

"Three months," she says calmly. Her yellow hair turns first brown, then the color of rust.

"Three!" Mother gasps. "You skipped right over four!"

The girl shrugs.

Father can only stare, speechless now. Alexander walks over to him and guides him back to his horse. Then he turns back to the witch, for clearly that is what she is. Humbly, so as not to anger her further, Alexander asks, "How will we know if a girl loves him?"

She rolls her eyes as though it is a silly question. "She will give him a kiss, of course."

"But how can we take our son back to the castle like this?" Mother shrieks. "What will people say when they see him? And if they see us with him, they will think we cannot even protect our own son, let alone an entire kingdom!"

"I cannot help what people will say or do when they see *him*," she says calmly, "but the rest of you I can take care of."

In a blink, the three of them are gone. Simply vanished!

I turn in circles (not easy with my new bulk and height) and call out for them. "Mother! Father! Alexander!"

"Riley?" Alexander replies. "Do you hurt? Are you in pain?"

I turn around again, but see no one. "Where . . . where are you?"

"Why would you ask that of me? I am right next to you."

"But . . . I cannot see you. I cannot see any of you!"

"What are you talking about, brother? I can see myself perfectly well. And Mother and Father, too."

I feel a tug on my hand and jump, nearly smacking my head on a low branch. I am not quite as tall as a giraffe, thankfully. Perhaps a baby one.

"It is only me," Alexander says, taking my hand again. This time I do not pull away. He places something round and hard into my palm, which I close around it. My hands might be larger, and the skin thicker, but I recognize the feel of Alexander's gold ring with our family's crest upon it. He never takes it off.

"So we are invisible to everyone but ourselves?" Mother asks, fuming. "*That* is your solution to this problem?"

The girl shrugs. "You were concerned what others would think when they saw you with such a creature. Now they will not see you at all. I could turn you all into beasts if you would prefer."

Only silence comes from Mother's direction now.

"Prince Riley, you have three months," the girl says, beginning to walk along the stream. The buffalo follows, his head so low his horns nearly drag on the ground. "If you fail, which, of course, you will, your family shall remain invisible. When your time is nearly up, you shall be drawn to me, and I shall add you to my collection."

The buffalo yelps and the girl smacks him with the back of her hand. The sudden realization hits me that the buffalo may not always have been a buffalo! My family must have come to the same conclusion, because no one utters a sound until they are both lost from view. Then my family surrounds me in a long, tight hug that I can feel, even if I cannot see it.

"We cannot go to the Harvest Ball like this," Mother moans, sounding more defeated than I have ever heard her. "I cannot bear to think of all the worry when we do not show. And Riley was the ceremonial symbol of the harvest!"

"Riley was the *what*?" Alexander asks, loosening his grip in the family embrace.

"Never mind that," I reply hurriedly.

Mother continues to wail. "And how will we get home? Riley would never fit atop a horse!"

"I have a theory," Alexander says. "Perhaps we shall wake at any moment to find this all a dream!"

"Yes!" Father agrees. "Mayhap we are all back in the carriage, dreaming still! Let us lie down in this tall grass and close our eyes."

It takes a moment to find a way to lie down where some part of my enormous body does not crush a leg or head of one of my family members in the process. When we have figured it out, Mother says fervently, "Good night, and may we all wake as good as new."

"Or better," Alexander declares.

CHAPTER SEVENTEEN

◦⊃ Beauty ⊂◦

I have scarcely finished telling Clarissa of recent events, when Veronica bursts through the apothecary door, just as she did an hour earlier. Only this time she is wearing a smile that shows her small white teeth. I should probably add teeth brushing to my list of grooming habits that I need to work on.

She runs up to me and grabs my hand. "I am so pleased you are coming!"

I glance questioningly at the apothecary, who shrugs and returns to grinding a pearl into fine powder. "I have not yet asked my father," I reply, pulling my hand back. "So I cannot say for certain."

"And as her older sister," Clarissa says, "I am not certain I am comfortable with this arrangement."

She turns toward Clarissa. "You are quite beautiful," she says.

"Thank you for noticing," Clarissa replies. My sister is never one for simply saying *thank you*.

"But there are things you do not understand in the world," Veronica says, sounding older than her years. "Forces are at work."

"Forces?" Clarissa repeats, sounding doubtful. "What kind of forces?"

Although no one else is in the store, Veronica looks left, then right, then leans close before replying. "You have read the old fairy tales? If you can read, of course."

"I can read," Clarissa snaps. "And yes, I know of the tales. But that is all they are, just stories."

Veronica shakes her head. "That is what I used to think as well. But the stories are true. At least some of them."

"Like the one about the girl who slept a hundred years?" I ask. "I do not see how that could be true."

She nods. "But it is."

I can tell by the way her eyes are darkening that Clarissa is getting annoyed. She may be a romantic when it comes to love, but she has little patience for make-believe. "Is that so?" she asks. "How about the one where the girl's hair grew so long you could climb up it? I have been growing my hair since I was six, and it does not even reach my waist."

Veronica shakes her head sadly, like she cannot believe she has to deal with such a silly question. "When magic is at play, the impossible can happen."

"Like witches and fairies?" Clarissa asks. "Goblins and ghosts and trolls?"

"All real."

"Pish-posh," Clarissa says, stomping off.

Veronica opens her mouth to reply but then straightens up and says, "I must go now and prepare. We shall leave three days hence. Let us gather in the courtyard of the monastery, where first we met."

"If I go, which I still have not agreed to, what would I bring with me?"

"I shall bring you a list tomorrow," she says.

"I should warn you, I have very few possessions."

"Whatever you do not have shall be provided for you," Veronica says. She leans close again, so close I can smell her flowery scent. I cannot help thinking of what the apothecary said about how he makes the perfumes. I wonder if Veronica knows that, and if she did, if she would still wear it.

"Be prepared, Beauty," she says in a low voice. "For a quest changes a person." And with that cryptic message, she slips out the door.

"And you say *I* am dramatic!" Clarissa exclaims.

I stand in the doorway and watch Veronica run down the street. Her legs move swiftly, almost as fast as mine. I suspect she was holding back when we first ran to check on her grandfather. Master Werlin would never have kept up. But I can keep up with her.

I understand now why her grandfather wanted me to accompany her. Someone who believes in fairy tales and mysterious forces might forget her own basic needs. He needs me to make sure she is fed, clothed properly, and given a safe place to sleep. I protect Veronica, and Handsome protects us both.

Master Werlin sets down his tools. "It does not surprise me that she wishes to believe in the old stories. Her own is a sad one."

Clarissa looks up from the glass jar she is rinsing. She is never one to miss any gossip.

"Her father caught a terrible fever right after she was born," Master Werlin says. "He only lasted another month. Then a few years later, her mother left on what was supposed to be a short trip. Her empty pack was later found in the woods, along with her shoes. Search parties were formed, but no sign of her has ever turned up. Everyone believes her dead, of course, either at the hands of bandits or wolves, but the girl holds out hope. Now we know why her mother left. At least Bartholomew's version of events."

"Is that what the quest is, then?" I ask. "She wants to find her mother?"

He shrugs. "Likely so."

Clarissa and I exchange a look. I am certain we are both thinking about the lengths we would go to if a chance existed that our own mother was still alive. I resolve to do my best to help the girl. Not that I believe her mother still lives, but perhaps I can help her accept her loss and move on. Living in the past is not living.

Clarissa appears beside me. She lays her hand gently on my arm. Her expression is both loving and serious. I turn toward her, anticipating some older-sister wisdom and encouragement. Instead, she says, "Please tell me you are bringing a comb on your journey. How do you expect Handsome to fall in love with you and break his engagement if you look like that? And would it kill you to powder your nose every once in a while? You shine brighter than the full moon on a clear night."

I groan and put my head down on the counter. The apothecary laughs. "Oh, yes," he says, "this is going to be fun."

CHAPTER EIGHTEEN

⤛ Beast ⤜

I stare at the back of my eyelids, trying to force myself to slumber. Or continue slumbering, whatever the case may be. Dreaming is the only explanation for what has just happened to us. As Freddy said this morning (which feels a lifetime ago), fairies and witches simply do not exist.

A moment later, I hear the unmistakable voices of the guards calling our names. My heart sinks. "There are the horses!" Parker shouts. I reluctantly open my eyes and hear rustling in the grass beside me. The others must be sitting up, too. Someone, I cannot tell who, grips my arm.

"You must hide," Mother whispers, the panic plain in her voice.

I turn my head in all directions but see nowhere I could go. I am wider than any of the trees, and taller than any of the bushes that line the riverbank. Besides, it is too late. Parker and the two guards at his side have spotted me. Shouts fill the air. "Who are you? *What* are you? Where is the royal family? What have you done with them?"

I shrink down, not daring to show them my full height. Do I truly look so unrecognizable? Parker has been guarding my family since I was born.

"Do not tell them who you are," Father whispers.

"Tell them not to fear," Alexander adds. "We do not want you to be attacked."

I clear my throat, but the mere sound makes the guards jump back. "Do not be frightened," I tell them, holding up my arms. They gasp. I quickly lower them. "I mean you no harm. I have not seen the royal family of which you speak." This is both a fib, and not a fib. Invisibility is tricky that way.

"We have searched for hours," Parker says. "King Rubin's men have searched, too. There has been no sign of them, and you have their horses! You *must* have seen them."

His words surprise me greatly. *Hours* have passed since we went ahead of the caravan? "I have not seen them," I repeat. And then I add, "The horses came alone."

"The beast is lying!" one of the younger guards points at me. "He has Prince Alexander's ring on his finger!"

I look down at my hand. I had slipped the ring over the first knuckle on my pinky, the only place it would fit. That was foolish of me.

"Seize him!" Parker orders. "We shall bring him to the castle dungeon until we learn the truth. King Rubin's men will continue to scour the area."

"Do as they say," Mother whispers as the guards approach from all sides. "This is our chance to get home."

So I stand up. This has the effect of stopping the guards in their tracks, which gives my family time to step away before the guards approach. Even though I could easily knock them aside with my ox-like strength, I allow them to grab my wrists and tie them behind my back.

They lead me to the road where the other members of the caravan are gathered, waiting to go. Upon seeing me, shouts and gasps again fill the air. Clea screams and faints dead away. One of the coachmen tries to catch her, but he cannot take his eyes from me and she hits the ground. The bump on her head shall hurt for a few days, I am sure.

Parker tells everyone not to panic and to ready themselves to leave upon his command. The guards herd me toward our coach, although there is no chance of me fitting through the door. They argue amongst themselves before deciding I shall have to be strapped to the top of the carriage. Then they argue about how they are going to get me up there, until finally I offer to climb. Although being tied to the top of a carriage was not how I intended to return home, it is better than being bumped around inside it.

The coachman must add a horse from one of the other coaches in order to pull my extra weight. While they are doing this, I take a moment to look around for any signs of my family. Out of the corner of my eye, I spot the door of one of the coaches opening. Then the carriage lowers a few inches and the door closes. They have made it inside! I think it is the one carrying the passed-out Clea. I hope for her sake she does not awaken before we reach the castle. She will no doubt believe she is traveling with three ghosts and faint dead away again.

The best part of the ride is getting to see the stars as they dot the sky. The worst part is not being able to push the tangled hair out of my face. Why could not Mother have joked about me having hair like a tiger rather than a lion? Then it would be nice and short, and the wind would not blow it into my mouth.

It is fully nightfall by the time we return to the castle. The guards are already leading me up to the main gate when the sound of our arrival reaches the occupants inside. A steady stream gathers to greet the caravan. Upon seeing what is before them, the maids, footmen, cooks, falconer, squires, pages, knights, jester, groomsmen, and others who the darkness hides from view work themselves into such a frenzy that I fear for their safety. It only takes a moment for word to spread that the royal family is missing, that the beast (*me!*) was found with the elder prince's gold ring, and that I likely ate the entire family.

Honestly! The tales people come up with! "I did *not* eat them!" I shout in my new, deeper voice. My words echo off the stones, making them sound even louder than I had intended. The crowd shrinks back, their faces masks of horror. I realize I have stepped into view of the torches that line the castle entrance. At once, the crowd streams past me, running away from the castle at top speed. I would have expected more from our loyal subjects. Certainly I look odd. A bit larger than the average man, and perhaps I have more hair, and my clothes and boots are in tatters, but this extreme reaction seems quite uncalled for.

"Wait!" Parker calls out. "We have the beast restrained! You are not in danger!"

But they do not wait. Nor do they look back. The coachmen, having unhinged the horses, now hop upon their backs and take off as well.

"Sorry," the three other guards tell Parker, before they, too, hurry down the path to the road.

Parker scowls. "Cowards!" His hold tightens on my arm. "I shall deal with you myself!"

I am so very weary. "Parker, it is I, Prince Riley."

Parker whirls around to see what kind of trick this is. Finding nothing, his face darkens. "How *dare* you jest with me! You shall rot in the dungeons for what you have done to the young prince and his family. If it were up to me, you would meet the hangman tomorrow!"

I open my mouth to argue, but a hard pinch on my bottom makes me yelp instead. "Do not tell him who you are!" Alexander whispers up at me. He shall pay for that pinch.

Parker grabs a torch from the wall and pushes me roughly through the now-unguarded gate, and down the long flights of stairs to the dungeons. I shiver, even though my newly furry skin provides ample protection from the dank and drafty hallways. I usually avoid the dungeons at all cost, even though no one has been imprisoned here since my grandfather was king.

Finally, we wind up at the farthermost cell, where Parker orders me to sit down against the wall. I barely fit on the narrow bench. "I am innocent, I tell you."

He must be too angry to be fearful, because he puts his face right up to mine. His hot, angry breath fills the space between us. "Then tell me exactly where the royal family is."

Probably right behind you, I want to tell him. Instead, I grit my teeth. "I cannot."

"As I expected," he says, slamming the door behind him and leaving me in utter darkness. I hear the wooden bars crisscross into place before he storms off down the hall. Even if my family were *not* invisible, I would not be able to see them now.

"I am assuming," I whisper into the inky blackness, "that you spent the ride devising a most excellent plan, because I do not intend to spend the night in this scary, wet, dark place while my comfortable bed lies empty."

A warm hand begins to stroke my tangled mane. "We have a plan, dear Riley," Mother says. "Fear not."

I cross my arms, careful not to scratch myself, or her, in the process. "Plus," I add, "I am very, very hungry. My new stomach must be the size of an elephant's."

"Please do not eat us," Alexander begs, barely concealing his mirth.

"Hush, Alexander," Mother scolds. "This is no time to tease your brother." She abruptly pulls her hand away from my hair and jumps from the bench. "Did someone just *tickle me?*"

Father laughs. "So sorry, my dearest. The dark is so total. I could not resist."

I sigh. Being invisible is a practical joker's greatest wish. I fear for the tricks he shall come up with now. Leave it to Father to find something positive about this nightmare. "Mother," I call out into the blackness. "Why would you not allow me to tell Parker of our situation? He has always been most loyal to the kingdom."

Father sits down beside me. I can tell because he says, "I am sitting down beside you now." Then he says, "I know it is frustrating, but we do have a plan. Neither Parker, nor anyone else in the kingdom, can know what has befallen us. If everyone in the town thought their leaders invisible and their prince turned into a beast, fear and mistrust would take over. Our castle and lands would be overrun. We must let them believe you are a fearsome creature from lands far away, one who has terrified nations, laid waste to civilizations, plundered villages, ravaged —"

"I get it. I am an evil, horrendous beast! But are you certain this is the answer?"

"This is the best plan we have for now," he says in the same firm, kingly voice he uses on his subjects when he wants them to believe and trust him. "Once the plan is in place we must figure out a way to change you back, and in doing so, to restore ourselves as well."

"But how can we do that from the dungeon?"

"You shall be free by dawn," Mother promises, sitting down on my other side and carefully — ever so carefully — taking my hand (paw?) in hers. "On the trip home, your father wrote a letter to Parker." She presses a folded sheet of parchment into my palm. I cannot help wishing for light in the room so that I could see the letter appear as if out of nowhere.

"When he returns," she says, "give him the letter. He knows well your father's handwriting, so he shall not doubt it. It informs him to alert everyone that the royal family is safe, and instructs him to give you free reign of the castle, to question you not, and to guard against any intruders who may do you harm. He is to clear the castle of all inhabitants, and to ensure they have places to stay elsewhere. Judging from how many people already ran away, this should not be a difficult task. He must make certain that large meals are delivered fresh every day, and that the fires are kept burning throughout the castle. He is to send all the knights to their outposts in the surrounding villages to make sure everything runs smoothly in our absence. The letter promises that if he obeys these rules, he shall be handsomely rewarded, and that you shall return the royal family unharmed in three months' time."

I let her words sink in. "It is a good plan. But how can I promise your safe return? Do any of you truly believe I can get a girl to love me in only three months?"

No one replies. They do not have to. We all know the answer.

CHAPTER NINETEEN

∽ Beauty ∾

Clarissa has taken to following me around with a powder puff. It was bad enough at home, when I awoke to find her putting the finishing touches on what I was horrified to discover later was a full face of makeup. Only now she is doing it at the store.

"But your forehead shines like the sun," she complains.

"I thought it was the full moon," I reply, darting out of her way.

"It is even brighter today. One more dab," she begs. I catch her arm as it reaches across the counter toward my face. She wrestles free and replaces the puff inside the powder container with a huff.

Master Werlin finally suggests I leave for a while so Clarissa can focus. I agree with him. If Clarissa is going to be my replacement, she needs to pay attention to his lessons without stopping to tie back my hair or coat my "lackluster" lips with beetle-encrusted lipstick. I want to warn him not to expect her to focus on the lessons for more than a few minutes at a time, but he will find that out on his own. He gives me a list of items to pick up from various vendors — beakers, a ladle, a spool of thread — and sends me on my way.

I return to the shop no more than an hour later, to find

a small brown-haired girl waiting out front. "Did you not hear me calling you? What, did you think I meant someone *else* named Beauty?"

I stop and squint down at her. I have never seen this girl before in my life.

CHAPTER TWENTY

↢ Beast ↣

I awake on the cold, hard floor. With no windows, I cannot tell the time. It must still be before dawn, though, since Parker has not yet returned. The others are curled up around me, using the heat from my body to derive what little warmth they can. Father's snoring and Mother's gentle wheezing bring me comfort. They could be sleeping in their own soft beds but chose to be locked down here with me.

"Are you awake, brother?" Alexander whispers.

"Yes," I reply, as softly as I can. It is still loud enough to cause both my parents to stir, but on they slumber.

"I am terribly sorry for telling the witch you did not mind being a beast. That was thoughtless of me."

"You could not have known she was a witch. She seemed so lovely."

"Perhaps, but we had been warned against strangers and odd goings-on in the woods. I should not have been so trusting, and so careless with my words. If I am to be king one day, I must think more clearly."

"Do not be so hard on yourself," I tell him. "She bewitched all of us. Remember how well I danced?"

He laughs. "Perhaps you are right. Still, I pledge to help you return to your normal, only mildly beastly self."

"I would kick you, but I do not yet know my own strength. I cannot risk hurting the future king."

He laughs and skitters across the room. "You would have to find me first."

I smile for the first time since my dance with the girl. (Or witch. Or evil fairy. Or whatever she is.) The smiling would feel better, however, if the sharp point on the tip of my nose didn't dig into my upper lip. Careful not to wake my parents, I lift my hand to my face. My nose still feels like my own, up until the time it curves downward to resemble . . . what was it? Oh, yes, a hawk. Perhaps I should be a little angrier with Alexander after all. I'm about to start taking inventory of the rest of my face when he starts shaking our parents awake.

"Parker is here!" he cries in a loud whisper. "Wake up!"

We all scramble to our feet (an act I find difficult since my sense of balance is off-kilter) and the others leave my side. I cannot tell where they are running to, but I know it is away from me.

The door creaks open, slowly at first, until it is clear I am not charging forth in an effort to escape. Light seeps in from the hallway and I glance quickly behind me, hoping against hope that I will see my family. But all I find is the empty bench lining the moldy stone wall.

Parker is not alone. The light of the lantern he is holding aloft reveals Ulmer, the bailiff, has accompanied him. I have never liked Ulmer much, but Father trusts him with the day-to-day business of running the castle. I find him to be a squirrelly little man, always darting around, his beady eyes missing nothing. If he truly were a squirrel, right now his tail would be twitching quite fiercely. I remember I am supposed to be inspiring fear, so I clench my fists and growl. He takes one look at me and backs up into the hall.

I shall have to remember not to clench my fists again, as I have once more drawn blood. Stupid nails!

"Are you not going to question him?" Parker demands. "He likely ate the royal family!"

"I DID NOT EAT ANYONE!" I bellow.

That does it. The bailiff turns and runs, the sounds of his footfalls quickly disappearing down the hall. Parker grunts in disgust and turns back to face me. Before he can say anything, I reach into my pocket and pull out the letter from Father.

"This is for you." I attempt to look both sincere and fearsome at the same time. Instead, I probably look like I need to empty my bladder. Which I do.

He takes the letter and throws it to the ground. "I am not falling for any of your tricks, Beast."

I hear a small cough behind me, but do my best not to react. Parker's eyes dart over, see nothing, and return to me. I growl and puff out my chest. In my deepest voice I say, "I suggest you take it. It is from King Silas."

"If this is a trick, I shall have you strung up in the courtyard. The loyal townsfolk shall throw rotten meat at your feet. And then the wild animals shall pick apart your bones for supper."

Parker always did have an active imagination. I do not reply. As a prince, I have never had such strong words flung my way before. I merely point to the letter.

Without taking his eyes from my face, he bends to retrieve it. "Stand back," he orders, then begins to read. His eyes widen in surprise, the occasional grunt escapes, but by the end his face smooths into a mask of grudging acceptance.

A few moments later, he is leading me through the wing of the castle where most of the bedchambers are located.

Every last person has fled from the castle, rendering it silent save for the wind whistling through the stones. Parker halts in front of a large guest room. "You shall stay here."

I shake my head. "I would rather have the room of Prince Riley."

"No, I cannot allow that. The prince does not deserve to have a beast in his private chambers."

"If my demands are well met," I promise him, "the prince will return to find his chambers just as he left them — you need not worry."

Parker glares at me but says, "Last room at the end of the hall."

"Thank you. Please see to it that a full meal is laid out in the king's private dining room as soon as possible. That is where I shall take all my meals. I do not wish to be disturbed while dining, or at any other time. If I need you, I shall find you. Thank you, that is all."

He hesitates, looking for all the world as though he would like nothing better than to see the hangman's noose around my neck. Finally, he gives one sharp nod and strides away without looking back. When I hear him reach the floor below, I lean against the wall and close my eyes. With Parker standing guard outside, and no one allowed in the castle, I shall be utterly alone. As much as I enjoy being by myself in the lab, or atop the tower roof, this is quite different.

"Please, Parker, thank you, Parker," Alexander mocks. "I am fairly certain a terrifying beast such as yourself would not be so polite."

When one's family is invisible, I suppose *feeling* alone and actually *being* alone are two very different things. I growl. "We are going to have to get you a collar with a bell."

"You are the one who needs a collar," he replies. "I believe you are starting to shed."

"Is that so? At least I still cast a shadow."

"Stop teasing each other," Mother scolds.

"You did an excellent job, Riley," Father says, patting my arm. It feels strange watching the fur ripple under his invisible hand. "If Parker follows his orders," he continues, "we may be able to live comfortably while —"

A scraping sound from somewhere down the hall stops Father from finishing his thought.

"That came from your chambers," Mother whispers shakily. It takes a lot to shake up the queen.

I nod, not daring to speak. My heart speeds up as I creep down the hall. I have little doubt that I shall find the witch girl awaiting me, ready to add me to her collection since my other option is hopeless. With a deep breath, I fling open the door.

"You are home early from the ball, Prince Riley," Godfrey says, a towel slung over his shoulder. "Are you ready for your bath?"

CHAPTER TWENTY-ONE

∽ Beauty ᔰ

"How do you know my name?" I ask the dark-haired girl. She looks vaguely familiar now. Perhaps she used to live near my old house?

"Beauty!" the girl says in an exasperated tone. "It is me! Veronica!"

My eyes widen as the image of white-haired Veronica adjusts into this one. "But how . . . why . . ."

She laughs now. "'Twas your sister's idea, actually."

"Clarissa did this to you?" No doubt the note of horror in my voice is evident. One cannot go around changing a child's hair color and expect to keep their job. My stomach knots into a ball.

"Master Werlin applied the dye," she says, "but Clarissa had the idea of it. I went to the shop to see you this morn, and Clarissa said that my hair is so bright that it will catch the eye of everyone we pass. She said that the point of a quest is to blend into the crowd in order to find the information we need."

"Clarissa said that?"

Veronica nods. "Well, I believe her exact words were: 'You should not have hair that can be spotted from a rooftop thirty miles away.' And she was right! Master Werlin agreed to dye it. He mixed chestnut bark with some foul-smelling paste, put it all over my head, and here I am."

Relieved that Clarissa (and, by association, *me*) still has a job, I stand back to get a good look. "Well, you certainly appear different." She still has that fairy quality, the sharp features, the tiny frame, but without the white hair, she looks a lot more earthbound, more like any other child one might see on the street. I can see the sense in it, though. I feel a touch of pride that Clarissa saw the truth of it first, before Veronica herself.

"By the way," she says, "a large chunk of Clarissa's hair is now green."

"Did you say 'green'?"

She nods. "Quite a bright green, in fact."

I sigh. I hope it washes out easily, or else Papa will not be pleased.

"Anyway," Veronica says, pulling a rolled-up piece of parchment from a large pouch across her shoulder. "I came to the shop to give you the list of supplies you will need for our quest."

I put down the bags of supplies in my arms, and she hands me the scroll. The list is written in a neat but childish hand, on very soft parchment, something only a well-off person could afford. As a lover of books and paper, I find myself running my hands over it, feeling its smoothness. She is watching me with curiosity.

"You seem more interested in my paper than in the words on it."

"My father is a seller of books," I explain. "Or he was, anyway, before the fire. Sometimes, if he could not sell one of his books, he would let me take it apart. Then I would use the bindings to make new books." My mind flits back to the shelf in my old room, lined with books of my own making. I could spend hours lacing the pages together, gluing on the spines, decorating the covers.

Veronica waves her hand before my face, bringing my attention back. "This paper is of the highest quality," I tell her. "I have rarely seen its equal."

"One of the scribes at the monastery gave me a few pieces. He spends all day in that damp, dreary room, and I think he is happy for my company. Once he even let me copy a few words onto the page he was working on."

Her comment reminds me of the fact that she lives at the monastery, apart from her beloved grandfather. "The scribe sounds kind," I say, not knowing what else to say. "Are all the monks like that?"

She shakes her head. "They are not *un*kind, of course. They mostly keep to themselves. Having a child underfoot is not always looked upon as a positive thing. And a girl child, at that."

I do not want to press her further, so I hold up the paper to read her list.

A traveling cloak, thick-soled boots, breeches, a dress, tunics, thick stockings, knife, spoon, bowl, sleep sack, towel, notebook, ink, quill, sickness tablets, canteen, iron or brass cooking pot, dried and salted meats, dried fruits, nuts, beans, and a compass. I do not even know what that is.

I hand her back the paper. "I have none of these things."

"None?"

"Nothing but the boots on my feet." We both look down. I am embarrassed to see the nail of my left big toe, visible through the worn leather. All the walking to and from the new cottage has done much damage. "I am sorry," I tell her. "When our house burned down, we lost most everything. I understand if you want to take someone else." The relief I feel when she shakes her head makes me realize how badly I need the freedom of this quest, even if it is only temporary.

"I told you I would provide what you need," she says, "and I shall." She picks up Master Werlin's bags and sticks them inside the shop. "Come. Let us go do some shopping."

I hesitate. If Clarissa could manage to color her hair green in only an hour, perhaps I should not leave her much longer.

"She will be fine," Veronica says, reading my mind. I let her pull me toward the market.

Turns out "some shopping" really means *let us buy everything on the list with a seemingly endless supply of coin*. I follow her from booth to booth as she loads us up with everything from hats to socks to a canteen to dried beef. "From where does all your money come?" I ask as she hands an entire pound to the cobbler without so much as a whimper.

In return he hands her a pair of boots. She piles them on top of my already full arms and mumbles something about her great-grandfather being a successful ship merchant who found unique objects and sold them for triple the price. I would pay more attention, but I am distracted by the boots. I have never owned boots as fine as these. Not that I care much for such fancy things, but the sturdy wooden soles and the thick leather will make the journey much easier.

We return to the shop to find Master Werlin covered from head to toe in a thick white powder. Clarissa is frantically rinsing out a rag in the sink. A green stripe runs the length of her hair. "I already apologized six times," she says. "I promise I shall never use the mixer again."

Veronica and I exchange a look.

"Do not even ask," the apothecary warns.

When Clarissa sees all the clothes and supplies in our arms, her eyes almost fly out of her head. She tosses Master Werlin the rag and runs over to us. "What have you got there?" She reaches out for the nearest item, a woolen tunic.

"Just a moment," I say, and plop it all down on the floor. Veronica adds the contents of her arms to the pile. Clarissa sits on her knees and pulls one item after the other off the floor. I watch her feeling the materials, running her hands over their surfaces in the same way I did to the fine parchment. My heart softens. She should be in our old house, surrounded by the things that made her happy. She should be going to parties and trying to find her true love, not stuck here trying to understand how different chemicals and minerals can either harm or heal depending on how you handle them. And yet she is trying so hard to hold it all together. Green stripe and powder-covered apothecary notwithstanding.

"Here," Veronica says, pulling a soft blue cloak from the pile. "This is for you. I thought it matched your eyes."

Clarissa takes it and looks up at her in surprise. "Truly?"

Veronica nods.

Clarissa swings the cloak around her shoulders and slips the button through the loop. She twirls around, beaming.

My eyes get glassy and I have to look away. "Thank you," I mouth to Veronica. She waves my thank-you away with a flick of her hand.

"I shall bring a large enough pack from Grandfather's house tomorrow," Veronica says. Without so much as a good-bye, she pushes through the door. She is halfway down the road before I catch up with her.

"I want to thank you properly."

"It was nothing," she says, stepping carefully over the mess a horse has left in the middle of the road. "I knew your sister would fancy the cloak."

I fall into step beside her. "Not just that. Thank you for all of it. I promise I will return everything. Except for the food, of course. That likely will not make it past the trip."

She shakes her head. "Everything is yours to keep."

"Truly?" I ask, reaching out to touch her arm. "But how could I ever repay you?"

She stops then, and looks up at me. I notice for the first time how dark and intense her brown eyes are. "You can repay me," she says in her usual matter-of-fact way, "by helping me find my crystal."

"Your crystal?" I repeat, looking on the ground by our feet. I am good at spotting small objects but do not see anything shiny in the dry dirt. "Did you lose it just now?"

She shakes her head and starts walking again. For a girl with short legs, she truly is speedy. I hurry alongside her.

"The crystal is pink," she explains. "The size and shape of a strawberry. I was two years of age when last I held it. It is valuable beyond measure. Our quest is to find it."

I nearly trip over my feet. "We are searching for a price-less *stone*? I thought we were trying to find your mother."

She stops and fixes those eyes on me again. "If we find the crystal, we will find my mother."

CHAPTER TWENTY-TWO

↤ Beast ↦

Godfrey! I assumed everyone had run last night, even him. After all, a monster had entered the castle. One does not usually stick around to see what happens next. "Er, one moment, Godfrey." I back out of the room and close the door. "What should I do?" I whisper to the seemingly empty hall. "If he sees me like this, it would be the end of him. He is not a young man."

"He is very nearly blind," Alexander says. "Mayhap he will not notice?"

"I think he will notice when he tries to dress me and all my clothes are ten times too small!"

"You must tell Godfrey you are not in need of his services anymore," Father says, his voice breaking. "Seeing you this way would distress him too greatly."

I cross my arms. "He has been with our family forever. I cannot send him away."

The door behind me creaks open to reveal Godfrey, holding the towel and a ball of lavender soap. "Indeed, Prince Riley, you cannot."

I hear my family scramble out of the way as Godfrey steps into the hallway.

"There is no need to hide," he says loudly. "I know you are all here."

No one replies.

"I can hear through walls, remember? I know what is going on."

"You . . . you do?" I ask.

"Your voice is deeper, true." He looks directly at me, squints, and gives me a once-over. "You have grown considerably taller. And quite a bit wider." He reaches up to touch my head, then lets his hand trail down my arm. "And quite a bit more hairy."

"Indeed I have," I reply, surprised. "Are you not frightened? An evil magic is afoot, and I am quite the beast. If you could see better, you might run from me like everyone else."

"I am old," he replies with a shrug. "I have seen many things, including some that cannot readily be explained. I am your chamberlain. I always have been, and I always shall be."

Tears sting my eyes. "Thank you, Godfrey." I want to thank him for still treating me like a person, but I am not so good with my words.

He leans around me and squints down the hall. "I can hear you breathing, King Silas. And the queen and Prince Alexander, too. Where are you hiding?"

Since there is no use pretending with him, I say, "Actually, Godfrey, they are not hiding at all. They are right beside me."

He shakes his head. "I may see most poorly, sire, but even I can tell the hallway is empty besides you and me."

"'Tis true, I'm afraid," Mother says. "We can see ourselves but are invisible to everyone else." Godfrey twists first to the left, then the right, then behind him. Seeing nothing, he turns in all directions again. Before he can comment on this unexpected development, Mother's voice hardens. "Alexander! Put your vest back on!"

"But why? No one can see us!"

"*I* can see you. It is not proper. You are still a prince!"

I can't help but smile as Alexander grumbles.

"I am sorry, Prince Riley," Godfrey says, thrusting my towel and soap at me. "But I cannot stay in these circumstances. This is a deep, old magic, and I must not be around it."

My heart sinks. Having Godfrey here made everything a little less frightening.

"Dearest Godfrey," Father says, sadness lacing his voice, "we understand. We never meant to get you involved. We shall miss —"

"I am merely jesting with you all, sire," Godfrey says in the general direction of where Father's voice came from. "My place is at your side."

Father laughs his big booming laugh. "Good one, old man."

Godfrey chuckles. "I could not have been your chamberlain for all those years without picking up a trick or two."

"I could eat you, you know," I tell him, handing him back the towel and soap. "I have been motivated by less."

Behind me, Father chuckles.

"I assure you," Godfrey says, "I would be quite stringy and bland. Come, let us get you washed up and put some real food into your ample belly."

I follow him back into my chambers, and hear the rest of my family trail behind. I stop. Alexander bumps into me. "Ow! You are quite a bit harder than you used to be. It's like walking into a wall!"

"We must have some ground rules," I proclaim. "Just because you are invisible does not mean I need to have you sharing my bath. Or sneaking up on me. There is such a thing as privacy."

"He is correct, of course," Father says. "As tempting as it is to play around, we must be sure to make our presence known to Riley and Godfrey at all times. Else they would be at a terrible disadvantage."

"Agreed," Mother says. "We shall announce our presence upon entering a room, unless a stranger is in the midst."

"Where is the fun in that?" Alexander asks.

Ignoring him, I nod. "Thank you for the courtesy. In return I shall refrain from eating all of you for supper."

"Your bark is worse than your bite," Alexander teases.

"Try me," I reply.

"Come, Prince," Godfrey says, leading me over to the tub in the corner of the room. "You smell a bit . . . how shall I put it . . . *ripe*."

I am about to comment on that remark, when I approach the mirror and catch sight of my reflection. For the second time in two days, I am shocked at what I see in the glass.

I had thought being dressed like a roasted pig with vegetables was bad. This is *so much worse*.

CHAPTER TWENTY-THREE

∽ Beauty ∾

I can hear the monks chanting their morning prayers while we are still half a block from the monastery. I used to love hearing them sing when I was younger. I am tempted to close my eyes and listen now, but time is of the essence. We enter the courtyard to find the others already gathered.

Handsome is wearing a large pack looped over both shoulders, a wide-brimmed hat, and a canteen attached to his belt. He certainly looks ready to travel. I had to convince Papa that it would not be practical to wear a dress, and he had finally relented. I am pleased to see that Veronica is in breeches, too.

Veronica's grandfather and Papa shake hands. Clarissa gives me a tight hug, engulfing me in her new cloak. She even wears it to sleep. "Be safe," she says. "Have fun, make friends, and bring me something. A nice hat, perhaps. I could use a hat."

I laugh. "You will have a whole pound a week to buy a hat. You could buy six hats for that."

She grins. "You are right! I forgot."

"If you do not get fired, that is."

She pretends to pout. "I am much more careful now."

This is true. Yesterday, she did not set a single thing ablaze, nor turn anything (or anyone) a different color.

Although it *had* taken Master Werlin an entire morning to figure out the correct combination of oils and minerals to get the green color from her hair.

"Thank you for taking over my job until I get back," I tell her. "It is very kind of you."

"I enjoy it," she insists. "It makes me feel useful."

"Perchance the boy of your dreams will come into the store while I am gone."

She smiles. "If he does, I shall do my best not to give him an ointment to make his hair fall out."

"That sounds wise." I hug her again until Papa pulls me aside.

"Beauty, I know you are not a quitter, well, except for a job or two, but if you do not feel safe at any point, I want you to come home."

"I know, Papa. But I gave my word that I would see this through."

He reaches for my hand. "If it is not safe for you, it will not be safe for the little girl, either. It may fall to you to convince her of that."

I nod. He is right. Perhaps that is another reason her grandfather chose me.

"I am glad Handsome will be there," Papa says, glancing over at him. "He will protect you both."

"I am glad, too," I reply. I reach up to touch my mother's old locket, which I had hung around my neck before leaving the house. Perhaps somehow she is protecting me, too.

"We must get started," Veronica says, appearing at my side.

Papa gives me one last hug. "Send word if you can."

"I will. Do not worry about me."

He nods, but I can tell by the anxious way he is twisting his hat in his hands that he is going to worry no matter what.

When everyone else has gone, Handsome reaches into his pocket and pulls out what I thought was a pocket watch. Instead, it has a single black arrow, bobbing around in what looks like water. The letters N, E, S, and W are spaced evenly around the edges. He holds it faceup in front of him, then shifts his feet until the arrow points at the N. "All right, I have found north. Shall we set out?"

Veronica shakes her head. "We do not need the compass yet. We have one last thing to attend to here."

"Here where?" Handsome asks.

"Here," she repeats. "At the monastery. In the library."

We do not move. Outsiders simply do not go into the monastery library.

She pushes our bags with her feet until they are nearly hidden by a bunch of shrubs behind the bench. "Come."

"I have not lived in this town long," Handsome says, "but I do not think we are supposed to go in there."

"I *have* lived here long," I say, "and I *know* we are not supposed to."

"It will be fine," Veronica promises. "You are with me." She heads to the front door. We have no choice but to follow.

I turn to Handsome. "I have a feeling this will not be the last time she will be leading us into places we are not supposed to go."

"No doubt. We might as well get used to it."

Inside, the front entryway is very simple. Stone and wood, simple religious decorations hanging from the walls, along with robes from metal hooks. It feels drafty, although

I can see no windows. Definitely not the cheeriest place for a young girl to grow up.

The chanting is much louder from inside. I do not see any monks milling about, so they must all be in the service.

"Take this," she says, tossing a robe to each of us.

We grab for them before they hit the ground. "What do we need these for?" Handsome asks.

"Just put them on."

"You're the boss," he says, slipping it over his head. I do the same. Mine is too long and drags along the stone floor.

"Now flip up the hoods."

We flip. Again, mine is too large and covers most of my face. When I point this out, Veronica says, "Good. We do not want them to know you are a girl."

Before I can ask why, she takes off around a corner.

Handsome groans. "We have not even traveled ten yards and I already want to leave her behind."

I laugh. "Remember, we are doing this to help her."

He grumbles but hurries along behind me. We catch up with her outside a large wooden door. A symbol of a book inlaid with white marble is carved into it. I cannot help tracing it with my finger.

"Do not speak if anyone is inside," Veronica warns. "I shall answer in your stead."

"Wait," Handsome says, reaching out for her. His arm gets caught under his robe. "Can't you tell us what we're doing here?"

"We do not have time for questions," she replies. "Services will end any moment."

Before either of us can ask what we are doing, she pushes us through the door, slips in behind, and then shuts it right away. The library looks no different from what we have seen so far, other than the long tables and shelves of books. I have seen paintings of great libraries, with marble floors and chandeliers and stained-glass windows. This is not one of them. But the stacks are full, and the books lend a slight air of coziness to the room.

A quick glance ensures us we are alone in the room. "What are we doing here?" Handsome asks. "If you forgot to pack a book, could you not have retrieved it on your own?"

She shakes her head. "I am not allowed in here. Only monks are."

Before I can point out that we are not actually monks, the door swings open. Handsome and I instinctively tug on our hoods to hide our faces even more.

"Friar Tal," Veronica says, hurrying over to the wide man in the brown robe. "These two monks from the next parish over requested to see our library. Everyone was in the service, so I hope you do not mind that I led them here."

"Not at all, child," he says, patting her head. "What else could you have done?"

"They have taken a vow of silence," she adds.

The monk looks over at us. We bow our heads in greeting but do not look up.

"I just came in for an extra prayer book," he says. "But I shall return in a few moments and will help them find what they need."

"Thank you," she says.

He ruffles her hair. I am glad to see the kindness he shows her. Even when she is lying.

When the door clicks shut behind him, she says, "We must be gone before he returns." She runs past us and begins pulling books off the shelves, then shoving them back in.

"Veronica," I say, reaching for her arm. Of course, mine gets caught inside my robe, too. "What are you looking for? We cannot help you unless you tell us."

"A book," she replies, continuing her frantic search.

"Obviously. But what book?"

"I do not know for certain," she admits. "Look for a dark blue cover, leather I am guessing, with a symbol of a cat on it."

"Does it have a title?" I ask.

"If it does, I do not know it."

We split up and each start at a different spot. I knew the monks had a lot of books, but I did not know they had so many fine ones. A few I even recognize from Papa's collection. Perhaps by the time I return from the quest, his business will have picked up again. I know it vexes him greatly.

I linger too long over a particularly beautiful book with metal hinges and rose quartz encrusted on the cover. "Beauty!" Veronica hisses from the next shelf over. "Keep looking!"

"Sorry," I mutter, quickly moving along to a section of newer books. These have pages made of bark instead of vellum or parchment. It is odd that either a goat or a sheep or a tree has to give its life so people can read. Papa has sold a few books with cotton pages, but they are rare and hard to come by.

"I think I found it!" Handsome says, probably too loudly for Veronica's comfort.

He holds up a slim volume. As I get closer, I see the words *How to Rid Your Home of Mice* engraved in gold lettering across the cover. An unmistakable drawing of a cat lies beneath the title.

"Sounds like a fascinating book," Handsome jokes.

Veronica snatches it from his hand. "This is it! Now let us be gone from here." She pushes open the door and the sound of singing returns.

We only make it halfway to the entry hall when the song ends and a loud shuffling sound begins to fill the hallway we just passed.

Veronica clutches the book to her chest. "You must hide me," she says, panic in her eyes.

Handsome does not pause. He swoops her under his robe, where she steps up onto his feet. He closes the robe around her so that only her eyes are visible. With our hoods down, we shuffle toward the door. I can hear the hallway filling behind us, but we do not stop until we have shut the door behind us.

Handsome grabs all of our bags from behind the hedge. We run at top speed down the road, through the alley that runs behind the bathhouse, and into the woods at the northern tip of the village. I can see he has that compass out again, and is holding it in front of him as he guides us through the woods, the bags bouncing against his back in a way that looks most uncomfortable. Even though I am not quite sure what just happened, or why we are running away from the very place Veronica calls home, it still feels good to run at all.

Finally, Handsome signals we have gone far enough, and my heart slowly stops pounding. We are deep into the woods now, in an area I do not recognize. I flip back my hood. Panting, I ask, "Did we, or did we not, just steal a book from the monastery?"

Veronica nods, plopping down on a log. "We did."

"And why, exactly, did we do that?" Handsome asks, tossing the bags off his back and sitting beside her.

"Because we need it."

"Surely they would have lent it to you," I point out. "You said you have friends amongst them."

She shakes her head. "I could not have asked. Not for this one."

"Why?" Handsome asks. "They do not want you to learn how to rid your house of mice?"

She rolls her eyes. "The book is not really about that."

"No?" I look at her, confused. "What is it, then?"

She pulls it out from under her tunic, where she had tucked it during our escape. She looks both ways, but no one, of course, is near. Not for many miles. She gathers us close anyway, and whispers, "Inside this book lies a map. Or at least that is what I have long hoped."

"I already have maps of the surrounding villages," Handsome says. "Safe paths through the forests, locations of inns, all that. Your grandfather gave them to me."

Veronica shakes her head. "This would be a different kind of map. My mother hid that book in the monastery for safekeeping. She swore me not to retrieve it until I was ready to use it."

We both look at her in surprise.

"She told me not to tell anyone, not even Grandfather or the monks. It is the last thing she said to me before she left."

We are silent for a moment, and then Handsome says, "Well, let's see it, then, shall we?"

Veronica takes a deep breath, unwinds the leather cord around the book, and opens the front cover. The title repeats again on the first page. She flips through pages of text and the occasional illustration of a cat catching a mouse by various methods. When she reaches the end, she starts again.

Then she holds the book by the covers and shakes it. Only dust and two long-dead beetles fall from the pages.

She throws the book to the ground, where it skids to a stop under some rotting leaves. "Nothing! Or else someone has taken it already! We stole the book from the monks for nothing!" She storms off, stomping her boots and flailing her arms.

"Um, do you think we should point out that we also stole two robes?" Handsome asks, lifting up the edges of the robes we both still wear.

"We may want to wait until she calms down."

Veronica storms past us again, kicking up leaves and dirt and muttering swears normally not heard outside of an ale-house at closing time.

"And when do you think that will be?" Handsome asks, eyeing her warily.

"Hopefully before nightfall. I do not relish sleeping in the woods."

Finally, Veronica's anger and frustration turn into quiet tears. Handsome scoops her up into his arms, where she soon falls asleep. I slip the discarded book into my own bag, then strap both my pack and hers around my shoulders. Onward through the woods we trudge. Map or no map, we are on a quest. And we are not quitters.

CHAPTER TWENTY-FOUR

← Beast →

Three days have passed since I was turned into the beast, and I have left my room only to eat. I have not even visited my lab, or the library, or the tallest tower to gaze at the heavens. Mother says I am depressed and has instructed everyone to "give me time to adjust to the shock." I do not know that one can ever adjust to the shock of looking into the mirror and seeing a wholly unfamiliar — and utterly beastlike — face staring back.

Before I saw myself in the glass, I had imagined that although my facial features were changed, I still resembled my old self. But that is not the case. Mother swears that when I smile, the old me comes across. But I have not smiled, so I cannot attest to the truth of that.

Meals have been very silent occasions. My family cannot talk, of course, since although the door to where we eat is closed, the occasional servant scampers in or out to clear the plates. Parker must be paying them a goodly sum to do this job. Never has one of them looked me in the eye, or questioned why I wanted so many plates and ate so quickly. I am certain they never guessed they were actually feeding four people.

Even Godfrey has left me alone, coming in only to bring water or the occasional book that goes unread on my nightstand. When he alerted Parker that Godfrey would be staying,

Parker tried to get him to change his mind. But Godfrey stood firm, declaring that he would not feel right if Prince Riley were to return home to the castle only to find him gone. He would serve the beast in the hopes of learning more of the royal family's whereabouts. Parker finally relented, loading Godfrey's arms full of enough weapons to hold off a small army. They lie piled in a corner of my chambers.

The door creaks open. "It is only me," Mother announces. She and Father have held good to their word, always making their presence known. Alexander has been less obedient. Once he snuck up behind me at the dinner table and stuck a celery stalk into my ear. Even Father admonished him for that.

I force myself to open my eyes and rub the sleep out of them. I no longer scratch myself by mistake, thanks to the gloves I now wear at all times. Mother tried cutting the long nails, but they grew right back. Same with shaving the fur off my arms, cutting my wild mane, or trimming my bushy eyebrows.

My bed groans as I push myself into a sitting position. I have already broken two beds. We have reinforced this one with extra wood, but I still fear I may wind up crashing through it.

"Is it time for breakfast already?" I glance out the window and see that the sun has only just risen. Concern floods me. "Is everything all right? Has something happened?"

The bed creaks as Mother sits down and takes my gloved hand in hers. "We are fine, do not worry. You will shortly have company, however."

I quickly draw the blanket up to my chest. "Company? But I thought no one is supposed to see me like this."

"Do not be nervous. It is only the castle doctor. Godfrey has gone to fetch him from his home in the village. He will warn the doctor to uphold the same level of respect and confidentiality that he would give a real member of the royal family."

I am less than encouraged at this news. "But what if he gives me poison in the guise of medicine? I am certain no one would punish him for ridding the kingdom of the fearsome beast."

"He shall not give you poison," she promises. "We will be certain of that. Our hope is that he knows of some remedy for your, er, situation. Also, I have sewn you some proper attire. I am no seamstress, and have no wish to use a needle ever again, but they shall do for now." Mother places a heavy pile of clothes on top of my lap. As they leave her hands, they fade into view. It has been three days, but I have not gotten used to that sight. Early on, Father had tried to amuse me by having me guess what random object he would "pull from the air" next, but even that could not make me feel better.

"All right," I tell her. "I shall hope for the best. Thank you for the clothes."

She chuckles and pats my leg before standing up. "'Tis good that you cannot see the bandages on my fingers."

We feared it would be too hard to explain to the doctor why the beast chose to live in *my* room instead of the much grander chambers of my parents, so I am now awaiting his arrival in the library. It feels a lifetime ago that I last hid in here, wearing that horrid Harvest Ball outfit. My invisible family is hiding somewhere amongst the rows of books. I haven't been able to focus on reading since my transformation, but seeing all these books now is truly making me miss it. The shelves are full of handsome leather- and velvet-bound books, some with clasps of silver, some tied closed with threads of fine silk. A yellow sun and white moon dance in the colored-glass windowpane, and I stand anxiously beside it. Or should I say, above it, since I am now taller than the top of the window.

The doctor, who has attended me since the day of my birth, takes one look at me now and backs away until he is up against the farthest bookshelf. The handle of the leather case he always carries slips from his hand, sending it thumping to the ground. He wraps his crimson cloak tight around his large belly and stares. I have never seen this usually arrogant and decisive man quiver before any challenge in the past. Between Alexander and me, we have presented him with all manner of rashes, coughs, broken bones, and wounds so deep we feared they would never stop bleeding. He always managed to heal us, or at least he usually did not make us worse. Probably I should not be so hard on him. I doubt "How to Cure a Beast" was taught in his medical texts.

"I had heard the rumors of a beast in the castle," he says, his voice cautious. "I had thought the tales exaggerated. I see they were not."

"He will not hurt you," Godfrey assures him. "He asks only that you try to restore him."

The doctor's eyes widen. "Restore him? Restore him to what? Did he used to be a *person*? Who is he?" He inches a bit closer to me.

Godfrey makes a sound, then closes his mouth. I can tell he is worried that he has said too much. I clear my throat and the doctor's attention snaps back to me. I make my voice as deep as possible so he does not recognize it. "I hail from a faraway land and have hidden away in this castle for reasons of my own. I mean you no harm, but I do demand that you do everything in your power to heal me. To un-beastify me, as it were."

The doctor inches closer. "If I give you aid, will the royal family be returned safely?"

I hesitate, not sure I can promise to restore the others to the visible world. The doctor picks up his bag and turns to leave. "Wait. I can promise you they will be unharmed. That will have to suffice."

The doctor pauses. "I suppose if I can un-beastify a beast, my name will be known far and wide. I might even gain a position in a kingdom much larger and more presti-gious than this one."

Across the room, a book falls off the shelf, and we all jump. I have no doubt one of my family members did not approve of the doctor's comment. Godfrey hurries over to replace the book.

"That is certainly true," I am quick to reply, "and I will personally sing your praises far and wide as I travel the world." I almost choke on those last words, for I have no doubt that if this ordeal ever ends, Mother will not let me stray farther than the grounds of the castle for many years to come.

"I shall do my best," the doctor says, flipping open his medical case. He directs me to lie down on the large rug in the center of the library floor. Godfrey places a pillow from the couch under my head.

The doctor kneels down beside me and inspects my body from head to foot. "Never seen anything akin to this," he says over and over. "Hair like a lion's mane! A nose like a hawk! How truly bizarre."

"Yes, yes," I say, "I know. I am a one-of-a-kind monster. Can we move on with the healing, please?"

With one last lingering gaze at my long fingernails, he reaches into his bag and pulls out his astrolabe. It is not as fine as my own, but I am used to him consulting the stars before determining his healing method. "If I were here at night, I would check the stars' positions for you," he says, "although I am not sure if your kind is even governed by the movement of the stars."

I bristle at being referred to as "your kind," but I say nothing. He leans over and tentatively lays the back of his palm against my forehead.

"You feel a bit feverish. I shall give you something to lessen it."

Before I can explain that all this hair makes me hot, he has reached into his bag and pulled out a tin of lemon balm. He rubs it on my forehead, which quickly begins to tingle. It smells pleasant enough, although my entire face is now beginning to sweat. What is *in* that stuff? He reaches back into his bag and fishes around for another moment. The sweating worsens. Finally, he pulls out a glass jar filled with, *gulp*, leeches!

"This will not hurt," he says, pulling off the lid. The leeches twist and turn in the jar, causing my stomach to do the same.

"Well, it will not hurt *much*," he amends his statement. "The leeches will suck out the impure blood. When your humors are balanced, you shall be healed. Hopefully."

I shut my eyes tight as he places the leeches on my arms and legs. Fortunately (or unfortunately), only my face is pouring water, so the leeches have no trouble holding fast. I grimace, expecting the usual discomfort. But my skin must be much thicker than it used to be, for it truly does not hurt at all. I open one eye and peek down at my arm. Three leeches suck greedily from spots between the patches of fur. Their once lean and flat bodies grow round and plump as I watch. In fact, the leeches are filling up so quickly, they lose their hold on my body and begin to fall off.

"Er, is that supposed to happen?" I ask.

The doctor reaches to the floor and grasps one between his thumb and forefinger. He places it in his palm, where it immediately twitches its little sucker things and rolls over, dead. He bounces it in his palm. It remains dead. "Fascinating!"

I have a hard time agreeing with that assessment.

"It should take *hours* to fill up," he says, picking the rest of the dead leeches from the rug. "Perhaps I need larger ones."

I sit up. "Perhaps we need to try something else."

"How are your bowels?" he asks.

My face grows even hotter at his question. I have to push the now-stringy and wet mane of hair from my eyes. "Excuse me?"

From the back of the room I swear I hear Alexander stifling a laugh.

"Your bowels," he repeats. "And your urine?"

I am used to the doctor asking me these questions when I am ill, but I am not usually surrounded by my entire family at the time. Will the humiliations never end? "They are fine, I guess."

"All right, then." He begins repacking his bag. "I shall visit the apothecary in the village and return tomorrow with a special elixir. It may not taste very good going down, but if you can keep it in for even a few moments, it just might work."

I nod, although the thought of swallowing one of his stomach-turning concoctions does not thrill me. Alexander has a theory that the worse it tastes, the better it works. We shall see.

Godfrey escorts the doctor back downstairs.

"You have earned a new title," Alexander says, suddenly close by my side. "Prince Riley, Leech Killer."

I growl as I wipe the sticky balm off my forehead with the sleeve of my shirt. "When you expect it least, I shall sit on you."

"And how do you expect to find me?" he teases.

"Easy. I shall simply follow the stench of the sausage you ate for breakfast."

Alexander and I start playfully pushing each other like we used to when we were kids. Or more accurately, I am pushing him, while he cannot budge me an inch.

"Well," Father says to Mother as we tumble past them, "at least he's out of bed."

CHAPTER TWENTY-FIVE

∽ Beauty ∾

The path through the northern woods takes us to a small clearing, ringed with apple trees. I immediately recognize the mermaid fountain in the center of the clearing. The setting sun turns the water a brilliant orange. Papa brought us to this town once to pick up a shipment of books. I had said the fountain seemed a waste of water, and he said that art was never a waste. This had surprised me coming from him, since I have never seen him crack a book open other than to inspect it for sale. But since then I have always stopped to admire fine craftsmanship when I come across it.

We rest on the low stone wall around the fountain and watch the water rush from the mermaid's mouth. Carved from some kind of white stone, she appears to rise out of the sea, the waves foaming beneath her.

"It is lovely," Handsome says. "I have not seen its equal."

"Nor I," Veronica says. These are the first words she has said since discovering the map was missing from the book. Even when we had stopped for lunch she sat by herself, eating from her pack in silence. Handsome had asked what her plan was, now that she did not have the map to guide her. But in response she had just turned her back. We decided it best to keep heading north, since that is how we started out. This is the first town we have come to.

"I visited this spot with my father once," I tell them. "He said the fountain was here before the town was even built."

"How is that possible?" asks Handsome. "Who would have built it, then?"

I shake my head. "He did not know."

"I do," Veronica says softly. "I know who built it." She leans forward in that dramatic way of hers and says, "The fairies."

"The fairies?" Handsome repeats. "That truly is something." I can tell he is trying to keep the doubt from his voice. He does not believe in that stuff any more than I.

Veronica reaches into the fountain and lets her hand trail through the water. "Grandfather says carving statues is a favorite hobby of fairies."

"I did not realize fairies had hobbies," I say, keeping my eyes away from Handsome for fear he will make me laugh.

"Oh, yes," she replies. "And they like to dance."

"Like this?" Handsome says, grabbing Veronica's hands. He starts twirling her around the fountain, across the rough stones with the weeds growing up between them. She tries to pull away at first, but he holds firm. I start clapping to the soundless music, and eventually she gives in and allows herself to dance along with him. At one point he stops, but she keeps going. Around and around the fountain she dances, such a tiny little thing, so graceful. Her feet barely graze the ground as she bends and twirls. As she passes me, I see her eyes are closed.

Handsome sits beside me and we watch together. "How is she not hitting the sides of the wall?" I whisper.

"I do not know," he says, his voice hushed, too. "I did not know she could dance like that."

"I did not know *anyone* could dance like that." Faster and faster she goes, her brown hair whipping around her head. Then she suddenly bumps right into the side of the fountain, bounces off, and lands on her bottom. Handsome and I jump up to help her, but she pushes our hands away.

"Are you hurt?" I ask. "Master Werlin gave me a supply of ointments and bandages."

"I am fine," she says, standing up and dusting herself off. "Let us be on our way. I want to settle at an inn before suppertime."

We each take our own packs this time, although we both offer to help Veronica with hers. As Handsome's compass leads us into town, I turn to Veronica. "You never mentioned you could dance like that."

"I cannot dance," she replies.

"Pish-posh!" I say, which is one of Clarissa's favorite expressions. "I have never seen anyone dance as well as you."

She grunts. "Then you really must get out more."

"You do not accept compliments well, do you?"

She shrugs. "Grandfather is the only one to compliment me. And he loves me, so it is hard to take his words as truth."

"Well, I am not even certain I *like* you, let alone love you, so you can trust my words."

The corners of her mouth twitch into a smile.

As we approach the main street, more people appear. They look us up and down but do not seem surprised to see us. As though reading my mind, Handsome says, "This town is on the trade route between two larger villages. They are used to strangers here."

Men and women shout out as we pass. "Best eel in town! New shoes! Hair ribbons!" We pass them all by, although I would not have minded some fruit. I stop to admire a particularly bright red apple, but Veronica drags me away by my elbow.

We look up at the signs above the shops until we find the one with a picture of a bed. "Here we are," Handsome says. "The Welcome Inn."

Papa had warned me that innkeepers were a slippery lot. *"They will promise you a room worthy of a palace, but it will turn out to be nothing more than a wooden plank on the floor, next to twenty others."* He also made me promise to insist on a room with a lock, and never to tell anyone what room we are assigned. He gave me a list of a few inns to avoid at all costs. *"Taking your chances with the bandits in the woods would be a safer bet."* But a few received passable marks, including The Welcome Inn.

We find the portly innkeeper behind a large desk. He is adding up a pile of coin. It seems dangerous to me to have so much money lying about like that. I take a step closer and hear a growl behind me. A very large (VERY LARGE) man wags his finger *no* at me. I step back again. Now I see why the innkeeper is not worried.

When he is done counting, he slips it all into a pouch around his waist, and cinches it closed. "What can I do for you children this fine eve?"

Handsome steps forward. "My, er, *cousins* and I would like a room, if you please."

I step up beside him. "My father, Alistair, is the bookseller from the village on the south side of the woods. He said you would know him and that you would give us the best room in the inn."

The man smiles. He is missing quite a few teeth. "How is old Alistair? Fallen on hard times, last I heard."

I nod. "He is doing his best."

"Book business is a tough one," the innkeeper says. "Can't stand reading myself." He gestures with his thumb to the huge bodyguard. "Now, Flavian here, he cannot get enough of books. Always got his nose in one."

We look at Flavian in surprise. He just grunts and pulls out a small book of poetry from his pocket. The book practically disappears in his huge hands. Flavian seems a very fancy name for a man with a shaved head and a hoop earring, but who am I to judge whether a name fits a person?

The innkeeper holds out his hand. "For three shillings you can have the best room I got and dinner before you turn in."

Veronica crosses her arms. "How much is the worst room?"

He winks. "Three shillings."

"Then what is the difference between the best room and the worst room?" she asks.

"Well, those who don't mind a little lice and fleas take the worst room."

Veronica drops three shillings into the innkeeper's palm. "Best, please."

After a dinner of weak vegetable stew that did not fill any of our bellies, we settle onto our pallets of straw. The thin blanket underneath me does little to protect my back from the pointy edges. While the room is tiny and damp, and the ceiling is so low that it grazes the top of Handsome's head, it does appear pest free.

Veronica and Handsome fall asleep as soon as they lay down their heads. I had finally adjusted to sleeping in the silence of our new house, and now I am in the middle of a busy town again and the noises are keeping me awake. It does not help that an alehouse below the inn is open all night, or that a pack of wild dogs has not stopped barking in the distance since the sun went down.

I reach for my bag in the dark and pull out the monk's robe. I spread it atop the blanket and lie back down.

But still I toss and turn. I pull the robe's hood up over my ears, but I can still hear the noise, both inside my head and outside the walls. At home, it used to make me feel better to embrace one of my books. Now the only books anywhere nearby belong to a giant of a bodyguard down below. He does not look like the sharing type.

I stare at the low, cobwebbed ceiling for a few moments longer before I remember that I *do* have a book! The one we stole! I reach into my pack again and feel around until I find it. Lying back down, I rest it upon my chest. Just the weight of it makes me feel better. I allow my hands to brush over the cover, feeling the indented letters in the leather, the still strong cord of leather wrapped around it to keep it securely closed. The book must not have gotten much use, because the covers are still soft and thick. Usually, by the time Papa gets his books, the stuffing material between the wooden boards and the fabric has flattened. But these are still quite puffy. I place the book under my head. Ah, almost as good as a real pillow. I may even be able to sleep now.

Then I jump out of bed and stand up so fast I slam my head into the ceiling. Handsome and Veronica startle awake at the noise. "What is it, Beauty?" Handsome asks as

I feel around my head for blood. "Are you all right? What happened?"

"I'm all right."

Veronica rubs her eyes. "Has dawn come already?"

I shake my head, an act that hurts. I push through the pain.

"Then why are we awake?" she snaps.

"Because I know where the map is!"

CHAPTER TWENTY-SIX

↤ Beast ↦

A knock on my door awakens me for the second morning in a row. "Mother?" I ask, pushing myself up as the door inches open. "Is the doctor back with the elixir already?" The door closes again, and I get a whiff of something I cannot identify. Is Mother bringing me breakfast in bed?

"It is Alexander," my brother whispers. "Mother and Father slumber still."

A glance out my window shows me that dawn has not yet arrived. I lie back down on my pillow. "What do you want, brother? I did not sleep well. I blame the leeches."

"I have something for you," he says.

"No, thank you," I reply, turning over. "The last time you said that, you gave me the measles."

"I was five!" he protests, pulling at my shoulder. "Sit up."

I groan. "What is it?"

He places the candle in a brass holder on my nightstand and I hear him rustling in a pocket. "Hold out your hand."

I am too tired to argue. He drops a small object onto my open, gloved palm. I bring it closer to my face. The faint candlelight reveals something that looks like a small bone, like a finger bone. Like a *person's* finger bone. Fully awake now, I quickly yank my hand away and the hard white object drops onto my bed. It gives a little bounce before settling into a fold of the blanket. I sit up and scoot a bit away from it. "What *is* that?"

"It's a finger bone," Alexander says plainly.

I stare at the spot his voice is coming from. "*Whose* finger bone?"

"Some saint, apparently. I got it from the pardoner last night. It cost me forty shillings, so it better work."

My eyes widen. "You left the castle?"

"Shh! Mother will hear you."

My mattress flattens as he sits down on the bed. "I went to visit my horses down at the stables," he explains. "I wanted to make certain they were being cared for properly. When I got there, I found the pardoner out front, selling pardons like they were the last plum pies on May Day. I was lucky he had any left."

"But how did you talk to him without revealing yourself?"

"It was the dead of night and easy to hide in the shadows," Alexander says. "The pardoner is well used to dealing with people who are unwilling to show their faces."

"I still do not understand. Who is buying all the pardons?"

He doesn't reply. The bed creaks a bit as he shifts.

"Alexander?"

In a low voice he says, "Everyone. And from what I overheard, it is because of you."

"*Me?*"

"Not *you*, of course. The beast."

"But I *am* the beast."

"All right, then. It *is* because of you. Sorry, brother."

"But I still do not understand."

"Well, from what I could gather, the townsfolk want to cleanse themselves of any wrongdoings in the hopes that you will spare their lives. I watched the cobbler purchase a whole shank bone! I am fairly certain that was from a cow."

"For what did he seek forgiveness? For making uncomfortable shoes?"

"He did not say."

Staring at the hollow bone, I ask, "But why did you buy *me* a pardon?"

"I figured if the doctor's elixir does not work, a pardon for your sins could be your only hope."

"My sins? What sins?"

He pauses for a moment. "Well, you are not a very good dancer. And you do not always pay attention in your lessons. And, well, you eat a lot of pies and nutbread."

I roll my eyes. "Those are not sins the last time I checked."

"True, they are not as bad as spreading falsehoods, or thievery, but . . . well . . ."

I put my hands on my furry hips. "You think I did something to deserve this, do you not?"

Silence again. It is becoming quite infuriating. "Alexander!"

"Honestly, brother, I do not know what to think. Why did the witch girl pick you, then? Why not me? Or Father?"

Now it is my turn to be without words. For I had not thought to ask that question of myself. I had figured it was simply bad luck. Could it have been more than that? Could I have done something to deserve this punishment? I did sneak an extra piece of ginger candy that Mother had laid out in the Great Hall for important guests. And I have led more than a few worms to an untimely death through my experiments. I clear my throat. "What do I have to do to earn the pardon?"

The mattress rises as Alexander stands. "You must bury the bone before dawn today. You must face southeast, whistle three times, and spit upon the ground."

"And my sins — if I have any — will be forgiven?"

"That's what the pardoner promised."

"Very well, I shall do it. But how will we get outside? Parker seems not to ever leave his post."

"The same way I did earlier," he says, lifting the candlestick holder from my bedside table. "Through the kitchen window."

Even if I were twice as short and half as wide, I would not come close to fitting through the kitchen window. Fortunately, the kitchen door is unguarded. Parker himself cannot watch every exit, and truly, I see no need at this point. Not one person has attempted to enter the castle since word of the beast apparently spread through town like wildfire.

"Shh," Alexander says as I close the kitchen door behind me. "Do you have to be so loud?"

"I am not making any noise," I insist.

"Your every step is like thunder," he whispers. "You lumber around like a giant. A giant on stilts."

"Yes, well, perhaps I am not the most graceful of creatures, but when was the last time you bathed? You smell like old cheese."

"I suppose it has been a while since I filled my tub," he admitted. "But the cistern is empty with no staff to fill it, and I would have to travel out to the well and then heat the water and lug it upstairs. Since no one but our parents can see how I look, I figured why go to all the trouble?"

"A small thing called consideration for those around you," I reply, making a show of pinching closed my beaklike nose. "I may not be able to see you, but I can still smell you."

"Fine," he grumbles. "I shall bathe tonight. Now let us get on with this. The sky is growing brighter."

I glance at the horizon, now empty of all but the brightest stars. Even without the stars to guide me, I know where southeast is. I face the carriage house, and step (*not* lumber!) over the dew-covered grass until I find a patch of loose, fairly dry earth. Kneeling down, I pull off my gloves and begin to dig. Finally, I have found a use for these long nails.

"Hurry," my brother says, his breath urgent (and smelly) in my ear.

I scoop out one last pile of dirt and place the bone in the hole. "How am I supposed to whistle without anyone hearing?"

"I shall make birdcalls at the same time," Alexander says. "That should mask the sound."

I nod. Alexander can imitate any bird with great skill. He begins to trill like a lark, and I jump in with my whistling. Turns out my pointy nose makes an excellent flute.

"Good work," he says as I quickly pack the dirt back into the hole. "Now spit upon the ground and let us be off."

I do as instructed, glad that Mother is safely in bed. She cannot abide spitting. An extra glob appears beside mine.

"I could not resist," Alexander says. "I have few pleasures these days."

I gather the saliva in my mouth, then spit once more. "One can never be too careful when hoping to be pardoned for one's wrongdoings."

Once again, a glob appears beside mine. "I agree," Alexander says.

"How long am I supposed to wait to see if it worked?" I ask.

"I had hoped it would have happened by now," he admits.

We wait beside the buried bone, taking turns spitting upon the small mound. Nothing happens. The sun is clearly visible above the distant fields by the time we sneak back inside, our mouths dry. I am still in my beast form, but at least the ground has been watered well today.

CHAPTER TWENTY-SEVEN

∽ Beauty ↩

Our room is so dark that we have no choice but to wait until daybreak to test my theory. We sleep fitfully, taking turns peeking out our window for the arrival of dawn. When it is obvious at one point that we are all awake, Handsome asks Veronica what the map will reveal, if we find it.

"I know not," she admits, her voice sounding tired. In the darkness, it is easier to remember how young she truly is. "My mother set out northeast, with two things — a copy of the map and her crystal. She did not return, and neither did they."

By the time dawn breaks through the shutters of our room, we are sitting on the floor, the book and Handsome's sharpest knife set out before us. The others elected me to do the cutting since I know the most about how books are made, and am less likely to cut through the map by mistake.

With a nod from Veronica, I lift the knife by the hilt, and dig the point into the top right corner of the front cover. I have learned from experience to hold the leather away while slicing downward in one long stroke. This gives me the greatest chance of keeping the leather in one piece. I then move left along the bottom until I reach the spine. Veronica reaches over and tries to grab some of the material inside, now made visible.

"Wait," I instruct, pulling back a bit. "Sometimes the padding is glued to the top. You do not want to rip it."

She pulls back and lets me continue. I finish the last cut. The leather is now attached only to the spine. I hold the book out to her, and she tentatively lifts off one strip of rag after another. A few scraps of parchment with splotches of ink follow, and then we are down to the oak binding. She sits back on her heels, her eyes filling with water.

"Do not despair of hope," Handsome says. "We still have the back."

Before any of her tears can fall, I am already cutting into the back cover. My heart starts beating a bit faster as I go, because I can already tell that whatever hides in this side is different from the other. This side has pockets of air around the edges, leading me to believe whatever is inside does not reach all the way to the corners.

This time even I cannot wait before reaching inside and pulling out the contents of the back cover. A single piece of parchment, folded in half, comes out in my hand. I hand it to Veronica, who takes it with just her fingertips, as if she fears breaking it with her very touch. Ever so slowly, she lays it on the floor, opens it, and smooths down the crease. Handsome and I lean over. If it is a map, it is the strangest map I have ever seen. Lines lead to nowhere, halves of words dot the page, strange symbols appear in no clear order.

"Is this the same one your mother had?" Handsome asks.

"I was only two," Veronica snaps. "I do not recall her map." She jumps to her feet (she is the only one amongst us who can stand fully upright in the room) and begins to pace. In the case of our tiny room, this means she walks three steps, turns around, and walks three back.

I hold the map (if it is a map) up to the sunlight, now growing stronger in the room. Whoever made this used a very old piece of vellum. The fine goat hairs add to the confusion of what is drawn upon it.

Handsome leans over my shoulder and we examine it together. "What do you think this means?" he asks, pointing to a large design that takes up the left side of the page.

"I do not know. A path through the woods?"

"I think it more resembles water," he says. "A river or a lake?"

"An underground city, perhaps?"

Veronica has stopped pacing to listen.

He beams at me. "Yes! And this large blob here with the zigzag through it? That must be a dragon guarding the gate!"

"For certain!" I say, trying to sound like I mean it.

Behind us, Veronica groans. "There be no such things as dragons!"

"So evil witches and tiny gnomes and magic boots exist," Handsome teases, "not to mention fairies. But you draw the line at dragons?"

"Just give it to me," she says, snatching it from our hands. "I shall figure it out."

"Suit yourself," he replies, lying back down on his pallet and closing his eyes. "Wake me when you know where we're going."

CHAPTER TWENTY-EIGHT

↤ Beast ↦

Three days pass before the doctor returns. "I apologize for the delay," he says, wiping his brow as he hurries into the library. "I had to travel far and wide for the correct ingredients. They are quite rare, you see." No stranger to rare ingredients, I am curious as to what he used. I open my mouth to ask, but shut it when I realize that while Prince Riley is familiar with the alchemical arts and the wares of the apothecary, the beast most likely is not. I cannot risk raising his suspicions.

The dark purple, sludge-like potion certainly smells bad enough to work. Since the pardoner's bone did nothing (in fact, upon further consideration, I am pretty certain it was a chicken leg), this is my last chance. "Cheers," I say, and shudder as the foul liquid makes its way down my throat. And then I wait, hoping not to empty the contents of my stomach upon the fancy carpet. The doctor and Godfrey inch closer. My family probably does, too, but who can tell?

"Hmm," the doctor says, pinching my forearm between his pudgy fingers. "Perhaps you are a bit less furry now?"

I am not.

"Your nose," he says, the hope evident in his voice. "It is a little less pointy?"

I reach up to touch it, then shake my head.

His face falls. "I am truly sorry to have failed you," he says, and I think he actually means it. Of course, he is probably afraid I will eat him now.

"It is not your fault," I assure him, even as my last ray of hope burns out. "Perhaps no man can undo the curses of a witch."

The doctor stumbles backward, grabbing his medicine bag and clutching it to his chest. "A witch! You said nothing of dark magic afoot. There is only one man I know of who knows the secrets of a witch's power."

Hope flutters in my chest. "Truly? What is his name?"

"Moravian S. Pilsner is the name," he replies. "But —"

"Can you tell me where to find him?" I ask, not wanting to hear any *buts*. "I shall reward you heavily."

"He is twenty years dead and gone," the doctor replies. Then he gives me one curt nod and scurries from the room. I sink into the nearest chair and rest my head in my hands.

The library is completely quiet. My fate, and all our fates, appear sealed. I debate crawling back into bed and dramatically throwing the blanket over my head, but truly, what good would it do? It would only upset my parents. They will lose me to the witch in a few short months. I need not make them worry more.

Father clears his throat. "I believe we have but one option left."

"What is that?" Alexander asks. "Flee to the countryside and hide in the forest for the rest of our lives?"

"We are the royal family," Father avows. "We do not flee or hide. What we shall do is quite simple." He pauses here for effect, then says, "We shall simply find a girl to fall in love with Riley."

At that, Alexander bursts out laughing. I would laugh, too, but I no longer seem capable of it.

"Where would we possibly find such a girl?" Mother asks. "She would have to be blind. No offense, dear," she says, patting me gently on the arm.

"None taken," I mutter.

"She does not have to be blind," Alexander says. "Only really, really, horrifically ugly. If Riley was her only hope of marriage —"

"I need some fresh air," I say, standing up abruptly. This results not only in the chair falling backward into a large vase but also in making me dizzy. Not willing to show weakness, I press on through the library doors, then pause on the stairs. I wait to see (or rather, *hear*) if they are following me, but the hallway remains quiet.

I am alone and glad of it.

Sadly, I cannot actually get any fresh air, at least not on the castle grounds. As far as I know, the tower balcony is still locked. Not that it would look good for a beast to be lording over the land from such a high vantage anyway. I shall have to make do with sitting by an open window.

I have not visited my lab since the explosion, nor have I given my experiments any thought. In light of what has happened to me, everything else — my bagpipes, my research into the unknown, even my interest in the stars — seems most unimportant.

But I now find myself eager to be in a familiar, comforting space that is all my own. I hurry up the two flights, careful not to trip over my own large feet as I ascend the narrow stairs. I still manage to bash my forehead against the door frame as I enter the lab. Thicker-headed now or not, I can already feel the swelling.

The lab seems larger than I remembered. After looking around, I realize it only appears larger because so many of my belongings are gone. All burnt to cinders, or shattered into tiny shards of glass and ceramic. Why did I ignore the first lesson Master Cedrick ever taught me? *"Always know the properties of your ingredients before you use them."* So what does Prince Riley, famous alchemist, do? He finds three unmarked bottles, mixes them together, and then heats them. I rub my wounded forehead.

The furnace is gone, of course, having crashed to the ground below, and a brick or two is still missing from the wall. The carpenters who fled upon the sight of me never returned to complete the repairs. They must have figured since the queen was missing, there was no reason to risk being a beast's dinner for one last brick.

All the rest of my worms are gone, too. Whether they were casualties of the explosion, or of the maids' brooms, I shall never know. It is just as well, since immortality will have to wait. I certainly do not wish to live forever in this condition.

The view outside the laboratory window is both familiar and strange. I am used to seeing much activity on the Great Lawn. Squires training, or children playing tug-of-war or leapfrog or lawn bowling, the sound of their laughter reaching me all the way up here. Not to mention all the workers who would normally be coming and going, busy with their daily tasks. The grounds are quiet now, as though someone spread a blanket over them. I allow myself to take a few deep breaths of air, grateful the winds are blowing away from the dung heap. I never realized how much I loved my home until now, when I am essentially a prisoner in it, unable to even claim my own name. I shall sorely miss it when I truly do become the prisoner of a witch talented enough to make me want to dance.

Me, dancing willingly! It is unnatural!

I turn to what is left of my stacks of notebooks and page through the hardened parchment. So many hours spent here, so many small discoveries, insights, tiny mysteries unfolded. My dreams of being a true scientist will never come true now. Of that I am sure. I lose myself in the notebooks as the shadows lengthen on the walls. It is nearly dinnertime, but I am not hungry.

A squeeze on my arm alerts me that I am no longer alone. I have long since stopped jumping at the unexpected touch or voice at my side. "Hello, Mother," I say, certain it is her by the scent of lilac and jasmine. At least someone in my family continues to care about their personal hygiene. Father has been getting pretty ripe.

"I am sorry to disturb you," she says, which are words that in all my years I have never heard from her. Everything is so changed now.

She takes a deep breath, and I steel myself for what is coming. "I advise you to take a long soak tonight, and perhaps allow Godfrey to do some . . . grooming?"

I sniff under my arms. Perhaps Father and Alexander are not the only ones to let themselves go.

"I am making some finer clothes for you," she continues, "and I expect you to be on your best, most charming behavior."

Did I miss something? I was never charming as Riley; I am much less so as the beast. "Why am I doing all this?"

Another deep breath. Then, "Because tomorrow you have a date."

"A *date*?"

"Three, actually. Godfrey went into the village and found three girls willing to meet the beast."

I am stunned at this turn of events. "But Godfrey can barely find the nose on his face."

"Alexander went along. He was Godfrey's eyes. He had been begging to get out of the castle anyway."

I groan. This day could not get any worse.

"Oh," she says, "and bring your dancing shoes."

CHAPTER TWENTY-NINE

∽ Beauty ∾

The sun will soon set on our third day at The Welcome Inn, and we are quickly wearing out our welcome. Veronica has complained to the innkeeper about the uncomfortable beds, the lack of lanterns in the hallway, the lack of soap in the latrine, the blandness of the stew, the rowdiness of the alehouse downstairs, and the general absence of anything interesting to do in this town. So far all the innkeeper has done to remedy the situation is to instruct the cook to toss a few chunks of meat into the stew. Considering their appearance coincided with the ceasing of the wild dogs' barking, we leave them on the bottom of our bowls.

Veronica has made an unlikely friend in the enormous bodyguard, Flavian. He said Veronica reminds him of his own daughter, who he had to leave behind in his search for work. Every time Veronica storms down to the innkeeper to complain about something, Flavian, clearly amused, slips her a ginger candy.

Although I would be hard-pressed to blame it on the innkeeper, this town truly is quite boring. We have been in every shop four times and visited every stall at least as many. While the baker here does make very delicious cinnamon buns, we were asked not to return due to Handsome being unable to keep telling the baker all the things he was doing wrong. We did stumble upon a lovely field of wildflowers, though, and have now amassed quite a large collection of lavender and lilies, and sprigs of sage, thyme, and rosemary. The sweet smell has successfully chased the dank one from our room.

But mostly our days have been filled with wandering the streets to see if anything on the map lines up with our surroundings. We have examined the map from all angles. We have held it close, stood far away, turned it in every direction, even held it up to a mirror to see if it revealed anything. It remains maddeningly undecipherable.

Besides the crowded dining hall, the only common area of The Welcome Inn is the few chairs set up before the large hearth near the front desk. For the past two nights, Flavian has kicked out whoever was sitting in the chairs so that we could warm ourselves by the low flames.

"I think this should be our last night here," Handsome says as we huddle close to the fire. The nights have gotten progressively cooler. "Even without the map's guidance, we must venture forth."

Veronica nods. "We shall leave after breakfast." As usual, she has the map spread out on her knees, as though it will suddenly start to make sense if she stares at it long enough.

A commotion behind us makes us all twist our heads. A tall, thin man in a fine waistcoat and stylish stockings relentlessly presses the innkeeper's bell while his groomsman drops one trunk on top of another. A boy who looks around my age orders the groomsman to be more careful.

During our time here we have seen many travelers come and go, but never any wealthy ones. Or if they were, they were wise enough to disguise their wealth.

The man takes a break from ringing the bell to storm over to the hearth. "Do any of you children know where the innkeeper is? My son and I have been traveling all day and we need a room for tonight. I need to know where to park my carriage. I need to eat. I need a bath."

"I hope you brought your own soap," Veronica mutters.

Handsome stands up. "You can park your carriage behind the inn. There are posts and water for the horses, too. I suggest you tip the guard well. He can be cranky."

The man goes out to his carriage while his son leans up against their pile of trunks and looks at us. Looks at the map, to be more precise. "What is that?" he asks, managing to sound both bored and interested at the same time.

"None of your concern," Veronica says, holding it away from the boy.

"I shall be the judge of that," he says, stepping toward her. She holds it farther away. I do not think she realizes how close her hand is to the fire behind her.

"Stop!" Handsome yells, stepping between Veronica and the boy. The boy looks shocked that someone would speak to him in such a manner, but he halts his approach. The two boys are so busy staring each other down that neither of them see what I see.

The map. It is . . . changing.

CHAPTER THIRTY

← Beast →

I have once again taken to bed, unsure if I will ever surface again. It has been two days since my dates, but their faces keep floating before my eyes, no matter how hard I squeeze them shut.

The first girl screamed and began pounding at the door the very second Godfrey escorted her into the drawing room. I tried to remain calm, and held off tugging at the waistcoat Mother made me wear even though it dug into my ribs relentlessly. Still, the girl would not even stay for tea and cookies, which I offered up in my most charming manner, having been coached by Mother for hours prior.

The second girl could hardly be called a girl at all. Truly, she was closer to Mother's age than my own. One eye was crossed, and the other floated around like a billiard ball. It took me a moment to find my voice, and by the time I did, she had emptied the tray of cookies into the large satchel across her shoulder and darted from the room.

And my third date? Well, I will never know because she never showed up. Now Godfrey and Alexander have set off to find girls outside of our kingdom. I do not expect them back for many days. In an attempt to cheer me up before leaving, Alexander promised to restock my laboratory along his journey. Although my heart was not in it, I gave him a list of supplies.

My door opens wide. "Get out of bed," Mother orders. My bagpipes appear out of nowhere and land on the end of my bed. I feel the mattress sag as she sits down beside them. "It is time to rejoin the living."

I shake my head. "It is hopeless. They will never find a girl to love me, and you heard the doctor, the only man who could have helped me is dead."

"If only he had written down what he knew," she says. "Alas, we must move forward and —"

Her words reach me slowly, but when they do, I jump out of bed, sending the bagpipes crashing to the ground. "That is it!" I cry. "He *did* write them down. I have seen his book!"

I hurriedly explain about finding *Fairies, Goblins, and Witches of the Western Kingdoms* while hiding in the castle library.

"And you believe this is the same man?" she asks.

"I do not recall for sure, but even if he was not the author, it is still a book about witches, the only one I have ever seen, and I have seen many books." I begin to pace excitedly.

"Riley, calm down before you stomp right through the floor."

But my thoughts are spinning fast. Once I am armed with the book and Alexander returns with my supplies, I should have all the material necessary to undo the spell. But they will be gone a fortnight! I stop pacing. "Mother! We must send a messenger to Godfrey and Alexander. We must tell them to alter their course and come home. You saw what happened yesterday with my dates. They will not find anyone. This is our only chance!"

"Be sensible, Riley. There is no way to reach them without sending out a search party in all directions. We are hardly prepared to do that now. Should be no more than a fortnight."

"But I cannot wait two *weeks*!" I tighten my lips. Princes do not cry. Unable to keep the quiver out of my voice, I whisper, "I do not want to go to the witch."

A moment later her arms wrap around my waist. I have not yet put on my gloves, so I dare not try to embrace her in return. Between my sharp talons and her invisibility, who knows what harm could be done.

"We do not want you to go, either," she says, her voice almost a whisper. "Who would tell me when to expect an eclipse? I might think the world was ending when the sun disappeared."

Once again, I am surprised at her words. "I did not know you listened when I blathered on about the stars."

"It is not blather," she says. "I admire your dedication to your hobbies. I do not claim to understand what you do up in your laboratory, but I respect your curiosity. You are like your father in that way. Your brother and I are the practical ones. That is not always the better way to be."

I do not correct her and tell her that what I do up there is not a hobby, for I am too warmed by her words. Who would have thought it would take a witch's curse to bring them forth?

When we pull apart, I ask, "Can we at least send Parker to see if they are still in our area? I would instruct him to ride only two days' distance at most."

After a short pause, she says, "All right, anything to get you out of that bed. Your room could use a good airing."

*   *   *

Parker leaves early the next morning. I think he is relieved to be away from me, even if only for the day or two the journey will take him.

Mother, Father, and I watch from behind the curtains in the Great Hall as he saddles up his horse and sets out. His nephew Valerian is now standing guard at the front entrance, nervously shifting his weight from leg to leg. Valerian shares neither his uncle's bravery nor his fierce loyalty to our family. Still, he is large and imposing, and I have no doubt Parker has instructed him well.

I am about to turn away from the door when, to my great surprise, a young woman appears on the walk. In lieu of a dress, she wears a long tunic, tied at the waist, stockings, and thick boots. A large brown sack across her shoulder bounces as she approaches the gate.

"Do you know this person, Lillian?" Father asks.

Mother must have shaken her head because Father says, "Nor do I."

While Father pushes open the window so we can hear, I peer closer, trying to get a good look at her face to see if I recognize her. When we were younger, Alexander and I used to play with the other children of the village, especially those whose parents worked at the castle. But her large, round eyes and wide mouth do not look familiar. Plus, her hair is red, and in our village that is a rarity. She is pretty, I suppose, from a purely scientific standpoint.

She stops when she sees Valerian.

"Who goes there?" he demands, barring her way. "State your purpose."

"I am here to see the beast," she says, her voice firm and direct. "He is expecting me."

"I have been told of no visitors," Valerian replies. "I cannot let you enter."

The girl hesitates only slightly before saying, "But we have a date. Rather, we were supposed to have a date yesterday, but I could not make it."

Mother grabs my arm. "Stop him from sending her away! She could be the one to break the spell!"

I groan. Another date! I might prefer to remain a beast forever. Mother's grip tightens. "All right, all right, but you are yanking on my fur."

She releases my arm and pats the fur back into place. "Sorry."

I have to admit, even with the strange garb, the girl does seem a much better candidate than any of the others. I push open the window farther, and stick out my head. "Er, hello?" I say. Then in a deeper voice I say, "I mean, hello there! I am the beast, and I should like the girl to enter."

Both of them turn toward me and freeze. Valerian clutches his chest. Honestly, that reaction is quite unnecessary. I am not THAT horrifying. The girl quickly recovers and steps right around Valerian, who is as still as a statue.

"Go open the door for her," Mother says. "And be charming."

I suppress another groan as I thud toward the castle's main entrance. The huge wooden door used to be a struggle for me to open; now it flings open quite easily. The girl is taller than she looked from inside, and a few years older, too. She tilts her head up and looks me directly in the eyes.

"You are the one who calls himself Beast?" she asks.

I nod. Who else would I be? "It wouldn't have been my

first choice for a name," I reply, trying to be charming. "But it seemed to fit."

She reaches across her chest and into her pack. "Sorry about this," she says, pulling out a long, silver dagger. "Nothing personal."

Then she throws it directly at my heart.

CHAPTER THIRTY-ONE

∽ Beauty ∾

If I had not been so shocked when I realized the heat of the flames had caused lines to appear on the map, I would have laughed. We had tried everything but setting it on fire, and then it turns out that was exactly what we had needed to do. When Handsome sees my expression, he turns to see what has me so enthralled. It takes him a moment to realize what he is looking at. Then he grabs Veronica and the map and runs from the room. I follow close after them, glancing back only to see the boy sneer and turn away.

"It is magic!" Veronica says breathlessly when we shut ourselves back in our room.

I lean close to the paper and sniff it. "I am pretty certain it is lemon juice."

"Whoever made this map," Handsome says, ducking under a beam to reach for it, "went to a lot of trouble to protect it."

We use the last rays of sun to examine it. Now the parchment clearly shows the woods; long, windy roads; a cliff; a seaport; and then a group of buildings—not quite a castle, more like a fancy estate where a high-ranking nobleman would live. At the very bottom of the map lies the mermaid fountain. At least we are in the right starting place.

Veronica is so happy that she does a little jig, kicking up her heels and clapping her hands. I do not relish ruining her mood, but I feel I must point out that nowhere on the map does it tell us what her mother's destination was. The buildings? The fountain? Somewhere in between?

Handsome leans closer to me and whispers, "I do not want to frighten Veronica, but I think that boy saw what happened with the map."

My eyes widen. "Do you think he would try to take it?"

"I do not know," Handsome says. "But he seems the sort to get what he wants."

"That he does," I have to agree.

"I can hear you," Veronica says, continuing to dance. "And you do not have to protect me. I am not a child."

Handsome and I share a small smile. Of course she is a child. He and I are not much past that ourselves.

Just then hushed voices outside our door bring her dance to a swift end. We spring into action. Handsome doublechecks that he had pushed the lock closed. Veronica and I run over to the wall and each peek through one of the eye-sized knots in the old wood. The holes are only waist high, so we cannot see too much. Still, it is enough to recognize the boy and his father. No one else around here dresses like that. They are each holding a towel and a ball of soap.

"The innkeeper refused to reveal their room number to me," the boy is saying. "But judging from their ratty clothes, they are in the poor section."

"We were lucky the best room at the inn was still available," his father says, reaching down to violently scratch his leg.

Veronica barely stifles a giggle.

"Shh!" Handsome warns, but he is smiling, too. His smile quickly fades with the boy's next words.

"I want that map."

"What makes you think it is valuable?"

"The way the girl protected it. If it were not a treasure map, she would have let me see it."

"All right," the father says, now scratching the other leg. "After we bathe, we shall find the children. Every innkeeper has his price." And off they go.

We step away from the wall, no one daring to speak until we hear the latrine door close firmly behind them.

"We must leave tonight," Veronica says. Neither of us argues with her. We rush to repack our bags. Veronica stops my hand as I am about to shove the monk's robe into my pack. "You should wear that. You, too, Handsome. In case the boy and his father are only pretending to bathe, or if their groomsman lies in wait."

"You are right," Handsome says, pulling his out.

"But where will we go once we leave the inn?" I ask, slipping the robe over my head and shoulders. "Darkness is soon upon us, and this is the only inn in town."

"I do not know," Veronica replies, slinging her pack over her shoulder. "We shall worry about that once we are clear of this place."

Handsome unlocks the door and peeks out. He steps through and waves us along. "One thing I must do first," he whispers, motioning for us to stay in the doorway. He tiptoes down to the end of the hall toward the latrine. I hold my breath. He is so close to them!

He slowly pushes the bolt across the door, successfully locking them inside. "Just buying us some time," he says with a wink.

"Nicely done," I say, nodding appreciatively.

And so one little girl and two hooded monks sneak down the stairs of The Welcome Inn, trying to look casual and no doubt failing miserably. Flavian takes one look at us, rolls his eyes, and waves for us to follow him. Having no better options, we let him lead us out the back door, where the horses and carriages are stored.

He holds open the door of the most opulent of the carriages. The doors are gilded with gold leaf, and the cushions are plush and firm. "Get in," he orders. "You can stay here until morn. When they come down to speak with the innkeeper, I will tell them you left long ago. They will never think to look in their own carriage. And the map? Nothing but a guide to the best places to collect berries."

"How do you know all this?" I ask, hurrying inside after Handsome.

"It is my job to know everything that goes on at the inn."

Veronica steps onto the carriage stairs and gives Flavian a hug. "You should go home to your daughter," she whispers into his oversize ear. "She would rather have you over whatever coin you make here." Then she slips something into his hand and jumps inside the carriage.

I wake to Handsome shaking my shoulder. "Time to go," he whispers. "Daybreak will soon be here, and we do not know when the boy and his father will be leaving."

I nod and stretch, feeling surprisingly well rested. The carriage was cozy and warm, and the bench as soft and plush as it had appeared. I do not know how much coin Veronica gave Flavian last night, but he not only stood guard outside all night, he brought us crescent rolls and warm butter for breakfast.

Veronica has decided that the group of buildings on the map is the place her mother most likely sought, so that is where we are headed. The first leg of the journey consists of miles and miles of road, which would take us weeks if we were to attempt to walk it. So instead we climb from our plush overnight lodging to a barely-holding-together-at-the-seams carriage-for-hire.

The new carriage comes with a grouchy coachman and a very gassy horse, but we are putting distance between us and The Welcome Inn, and that is a good thing. Veronica must have a seemingly endless supply of coin, because the coachman agreed to drive us as far as we need without asking questions.

We stop only when the coachman or his horse gets tired. One night we even sleep in a barn, with nothing but some scruffy farm animals to keep us warm. If I thought our horse had a bad odor, that was before I spent the night with a cow sleeping not an arm's length from my face.

On the third day, Handsome tries to make the time pass faster by making up stories about the welcome we shall receive when we arrive at the grand estate. Never mind that we do not even know who lives there, or why Veronica's mother wanted to go there, or even if that truly was her destination. "Splendid gardens and babbling brooks await us," he promises. "Feasts of grilled lamb and peach pies and cold cider. Private bathhouses where the water is topped with fragrant rose petals, and towels as soft as velvet. Servants to dress you in fine linens and —"

"And my mother shall be there to greet us," Veronica finishes.

Handsome hesitates, then says, "I hope you are right."

CHAPTER THIRTY-TWO

← Beast →

Time slows to a creeping halt as I watch the dagger grow ever nearer. I can see both edges spinning in the air, sharp enough to cut stone. I may be thicker skinned now, but I am not made of stone. It finally dawns on me to question why anyone would show up for a date when it is barely time for breakfast.

Some beastlike instinct I did not know I possessed takes over. I spring to the side, then leap upon the girl, holding down her flailing arms. Valerian finally springs into action as well. He places his boot on her chest and blows the whistle around his neck. While he waits for another guard to arrive, he yells down at her, "I do not like the beast, either, but that does not mean you can kill him!"

She raises her head and spits at his boot. "I have been hired to avenge the deaths of the royal family. You should let me finish the job."

Valerian shakes his head, keeping his boot right where it is. "My cousin told me the royal family is not dead yet. Had you killed the beast, you may have been responsible for their deaths."

I bend my head closer to the girl. "Who hired you?"

She struggles, but it is of no use. I am incredibly strong. "A group of loyal villagers, if you must know."

I can hear the pounding of hooves around the side of the castle. The guards will be here any second. The girl continues in vain to free herself.

"But why did you tell our guard you were here for a date?"

"That is what they told me to say. Apparently, some old man has been going through town asking for dates for the beast." She looks me up and down. "You may want to set your sights lower."

"First you try to kill me, then you insult me?"

"Enough chitchat," Mother hisses from my side. "Get back in the castle before the other guards see you and kill you themselves!"

The girl whirls her head to the side. "Who is there? I demand you unhand me!"

After being sure Valerian has her under control, I hurry back through the castle door. My parents soon arrive at my side and each place a hand on my back. "How bad is it?" Mother asks, the worry evident in every word.

Only then do I realize the dagger scratched my arm after all. "How bad is what? The wound or the date?"

Father chuckles.

"The wound hurts but a little. The fur protected me, I think. But I would have to say that was the worst date in the history of mankind."

"I would have to agree, son," Father says, sitting down beside me. "She is the sheriff's problem now."

"Let us hope he was not one of the 'loyal villagers'!" I reply.

"When Parker returns," Mother says, "he will have to remind the villagers that the royal family's safety depends on the beast." She dresses my wound (which truly would have been much worse had I been the old Prince Riley) but does not mention how I defended myself. I think my parents are a bit unsure how to handle that. I am, too. Had I not been wearing my gloves, I could have sliced her into pieces. I shudder. Not a nice thought.

"If you don't mind," I tell them, "I'd like to be alone." They do not argue, and I pull my sleeve down over the bandage and head up to the library. I run my gloved fingers along the spines of the books, trying to recall where I left it.

"Looking for this?" a small but steady voice asks.

I whirl around to find Freddy, the young page, standing before me, grinning. He holds out the book I had been searching for. I step backwards and an entire row of books tumble to the ground. Neither of us makes a move to pick them up.

"Why are you still here, in the castle?"

He shrugs. "I had nowhere else to go."

I remember his sad story. He really *didn't* have any place to go. "Why are you not scared of a beast such as myself?" I ask. "Rumor has it I eat people."

"Oh, you would not eat me," he says. "For I bring the book you seek. That, and the fact that we are friends, Prince Riley. It would be most unkind to eat a friend."

I smile, not even minding that the point of my nose digs into my lip. "How did you know it was me?"

He nods. "I was not completely sure until just now, when you came to find the book. I have been listening to you and your family, but the walls muffle your words. I believe I have put the story together now — you're a beast and your family is invisible and you need to find a girl to love you. Am I correct?"

"Indeed, that is the sorry state of my life these days. Remember when my biggest concern was looking foolish at the Harvest Ball?"

He laughs and I join in. I am so pleased he has shown up. I am in desperate need of a friend. "Where have you been hiding all this time?"

He points to the tapestry beside the one window. "There is a passage underneath that leads to a series of tunnels. I have been living in the tunnel behind the kitchen. It is quite cozy, actually."

Well, at least that explains how he always sneaks up on me. I wonder what else I don't know about my own home! "How come I have not heard of these tunnels?"

He shrugs. "The staff uses them to get around without bothering the royal family or their guests. I mean, *your* guests." He bows his head slightly. "You are still the prince, of course, although you do not look much like him."

I reach out to shake his hand. "I am very, very glad to see you, Freddy. Thank you for not running away from me like everyone else. You are much braver than you think."

His cheeks flush at the compliment. "I am glad to have a friend like you. I care not what shape you take." He steps back to size me up. "Although I must say you are quite the sight! I cannot wait to hear the story of how you became this way. But first let me give you this." He hands me the book. It feels much smaller in my huge hands. I open the front page and see Pilsner's name right there in big letters. I was right! He *did* write this! "Thank you! This will hopefully help me break the spell the witch cast upon me. You will have to start believing in them now."

He sighs. "I suppose I must. But I hope you will not pin all your hopes on that book."

"Why not?"

"Take a look."

I lay the book down on a table and turn past the author's name to the first page. Instead of words, strange symbols swim before my eyes. Numbers and triangles and many-sided figures, in no recognizable pattern. I flip the book closed.

"Rats."

CHAPTER THIRTY-THREE

∽ Beauty ∾

By our fourth day of travel, I feel like I have been cooped up in this stuffy carriage for half my life. With nothing but dirt and trees and one another to look at, it has been quite tedious. At midday, the coachman pulls into a village square around the size of our own. I see an apothecary shop outside my window and feel my first longing for home.

The coachman instructs us to find lunch and return promptly. Veronica catches me glancing at the apothecary shop and offers to get the food with Handsome so I can go look inside. For one so young, she has a gift for knowing what people need.

As I approach the shop, a blind man with a cane pushes the door open. I reach out to hold it open for him. I could swear I hear a male voice say thank you, but the old man's mouth did not move. I wait for someone else to come out behind him, but he is alone. Perhaps too many days with the same people simply has me wishing for the sound of new voices.

This apothecary shop is much smaller than Master Werlin's but even busier. I have to wait for the apothecary, a much younger man, to finish pulling a rotted tooth from a woman's mouth. I notice he does not bother to numb the area first by having her chew tarragon leaves. But unlike

Handsome at the baker's, I am able to hold my tongue. Until the poor woman yelps in pain and I blurt it out.

Then, just like Handsome, I am promptly escorted outside.

Two more days on the road and we finally reach the port town shown on the map. It feels good to stretch my legs and breathe the salty, fishy sea air. I have never seen such a large body of water and am both enthralled and overwhelmed by it. Papa has been to port towns before, and has told us tales of the blue waves bobbing up and down and crashing on the shore, and I have seen it in paintings, of course, but no one described the smell.

We easily scamper down the large rocks along the side of the cliff and walk along the sandy beach. The buildings from the map loom in the distance atop a cliff, too high and too far away to see in any detail. We watch the boats come and go, tilting our faces to the sun and feeling the warmth on our cheeks.

Veronica is the first to break away. She sits down on a large rock on the shoreline, unties her boots, and dangles her feet in the water like it is the most natural thing to do. I take a step back. Handsome hangs back, too, then unties his boots, rolls up his pant legs, and runs in!

"You must try this!" he cries, splashing like a child on a hot summer day. "It is lovely!"

I shake my head. I have spent many hours playing in the narrow river outside our village, but this is quite different. It is too deep, too vast.

Veronica takes out the map. "Do you think we should cross the sea, or go around the peninsula? The woods look very dense to me, perhaps impassable."

"The sea," Handsome shouts, scooping up water with his hands now.

"The woods?" I suggest, knowing already that I am outnumbered.

"The sea it is!" Veronica says. She folds up the map and heads down the shoreline to talk to the fishermen.

Handsome splashes around while I dig through my pack for any leftover mint or ginger to chew. We used up most of it during the endlessly bumpy carriage ride. Had I thought ahead to the boat portion of our travels, I would have doled it out more sparingly.

When next I look up, it is to find Veronica dragging a rowboat along the shallow sea. She stumbles and splashes every few steps but has that determined look on her face that I have grown to know well.

"No one will take us," Veronica announces when she reaches us. "Too many strange happenings, so they say. Sailors not returning. Noises and lights at odd hours."

"So you stole a boat?" Handsome asks, helping her drag it onto the sand.

"I am simply borrowing it," she says. "And I shall leave them some coin. But let us get in quickly before they return from lunch."

I toss the remaining ginger into my mouth, cringing at the sharp taste. Still, it is better than losing my last meal to the waves. Handsome piles our bags at one end, and we climb aboard. No doubt the journey was lovely, with fish splashing happily beneath us, the glint of sun on the water creating a kaleidoscope of colors. But since I do not open my eyes until the boat scrapes the bottom of the opposite shore, I cannot say with certainty.

As we crossed the sea, Veronica and Handsome had been talking about the wondrous artwork gracing the walls of the home we would soon enter. They tried to outdo each other with stories of fairies and mermaids swimming together in fountains of gold. Yet when we land, a hush falls upon them. I follow their gaze to the buildings, now only a stone's throw away. They are in ruins.

We climb out in silence, and in silence we explore the piles of stone and wood, the remnants of frescoes, the dried-up fountains with their cracked marble tiles. Veronica sits down hard on the ground, her feet hanging over the edge of what was once a brook, and is now only dust and twigs. She lays her head down on her arms and begins to weep.

Handsome and I remain behind her, each placing a hand on her shoulder. We stand like that for long moments, feeling the rise and fall of her sobs.

"My mother is not here," she finally says, voice cracking. "There is no sign she ever made it. I shall never know what she was searching for."

Handsome and I exchange a look. He motions with his eyes for me to say something. "But *you* made it here," I say, hoping they are the right words. "You did not give up, nor let anything or anyone stand in your way. Your mother would have been so proud."

She sniffs and wipes her eyes with the back of her hand. "But I hoped . . . *ouch!*"

"Are you all right?" I ask, crouching down beside her. "What happened?"

She leans over to examine her ankle. "That grasshopper just bit me!"

I look around in time to see a small green grasshopper hop away into the dried-out ravine.

"Grasshoppers do not bite," Handsome says. I am sure he would have teased her further had our current situation been different.

Veronica gets to her feet, wiping her eyes almost angrily. "Well, this one did!"

I watch the grasshopper hop down from rock to clump of brown grass to crumbly leaf, where it stops, no doubt unaware of the drama he is causing. Veronica storms off, ranting about evil grasshoppers and ruined buildings and the unfairness of it all. Handsome goes in pursuit.

Perhaps it is due to years of training in spotting small objects in my path, or perhaps because I am sitting alone with nothing to look at, or perhaps it is simple luck. But I am the one who spots the strawberry-size stone glowing in stark contrast to the brown leaf beside it.

I scramble down the side of the dried-up brook, afraid to take my eyes off the shining object. The grasshopper hops away as I push the leaf aside and reach for the stone. It is just as Veronica described it. A pure pink, dusty from its burial, but still vibrant and beautiful. A small, dirt-filled hole at the tip must have held a chain at one time. I hold the stone up to the sun, and a thousand streams of light shoot out from it. It is so pretty I have to force myself to lower it. For all its sharp edges, the stone feels warm and comfortable in my hand.

I find the others sitting on the remnants of a marble staircase, picking at pieces of tall grass growing between the stairs. Veronica seems to have calmed down. Handsome has a way of doing that. He must be an excellent older brother.

I hold out the stone. Veronica gasps and grabs it from my palm.

"My mother's crystal! Where did you find it?"

I point to the spot. "Under some leaves at the bottom of the brook. I was watching the grasshopper, and then I saw the stone."

She holds it close to her chest, her eyes shining, only not with tears this time. "So my mother *did* make it here!" Just as quickly, her eyes dim again. "But I do not understand. She never would have simply left it behind."

"Perhaps she lost it," Handsome suggests.

I think of how deep it was in the ravine. "Or perhaps she hid it. If the buildings still stood when she was here, that ravine would have been filled with water. Perhaps she threw it there to protect it?"

She considers my words. "Perhaps she did hide it," she says. "But these ruins look like they have been here for a century, not merely a few years."

"That is true," I admit.

"Either way," Veronica says, staring down at the stone. "Finding this means she is truly gone. It means we can go home."

Handsome touches her arm. "Are you all right?"

She nods. "Better I know the truth." To my surprise, she turns to me and puts her arms around my waist. "Thank you," she says.

I, not used to hugging anyone outside my family, pat her on the back in response. "Do not thank me. Thank your biting grasshopper."

She laughs. "Perhaps I will!"

But when we go to look for it, it is gone. I show Veronica the spot where I had first seen the stone. She climbs down and digs around the area until her hands are scraped up, but finds no other clues.

When we get down to the boat, I dig through my pack and pull out the leather cord that was wrapped around the book from the monastery. I loop the cord through the hole in the crystal and tie the ends together. Veronica solemnly slips the necklace over her head. The stone thumps against her tunic, looking as though it's been there forever. It occurs to me finally that her flowery scent is not perfume. It is simply the way she smells. I have no doubt I do not smell as sweet.

We are quiet as Handsome rows us back to the port. But it's a different kind of quiet than our time in the carriage. It's the kind of quiet that marks the end of something. This time I keep my eyes open, for who knows if I shall ever see the sea again. It is hard to believe the desolate, empty ruins are right atop the cliff. Down here is so vibrant. Boats of all sizes and shapes sail by, carrying people and fish and wooden crates to wherever their final destinations lay. The world is much bigger than I had supposed, with everyone busy leading their lives, working their way toward their futures.

It dawns on me that I have been rude by never asking Handsome about his future bride. I haven't been putting it off for any real reason, only the time never felt quite right and I have little practice in asking personal questions. But as Handsome steers us in between two small boats carrying stacks of fruit, I decide the time has come.

"What is she like?" I ask. "Your wife-to-be?"

He smiles. "Suzy is lovely. I have known her all my life. She is sweet and kind to everyone. She liked that you set that piglet free."

I am surprised, but pleasantly so. "You told her about that?"

He nods. "I had to go to my village with the baker to get some supplies. I was able to see her briefly."

He tells us more about Suzy, about how kind she is to animals, and how she loves dancing but only in large groups, and how she wants ten children. By the time we reach the shore, I have a clear image of a lovely young woman who I'm certain will make an excellent wife to my new friend.

This time, when the boat scrapes along the shore, I put my feet right in the water instead of waiting to get out on dry land. It is cold, but refreshing, and the sand is much softer underfoot than I had expected.

A red-faced fisherman paces the edge of the water, clearly the owner of the rowboat. Veronica quickly pacifies him with coin. We hurry past him onto the shore, our packs bouncing on our backs.

True to his word, the carriage driver awaits us in town. We stock up on food and drink, and settle back in for the journey. Handsome talks excitedly about how he will work on perfecting his bread recipe when he gets home and makes us promise to come for the wedding. I shall miss him, but I am happy for him.

The days pass much quicker this time, and when we are only a day away from home, Handsome points out the window and says, "My village is a few miles down that road."

I glance at Veronica, who nods. "You should go, then," I tell Handsome, leaning forward to rap on the window. The driver pulls to the side of the road. "Veronica and I will be fine on our own for one more day. It does not make sense for you to come back home with us only to leave again."

He shakes his head. "I told Veronica's grandfather that I would escort you both on this quest, and my job is finished only when I drop you safely at the door of the monastery."

Veronica shakes her head and pulls out her purse. "Your job is finished now. You are officially fired." She drops a pile of coin in his hand. Then she reaches out and places her hand over his. "Be well."

"Are you certain?" he asks, looking from her to his closed hand and back.

She smiles. "I will be fine, *cousin*. I am in good hands." Handsome leans over and gives her a long hug.

The driver holds the door open for Handsome. But before he slides out, he turns to me.

"I am truly honored to have shared this adventure with you, Beauty. One day you shall no doubt meet another boy who realizes how special you are. If marriage is what you decide you want, of course. Do not worry, you shall know your future when you find it."

My eyes sting with tears at his kindness. I want to tell him that by being my friend, he has made me a stronger person. But I do not know how to say these words.

We watch until he disappears down the road. It takes a while until the lump in my throat fades away.

CHAPTER THIRTY-FOUR

⤝ Beast ⤞

Since my tutor, Master Cedrick, has not been seen in the village since my arrival, the only person with a chance of being able to decipher the book is Alexander. And he is still on a wild goose chase to find me a girlfriend. His time would be much better spent doing, well, *anything* else. After my last date tried to stab me, I am fairly certain romance is not in my future. Unfortunately, Parker returned to the castle alone, so all I can do is wait.

Thank goodness Freddy is here to keep me from checking the windows every moment. He keeps me busy playing games and sharing stories, both in the castle and outside on the back lawn in the cover of darkness. We experiment with how fast I can run (faster than a horse!), how heavy an object I can lift (a table, and a fallen tree trunk), and how quickly I can climb the sides of the castle walls by wedging my nails between the stones (very quickly). Mother does not approve of that one at all.

Freddy continues to impress me. I worried when he was finally in the same room with my invisible parents he would find it too strange and retreat to the safety of the hidden tunnels. But he simply shrugged and said that sometimes he imagines his own parents are still with him, only they are invisible, too. That put things in perspective. At least mine are still with me, even though I cannot see them. (Which at this point may be a blessing, since according to Mother, Father has stopped wearing any pants over his knickers.)

I have just blown out my candle on the eleventh day of my brother's absence when I hear the carriage pull up outside. I throw back the blanket and jump out of bed. I am getting better with my balance and coordination, but still, the crash of my feet landing on the floor is loud enough to cause Freddy to run in from his guest room down the hall.

"Alexander is back!" I tell him. "He can read the book now!"

"Are you certain he will be able to?" Freddy asks as we race down the stairs in our slippers and nightclothes.

"He is the only person I know who speaks five languages. If he can't do it, no one can."

By the time we get downstairs, Godfrey has already come inside, and is resting on the couch. He is quite old for such a long journey, and I hope he is not unwell.

"Are you all right, Godfrey?" I ask. "Was the trip too much for you?"

He shakes his head. "It was actually quite exciting. It has been many, many years since I have visited the outer kingdoms. The different sounds, the smells of the local markets, all very new. And of course, everywhere I went, people thought me daft since I was always talking to someone who was not there."

I chuckle at that. "I imagine you were the talk of the town. Where is Alexander now?"

"I am right here, brother," Alexander replies, slapping me on the back. "And wait till I tell you what I have found! Or shall I say, who!"

"Never mind that," I say, "we have more important things to deal with."

"And who is this?" Alexander asks, no doubt meaning Freddy.

"Do you not remember him? He started as a castle page a few weeks before I became a beast."

"And he is still here because . . . ?"

"Long story. I remembered this book I saw in the library about witches, and Parker went to find you, and then I was stabbed by this girl, and then —"

"You were *stabbed*? By a *girl*?"

"That is not important. I have healed already."

"You were very brave," Mother says, squeezing my arm.

"Do tell," Alexander says.

"Later, I promise." I thrust the book open in front of where I imagine his eyes would be. "This was written by that expert on witches that the royal doctor told us about. Only it is in some strange language. If we can read it, maybe we can break the spell."

If he were to take the book, it would disappear. Instead, I slowly turn the pages for him. "Interesting," he murmurs, "most interesting."

"What does it say?" I ask, barely containing myself. Freddy and I push in closer.

"It is indeed instructions on how to break a witch's spell!"

"Hurrah!" I shout. "Did you get all the ingredients on my list? The minerals? The herbs?"

"I did indeed," he says. "It was at the apothecary's that I met your future bride, in fact."

I brush him off. "Enough with that. This is what we need to focus on."

"You won't need your herbs or minerals or crushed donkey horns or any of the odd things you had me buy. The solution is much simpler than that. Follow me."

Freddy and I exchange a glance. "Um, how can we do that when we can't see you?"

"Sorry. Heading to the kitchen. Invisible people first."

Freddy and I hang back to let my family pass. We leave Godfrey snoring comfortably on the couch.

"Lovely knickers, Father," Alexander says as they walk down the short hallway.

"Thank you, son. Nice haircut."

"Oh, do you like it?"

"It looks like you hired a blind man to cut it," Mother says.

Alexander laughs. "That would be Godfrey."

"Are they always like this?" Freddy asks as we follow behind.

I nod. "Mother is fighting a losing battle trying to keep the two of them presentable. Can't say I blame them. If I were invisible I probably would have given up on washing altogether."

We arrive at the kitchen to find various jars and jugs appearing on the counter with resounding thuds. "All right," Alexander says, "step up, please."

I stand beside the counter while Alexander scoops out a spoonful of mustard seeds, a half cup of curdled cream, and a pinch of saffron. Then he chops up a pickle and tosses in a wrinkled, half-rotted plum. He mixes it all together in a bowl and pushes it in front of me.

I pick up my spoon and hold it over the bowl of glop. I am not a picky eater, especially now when my stomach must be four times its regular size, but this looks truly unappetizing. "You want me to eat this? Are you certain this will break the witch's curse?"

"Not this alone," he says. "While you eat it, you must also hop on one foot while singing *She was a lovely lass*. Oh, and you should do it in the rain."

"But the sky is cloudless."

He pauses, then says, "In the absence of rain, the book said you may use spit."

I lay down my spoon. "I am beginning to suspect you could not read that book at all."

"Not a word of it," he replies. I do not need to see him to know he is grinning. And to think, he used to be the responsible prince, the one who worked hard and could be relied upon at all times. Father's jokes and tricks used to annoy him, and now he is playing them himself.

Alexander yelps. "Ouch! Honestly, Mother, I am too old for you to tug my ear."

"I am confused," Freddy says, turning toward me. "What is going on?"

I growl and step away from the counter. "Come, Freddy. Let us get some sleep. We shall simply have to figure out how to read the book on our own."

We turn on our heels and march from the room. "I'm sorry! It was just a joke," Alexander calls after us. "I was merely trying to lighten the mood."

"Even *I* would not have done that," Father says, although I detect a note of admiration in his voice for a trick well played.

I stop in the doorway. "What happened to your pledge to help me? You are poking fun instead."

"Ouch!" Alexander cries out as Mother expresses her disapproval again. "Enough with the pinching!"

"Stop acting like a child," Mother says, "and I will stop pinching your ear."

In a serious tone without any guile, he says, "You are right, brother, I am behaving horridly and I apologize. It has been a long trip and I missed being home. It was quite difficult remaining quiet and hidden in corners all the time so people wouldn't bump into the invisible boy."

"I had not thought of that," I admit, feeling a bit of my annoyance ebb away. "It must have been very hard indeed."

Freddy rolls his eyes at my ease of forgiveness, but I ignore it. The brotherly relationship is a complicated one; I do not expect him to understand.

"But I truly did find you a girl," Alexander says, dumping the bowl in one of the large copper sinks. "And I think you will like her."

I shake my head. "I think we have already proven that the witch knew no girl would ever love me. Your search was in vain. It is a hopeless, impossible task."

"And tonight we have proven that we have run out of options," he says, his voice rising. "Your book is a scribble of nonsense. I am fairly certain you do not want to live your life as a beast, and I am absolutely certain I want to be seen again by people other than our parents."

"Perhaps not until your hair grows out," Father whispers.

Freddy giggles. I do not think he likes Alexander much.

I hang my head. Lately I had been thinking only of my own fate, not theirs. "What is this girl like?"

"Well, I do not exactly know for certain," Alexander admits. "It was her older sister, Clarissa, whom Godfrey and I met at an apothecary shop over a three-day ride from here.

Well, truly only Godfrey met her, since I was busy trying not to knock over any jars of strange-looking roots or balls of mercury and give my presence away. But she and Godfrey were talking as he gave her our order. By this point in the trip we had given up asking girls to come back with us, so she and Godfrey were merely talking like old friends. He brings that out in people. I heard the girl say she was filling in for her younger sister, a girl near your age, who is working hard to support their family. Their father used to be a successful book merchant, but they have fallen on hard times. If the girl is anything like Clarissa, she is sweet and generous — Clarissa gave us a lot of extra things we hadn't even asked for — and quite a spectacular beauty. In fact, that is her name."

"The girl's name is *Beauty*? What kind of name is that?"

"A better name than *Beast*," he points out.

"But I did not choose my name."

"Neither, I am certain, did she."

I suppose he has a point. "All right, so this generous, sweet, beautiful girl, why would she come here?"

"Well, I have not quite worked out that part yet. She is apparently very dedicated to helping her father and sister. Getting her to leave them will not be easy."

I sigh. "Then why are we even having this conversation? I am going to bed."

Freddy shakes his head in Alexander's direction as if to say "shame on you" one last time before we exit.

"Welcome to our crazy castle, Freddy!" Alexander calls after us. Followed by, "Ouch, Mother!"

CHAPTER THIRTY-FIVE

∽ Beauty ᴄ∽

"Can I help you?" the innkeeper asks, chomping on an apple.

"We have returned," Veronica says. "We would like a room for one night."

He squints at us. "Have you visited The Welcome Inn before?"

"Now, now, do not tease the children," Flavian admonishes, striding in from the other room. He places a huge hand on both our shoulders. "These are honored guests!"

We smile up at him. The innkeeper shrugs. "If you say so. Then I shall give you my best room."

Veronica rolls her eyes. "We have heard *that* promise before. The last was not so great, to be honest."

"Ah," says the innkeeper, reaching for a key behind him. "But you have not seen the best of the best yet." He winks at Flavian, who grabs the key from him. Instead of leading us upstairs, this time we go down a long, narrow hallway leading off from the main room. "I shan't be here if you visit again," Flavian says as we walk. "I have found work closer to home."

"That is wonderful," Veronica says sincerely. I squeeze her hand. Her mother will not be coming home to her, but she is still happy that another little girl out there will get her father back.

Flavian stops at the last room on the end and pushes open the door. Real beds! A window that opens and shuts to let in the air! A bathtub! We look at each other and bound into the room, grinning wide.

"Where is your cousin?" Flavian asks as we flop onto the beds. I look up to see that he is still in the hallway. The ceiling is higher in this room than in our other, but not by much. He would never fit.

"He had to go home," Veronica replies with a giggle.

"That is too bad," Flavian says. "But no doubt you will see him soon at the next family meal." He winks. Clearly he never believed Handsome was our cousin.

"No doubt we shall," Veronica replies.

"Enjoy your stay," Flavian says, tossing the key to me. "And you do not need to worry about getting locked into the upstairs latrine by mistake. We had to take the bolt off the outside of the door after a father and son were accidentally locked in there last week. For twelve hours." He winks again and closes the door behind him.

We burst out laughing and it feels good. I shall have to remember to do it more often.

After a meal that tasted just as bad as the last time we were here, I help Veronica scrub the dye out of her hair. The tub water turns deep brown, but even so, we cannot get her hair as light as it was. Time will have to do that.

The next morning we stop for one last visit to the field of wildflowers. Most of these varieties do not grow at home. Veronica wants to collect them for her grandfather, and I for Clarissa. I shall bring some to the apothecary, too, for he uses them in many medicines. I pull out one perfect red rose, and add that to my pile. Roses always remind me of my mother, and I instinctively reach up to touch my mother's locket.

Handsome had given me his compass, so as long as we follow it south through the woods, we manage to stay on course. We talk about silly things like what Handsome's bride will wear to their wedding, and whether their cake will be made of flour and sugar like normal cakes, or from bread! This keeps our minds from worrying about meeting strangers. But in truth I am not very frightened. While I was glad for Handsome's protection, I am equally glad to be the one in charge now. I feel more at home in the world than I ever did. Plus, Veronica and I finally get to run as fast as we can without anyone slowing us down. We could certainly outrun any stranger. As we get closer, I get more and more excited to see Papa and Clarissa. I hope they fared all right without me.

We reach the outskirts of the village well before sunset. "Do you want to go to your grandfather's house first?" I ask Veronica.

She shakes her head. "I must return the robes, and repay the monks for the book. I doubt they would want it back now."

I laugh, remembering how we shredded it. "I think you are right. People will have to learn how to rid their house of mice some other way."

She smiles. "And you were right about the magic. I was silly to believe in the stuff of fairy tales."

"It is never silly to believe in wondrous things."

She hugs me good-bye and promises to bring my payment to the apothecary shop in the next few days. Before she turns away, I hand her the rose. "To remember our quest," I tell her.

She takes the rose and sticks it behind her ear. "I am not likely to forget it."

"Nor I." I swing my pack over my shoulder again and begin the trek home. It feels strange to be alone after all this time, but I find myself enjoying the solitude.

Papa and Clarissa are sitting at the table eating when I burst through the door. "I have returned!" I call out.

They both jump up and run over. Papa takes my pack and Clarissa hugs me tight. "We missed you!" she shouts.

"I missed you both, too." I hand her the flowers. Her cheeks look rosy and her dress is clean. She almost seems like her old self again. I glance around the room. They have made it look more like a home in my absence. A rug, a comfortable chair, even a picture on the wall. A few books are stacked by the front door, which means Papa must have at least started selling a bit again.

Clarissa goes to bring me a cup of water, and Papa pulls me aside. He looks tired around the eyes but otherwise much happier than when I left, and a little plumper, too.

"You look good!" he says, holding both of my hands in his. "A quest changes a person, you know."

I smile. "So I have heard."

I spend the rest of the evening telling them all about our adventures. When we lay in bed later, Clarissa tells me that one of her old friends came into the apothecary shop complaining of a large scrape where her horse kicked her in the shin. Clarissa was able to make up a poultice of vinegar and myrrh, and now her friend is as good as new and no longer ignoring her. At least I think that was the last thing she said, because I faded off to sleep at the end.

Although I do believe she has begun to enjoy the job, in the morning Clarissa easily hands over the smock she had taken to wearing to the shop to protect her clothes. Papa and I walk into town together, and he tells me how his business is slowly getting on its feet again. He tries to sound enthusiastic, but I can tell he is far from feeling secure again.

When I enter the shop, the first person I see is the butcher, sitting with his head back on a chair. If he recognizes me, he does not show it. He is busy chewing tarragon leaves while the apothecary readies his tooth-pulling tongs. I smile to myself.

"You have returned," the apothecary says with barely a glance. Then he rattles off a list of ten chores to do.

"I am glad to see you, too," I reply, tying my apron around my waist.

He grunts and gets to work on the butcher's mouth. I spend the day reorganizing the drawers again, occasionally finding a few ingredients in the wrong place. Nothing as bad (or deadly) as the burdock and nightshade incident, but I would not want an old man to come in for a rash and leave with a remedy for womanly cramps.

As much as I enjoy working here, my mind keeps straying to the open road. The shop, and the whole village actually, seems much smaller than when I left. I remember feeling that way upon our return from trips with Papa, although they were much shorter trips. He and Clarissa seem to have fared fine without me, but it is nice to have our family all together again.

The days pass pleasantly, if slowly. I've been avoiding the bakery since I know it will make me miss Handsome. But after I've been back nearly two weeks Papa asks me to pick up the barley rolls on my way home and I can avoid it no more. A small part of me wonders if I'll find Handsome inside, baking his famous rolls, but instead I find the baker teaching his new apprentice the proper way to take bread out of the oven. Judging by the wet compress the boy is holding around his hand, it is not by sticking your arm in.

I tell the baker how Handsome had gotten kicked out of another bakery when he tried to teach the man to bake better bread. He laughed. "North of the woods, you say? That baker is my cousin. He never takes my advice, either!" He gives me my rolls and tells me that Handsome has a solid future as a baker.

"I shall tell him that if I see him again."

"I am certain you will," the baker says. "How can two people named Beauty and Handsome stay apart?"

I smile and thank him for the bread. I do not know what part in my life Handsome will have in the future, but I hope the baker is right.

I arrive home to find Papa waiting at the door. "Come, I have news."

I hurry inside after him. "What is it? Is everything all right?"

Clarissa jumps up from the chair. "I forgot how boring it is at home all day! And Papa would not tell me why he is jumping around like a child on May Day until you got home."

"I wanted to tell you both at once," he says. "I have just received word of a shipment of books long thought lost. I have to pick it up myself, though, and it is far from here. I shan't return for near a week."

"Is this a big shipment, Papa?" Clarissa asks.

"Yes," Papa says. "In fact, it is such a big shipment that you can choose anything you like and I shall bring it home for you!"

"Truly, Papa?" Clarissa asks.

He nods. "Anything."

Clarissa beams at me in excitement and then says, "I would like a silver comb, hair ribbons in pink, yellow, and green, shoes with laces rather than buckles, a hat with an ostrich feather, a pencil for my brows, and a silk scarf."

"Is that all?" he jokes.

"Oh, and a tin of hard candies."

"All right," he says. "And for you, Beauty?"

I have no idea what to ask for. I look around the room and see the wildflowers I had brought back, now lying on a shelf next to the nub of a red candle. I think of the rose I gave Veronica to remind us of our journey, and of my mother's rose petal in the locket around my neck, turned to ash by the fire. "A red rose would be lovely."

"That is all you want?" he asks.

I nod. Clarissa rolls her eyes but says nothing.

When we awake in the morning, Papa is gone.

CHAPTER THIRTY-SIX

⤛ Beast ⤜

To keep myself occupied, I set up my laboratory with Freddy as my able assistant. It is now as good as new. Better, even, since Alexander picked up some items that I had not even thought to request. When I asked about them, he said the girl Clarissa gave them to Godfrey as a gift. "She said he reminded her of the grandfather she always wished she knew."

Godfrey does tend to bring that out in people.

So besides my usual stock of roots like sassafras and comfrey, arrowroot, motherwort, rose hips, oils of cinnamon and pine, holly, yellow ember flower, iron dust, ambrosia flowers, sulfur, carbon, and various other minerals, I now possess burdock leaves, wormgrass, a jar of horsehair, and three spider fangs. Oh, and a book about witches that I am tempted to use as kindling on the next cold night.

The castle is even more quiet than usual now as the days tick by into weeks. We are all wrapped up in our own thoughts. I am surprised when Alexander bursts into the lab late one afternoon, just as Freddy and I have figured out that mixing carbonate of copper with nettle oil will turn the fur on my arms a lovely shade of green.

"Riley! Stop what you are doing, you must heed my words. Do not come downstairs until tomorrow morning. I shall bring your meal up to you."

"Why?" I pick up a rag dipped in water and attempt to scrub the color off my fur.

"Because we have a very important guest and he must not see you. Not yet."

I stop scrubbing. Mother would never have a guest in the castle. Without our usual squad of servants, the place is quite messy. "A guest? Is Godfrey entertaining him?"

"No. *We* are. Mother, Father, and I."

"Excuse me?"

"It is complicated," he says. "You must trust us. If our plan works, Beauty will be arriving at our front door in little over a week!"

"Beauty! But I thought there was no way she would leave her family?"

"The less you know right now, the better. That way you will not slip up and say something you should not. But you must understand, this is our final chance. On my trip with Godfrey, a hundred girls must have turned down his invitation to meet the beast. He did not tell Beauty's sister about you. The element of surprise is still on our side."

"But I do not understand. The witch said the girl had to come willingly."

"I am betting that she will."

"But why would she do that?"

"Just put on your finest clothes tomorrow and be prepared to be a bit ruthless if it comes to that."

"Ruthless?"

"Mother will explain everything in the morning. When you return to your chambers you will have to tiptoe. None of your usual pounding on the floors. Our guest must think he is alone in the castle. I have already instructed Godfrey to keep out of sight."

"But I still —"

"And cover up that green fur."

"But —"

The door of the laboratory swings shut. He is gone.

"Interesting," Freddy says, nodding thoughtfully. "Very interesting."

By morning, I have to fight the urge to pace the floor of my chambers while I wait for Mother to fetch me. It has been hard to stay quiet, especially now that the time for my appearance draws near. Mother slid a list of instructions under my door last night. I have grave doubts that I will be able to do what they ask of me, but I cannot let them down.

A moment later, the door opens a crack. "It is time," she whispers. "Stand up tall. You tend to slouch."

I straighten my back, feeling the fabric on my waistcoat straining. Luckily, it does not tear. I glance one last time at the parchment, which I have already committed to memory. With a deep breath, I head downstairs. Sitting on the couch, twisting his hat back and forth in his hands, is a man around Father's age, although the deep lines on his face make him look much older. His overly large traveling cloak does little to hide his thin frame. A small brown pack sits on the floor beside him, with a single red rose draped across the top.

He jumps up when he sees me. His eyes widen in fear, but he sticks out his hand and attempts to keep it from trembling. My instinct is to shake it, but Mother warned me not to do anything to put him at ease. He eventually pulls his hand back.

"Sir," the man begins with a shaky voice. "I am truly sorry for intruding upon your castle. I had been given this address clearly by mistake, and after your guard alerted me to my error, I intended to return to my home, a long way from here. I picked a single rose from your beautiful garden for my daughter who asks for so little, and was about to climb back upon my horse when your guard invited me to rest by the fire."

I know Godfrey had instructed Parker to do all this when Beauty's father arrived, although our loyal guard must have hated leaving a stranger unattended in the castle. He will deserve a big raise when — or if — this ever ends.

The old man continues. "When I awoke from my nap, I did not see the guard — or anyone — until you came down just now. But a lavish feast had been laid out, so I partook of the meal and then slept once again. When I awoke this morning, the table had been cleared. I called out to my host to thank him or her, but no one appeared. When I tried the front door, it would not budge."

He looks so confused and scared that I am finding it hard to begin my speech. A quick pinch on my backside from Alexander, and I am ready. I clear my throat and try to sound as imposing as possible, like Father when he has to give an unpleasant order. "Sir, you have come into my home, rested at my hearth, eaten of my food, and stolen from my garden. I cannot simply let you leave. I am a beast, you see. A price must be paid."

His eyes widen. "But . . . but I have nothing to give. My luck as of late has been all bad."

"Then you must live here and maintain my castle for me. You look like a strong worker." That last part is clearly a fib, for he seems on his very last legs. "If you cannot do the labor, then it is off to the dungeons for you." Another fib, of course, but he does not know that.

His eyes grow huge. "For . . . for how long would I need to be here?"

Foolishly, I had not anticipated that question. "Until I decide otherwise," I reply.

He clutches his hat harder. "But I cannot. I have two daughters at home."

I pause before my next line until I sense another pinch coming. "Then you shall send your hardiest daughter in your place." I try not to cringe as I say this. Who would send his daughter to live with a scary beast?

"I could do no such thing!"

Mother figured he would say this, so I am prepared with my response. "Then my carriage shall return for you the next morn, after you have said your final farewells to your daughters. I will not send you home empty-handed, though. You may fill my carriage with as many fine jewels and objects as you like. We even have a large collection of rare books. Your daughters will be well taken care of for the rest of their lives. If I find you have fled, I shall take it all away and it shall be the dungeons for you."

His eyes open wide again. He begins to speak, falters, and then nods. He must know he will not get a better offer. He is gone by midday, along with two trunks filled with gold, jewels, and rare books. Mother had wept quietly as her jewelry was dropped into the first chest. Father remained silent as Beauty's father pulled book after book from the library shelves. The man must know his business well, for he chose the most valuable ones. I suppose it is only fair, since if the plan works, he will be surrendering what he holds most dear.

The whole experience has left me feeling beastly. I must go lie down.

CHAPTER THIRTY-SEVEN

∽ Beauty ⌒

A week has come and gone, and Papa has not yet returned. I can tell by the way Clarissa has cleaned every inch of the house that she, too, is worried. At night, to make the time go faster we play cards and Clarissa tells stories of how grand life will be when we are wealthy again.

On the eighth day of his absence, Veronica comes to the shop. She had dropped off a pouch of coins for me earlier in the week, but I had been on an errand. "It is good to see you," I say, meeting her halfway across the floor.

"And you," she says. Her hair is back to its regular color again, and I am struck at how different she looks. I quickly realize it is not only her hair that makes it so, it is her bearing in general. The crystal hangs from its string on her neck. She could have replaced the leather with something a lot nicer, but she did not.

"Is that what you sought on your quest?" the apothecary asks, coming to peer closer at the necklace.

She nods and holds it out to him. "It is rose quartz."

He shakes his head. "No, it is something much rarer than that. I have never seen so brilliant a stone. It is very special."

She lets it fall back. "I know."

The front door of the shop flies open and Clarissa runs in.

"Could not stay away, eh?" the apothecary asks.

But Clarissa ignores him, which is not like her. She is never rude. My heart picks up its beats and I grab hold of the counter.

"Beauty!" Clarissa says, grabbing my arm and pulling me toward the door. "You must come home. 'Tis Papa!"

I feel my hands grow icy, although the cauldron heats the shop quite well. "Is he all right? Has there been an accident?"

"He is home," Clarissa says. "But I have never seen him like this. You must come quickly."

"Is there anything I can do?" asks Veronica.

"Is he ill?" asks the apothecary.

Clarissa shakes her head. "'Tis a family matter only, I think." She pushes me ahead of her out the door before I have a chance to say anything to appease their worried faces.

My sister is pinching the cramp in her side by the time we reach the house. I would have run even faster, but did not want to leave her behind. In the old days, Clarissa never would have been able to run all the way to town and back as she did today. She is getting stronger.

Papa jumps up from the front step when he sees us. His face is completely devoid of color, his eyes wild with fear or pain, I cannot tell. He has twisted his hat so many times that it hangs in shreds in his hands. Yet still he twists it.

"Papa!" I run to him. "What is it? What happened?"

He stumbles over to the chair and nearly falls into it. "The beast! I took a mere flower from his garden and now I must return to his castle forever." He buries his head in his hands and begins to sob. Clarissa and I look at each other, stricken. Has Papa eaten some bad berries? Has he gone mad?

"What are you talking of, Papa?" I ask, kneeling beside him. "How can an animal have a castle?"

He shakes his head. "This was no animal. He was huge, taller than the tallest man! And wide as *two* men!"

"Not every large man is a beast," I tell him, thinking of Flavian. "He might appear a bear on the outside but be a kitten within."

"He was no kitten, nor a bear, either. 'Twas a talking beast, I tell you. With long hair and fur and nails as sharp as knives!" It takes him a while — with many interruptions for clarity by me and Clarissa — but he finally gets through the entire story. After a moment of stunned silence, we follow him to his bedroom behind the kitchen.

He takes a deep breath and pushes open the door. Our mouths drop in unison. Treasure — for that is what it must be called — covers the room nearly from floor to ceiling. Jewel-covered books and bracelets and rings and gold figurines. Fine robes and shoes and headpieces. And on top of it all, a crumpled red rose.

CHAPTER THIRTY-EIGHT

←· Beast ·→

For the next few days, we polish the silver and gold tea sets, scrape food and grime from in between stones, sweep the rushes under the tables and the cobwebs from the corners. I can easily reach the ones on the ceiling, so that becomes my main job. It is also my job to throw away all the objects I have either smashed or slashed by mistake. If it is the girl who chooses to come, I do not want to frighten her even more with the evidence of my strength.

Mother happily clips flowers from the gardens and places them in bowls around the castle. I have asked many times what we will do if Beauty's father returns instead of Beauty herself, but Mother says we will cross that bridge when we come to it. This does not make sense to me. If one does not know how one will cross a bridge, one best figure that out before one reaches it. Otherwise, it is just poor planning. But no one listens to me.

Mother spends most of her time turning the largest guest room into an explosion of pink. I think she always wanted a girl. She hangs large, ornate mirrors and colorful artwork on the walls, and drapes a silk canopy above the bed. Freddy proves to have an excellent eye for detail, and she has taken to asking him for advice on exactly where to place a decorative pillow or a washing basin.

When not busy running into town on an errand for Mother, Freddy has dedicated himself to figuring out how to rid my fur of its greenness, which has, if anything, gotten brighter. So far he has had no luck.

Alexander keeps me busy by coaching me on the right and wrong things to say to a girl. Asking her if she likes spiders and then tossing one on her is wrong. Asking if she likes flowers, and then pinning one behind her ear is right. Talking about myself is wrong. Asking about *her* is right. I am not to talk about the stars, unless it is to point out a pretty one and compare her to it. I am not to bore her with any scientific talk of alchemy, my experiments, or anything to do with the witch and the spell.

I am to chew on cinnamon sticks as often as possible to keep my breath smelling sweet. Apparently, as the beast, my larger mouth is more likely to collect morsels of food.

I am also not allowed to play the bagpipes due to them sounding "like a whole herd of buffalo groaning at once." I highly doubt Alexander has ever heard a buffalo groan in his whole life, let alone a herd of them.

Basically, I am supposed to keep my mouth shut most of the time. I do not know how doing, or *not* doing, these things is supposed to make her fall in love with me. But Alexander must know what he is talking about. He always has plenty of dates. Well, he used to before the witch brought a swift halt to his busy social life.

I have taken to hiding in any place large enough to conceal me.

CHAPTER THIRTY-NINE

∽ Beauty ᴄ∾

Clarissa reaches out to grab the wall to steady herself.

I find a corner of Papa's bed to sit on, speechless as well. And then I feel it. This is my future. Not Papa's, not Clarissa's. I stand up and put my hand on Papa's shaking arm. "He is clever, this man who pretends to be a beast. It was my fault you took the rose, Papa. It is me he wants. It is me he shall get."

"No!" Papa says, pulling away from my grasp. "I shall go back. You have your whole life ahead of you. I cannot let you give it to a beast!"

"Look at all this," I say, waving my hand around. "With these books and the money you could make from selling the rest, you can be the leading bookseller in all the king-doms. You can both move back into town, in the grandest house in the village. You have worked hard your whole life and sacrificed much for us. That is the life you should lead, not this one."

"And you?" Clarissa asks. "You will go live in a castle with a beast? In a cold, dark dungeon, no doubt? I hardly think so!"

"We cannot let Papa go!" I reply. "Look at him! He will surely die. I am strong and resourceful. I have traveled far, too, and saw no sign of magic, dark or otherwise. I do not believe in walking, talking, vengeful beasts. I shall unmask him — this man who has treated you so horribly — and return home, I promise."

Papa begins to weep, silently now. Clarissa opens her mouth to argue with me, but I know she sees the sense in my words.

None of us sleep more than a few moments that night. I have packed my belongings, and now I wait for the carriage to collect me. Clarissa has offered to go to the monastery to fetch Veronica so that I may say good-bye. She also assured me she would apologize to Master Werlin for my leave-taking. It seems I am not so reliable an assistant after all. As fine a job as Clarissa did while I was away on the quest, I do not think she will be returning to work at the shop. She and Papa will be busy making a new life for themselves.

Veronica runs in, followed by a panting Clarissa. Soon my lovely sister shall have horses again to carry her long distances, and shoes too fine to run through forests in. And hopefully, a young man she loves, to share her life with. Perhaps now that our family is wealthy again, some of her previous suitors will return.

"Well!" Veronica says, her hands on her hips. "I take you on one quest and suddenly you are brave enough to live with an evil beast in some faraway castle?"

I suppose I am indeed braver than when I left. But it is Veronica's willingness to march into her future that is allowing me to march into mine. My lips twitch into a smile. "Do not worry about me. I have a few tricks up my sleeve. If the beast gets out of control, I shall simply lock him in a latrine when he takes a bath!"

She laughs, then stops and studies me for a moment, searching my face for I know not what. Then she pulls her necklace over her head, reaches up, and slips it carefully over my hair. "I cannot take this," I argue. She only shushes me and pushes my arm back down. As the stone passes between our two faces, I can see Veronica bathed in a pure white light, like she is glowing from the inside. I startle for a moment, blinking. A strange trick of the light perhaps, but it continues. I see she is looking through the stone at me as well, her expression full of delight. She is still smiling as the stone falls upon my chest, right next to my mother's locket. It feels warm, even through the many layers of clothes Clarissa insisted I wear since winter is fast upon us. Veronica looks like her normal fairy-like self again, the bright light around her gone.

"Are you certain you want to give this to me?" I ask, clutching it. "You went to such great lengths to get it."

She nods. "You need it more than I right now. We shall see each other again, and you can return it to me then."

I do not see how I could "need" a necklace, but I do not want to insult her by arguing further. "I shall keep it safe for you," I promise. My throat is too tight to say any more. Veronica gives me one last fast embrace and runs out the door. Clarissa reaches for my hand. We stand together in the quiet until the clomping of the horses outside makes us all jump. Papa, unable to help it, cries out.

"Take good care of him," I whisper as I hug Clarissa tight. "You must promise not to worry for me. How bad could life in a castle be?"

She tries to smile, but does not quite make it. Papa hugs me so tight I am afraid he shall shatter the crystal. "I am so sorry," he whispers hoarsely.

"This is not your fault," I assure him, pulling away. "You were tricked. I shall make it right." I may sound brave, but for a split second I almost suggest we run away instead, leaving the riches and Papa's obligation to the beast far behind us.

But I cannot run from this. So I clamp my lips shut and allow the coachman to lead me to a carriage so grand it makes the one we slept in that night at the inn look like a child's plaything. This is the carriage of a king. Ornate patterns of gold and silver leaves twist and twirl around the dark, gleaming wood. The two white horses are twice as large as any I have ever seen, and they wear gilded harnesses and jewels down the front of their noses. Inside, the benches are covered in velvet and silk. I sink deep into the soft cushions, feeling uneasy. Why would a servant — for surely that is what I am to become — be treated like royalty?

Before I can do more than wave to my family out the window, the coachman yanks down the shades. "I am sorry, miss. I cannot let you see our path."

He shuts the door, leaving me in near-total darkness. I quickly lose track of time. From the noises outside I can tell when we are in a town or the woods, but other than that I am lost. We stop occasionally to stretch our legs and eat from a large basket of fruit and cheese. I ask about the beast, but the coachman only shakes his head. "Not my place to talk of him," he says. "I do not want to end up like the royal family."

Though they are strangers to me, I feel a chill that has nothing to do with the cold. "Why? What happened to the royal family?"

But he only shakes his head again and hurries me back into the carriage.

After three or four days of nonstop travel, we find ourselves in a terrible storm. The horses snort with the effort of pulling us through snowdrifts, and the wheels creak and groan. I pull my cloak tight around me and huddle against the seat. It dawns on me that my thirteenth birthday came and went sometime in the last day or two, with nothing to mark the occasion but darkness and the clanking of metal wheels.

Finally, the carriage stops completely. At first I assume we must be stuck in a drift, but when the coachman opens my door he says, "We are here. The beast's castle."

At first I do not move. Snow swirls on the ground here but does not cover the grass. Then I look up at the enormous stone and wooden entranceway before me, and the rows of windows behind it. I had not even thought of what a castle might look like, but this is surely the grandest in all the land.

I remember something Clarissa always said when we went to parties at the finest houses in the village. *"You cannot walk in empty-handed. A lady always has good manners."* We always brought a pie, or flowers, or a scarf. Even without a mother to guide us in such things, Papa always made sure we had social graces. Or that Clarissa did, at least. I force myself not to think of my family now. They are safe and shall not want for anything. I must focus on the task ahead if I am to succeed.

I shall show this "beast" that I am not afraid of him. I allow the coachman to help me out of the carriage, then I ask him to take me to the garden. I may be a prisoner here, but that is no reason to be rude.

CHAPTER FORTY

← Beast →

The day arrives sooner than I would have liked. I know I am supposed to hope a beautiful girl walks through the front door, but a part of me hopes it is her father, instead. Alexander can coach me all he wants, I will no doubt still be awkward and do all the wrong things. Having a girl living three rooms down from me has me in a panic.

A terrible early-winter storm sweeps in midday, and I worry that the carriage will get caught in the snow. I would feel dreadful if any harm came to the inhabitant. But as we all push our food around our dinner plates, Parker knocks on the door of the private dining room.

I wait till my invisible family drops their spoons. "Enter."

"Your . . . *guest* has arrived." He gnashes his teeth at the word "guest." I cannot blame him. I had told him that a young lady may be coming to stay here. He clearly does not approve. "She awaits you in the parlor."

"Hurrah!" Freddy shouts. "It is a *she*!" My stomach does a nervous flip. I am glad I did not eat much. I pick up my glass of water and drink deeply. It does nothing to appease the tightness in my throat.

"I shall be out in a moment," I tell Parker.

He nods curtly and closes the door behind him. Everyone starts talking at once. I put up my hand and say, "I do not want her sitting alone for long. She is likely frightened half to death already, and seeing me will only make it worse. I best get it over with."

"We will be right beside you," Mother promises.

I nod, grateful. Mother has asked Godfrey and Freddy to keep out of sight for a while. She fears their presence would cause the girl to ask questions that might lead to her figuring out who I am. We cannot risk that.

"Remember everything I taught you," Alexander says.

I nod again but am so nervous that all I can recall is that I should not throw a spider at her. I take a deep breath, stand straight, and then duck through the door. I see the girl before she sees me. She is standing beside a painting of the gardens behind the castle. We hid all of our family portraits, since we do not want Beauty to know about the "missing" royal family. Her village is so far away, she would not have heard of us, and we intend to keep it that way. It would be even harder to fall in love with a beast if you thought he ate a whole family.

I watch as she peers closely at the painting, then reaches out with a finger. Her other arm hangs at her side, grasping what looks like a handful of wet flowers. She is tall for a girl, and dressed in a well-made cloak. Her brown hair is pulled back to reveal a regular sort of face, square-shaped, with cheeks flushed from the weather, or the fire, or fear. As she admires the painting, her features relax into something that one might call pretty.

"*She* is called Beauty?" Alexander whispers. "Her name should be *Plain*."

"Shh!" I elbow him.

"Ow! That was my head!"

"Good!"

The girl turns slowly in our direction, lowering the finger she had been running down the length of a painted tree. I straighten up and tug on my waistcoat. Her eyes grow wide. I get the feeling she is examining every inch of me, taking in the fur not quite hidden by my long sleeves, the nails I cannot believe I forgot to cover with my gloves, the hawk-like nose, the wide face, the lion's mane of hair that Godfrey combed this morning until it gleamed. Now I feel foolish that I did not tie it back. I clear my throat. "Um, I am the beast. Welcome to my castle." And then, as I practiced a hundred times this week, I add, "The name Beauty suits you."

Her lips move in a twisty sort of way, and I fear she is either going to scream or throw up her last meal. Instead, she looks me directly in the face and laughs.

CHAPTER FORTY-ONE

∽ Beauty ℃

"Why are you laughing?" the beast asks, with what I think is a look of bewilderment, but I cannot be sure because of all the hair flopping in front of his face. He pushes it out of his eyes and asks again.

What should I tell him? That I find it hilarious that Papa would think this man is actually a beast when his costume is such obvious trickery? Or that I have waited my entire life for someone to say my name suits me, and then when someone does, it is someone like him? Or perhaps I should blame my laughter on nerves, like Handsome does. Instead, I hold out the flowers. "These are for you."

His bushy eyebrows rise. "You brought me flowers?"

I nod, then remember how possessive he is about his flowers. Papa picking that rose is what led to me being here. I hold my breath. Even a fake beast can be dangerous when angered.

But all he says is "Thank you. You might want to put them on the table. I do not want to stab you with my nails."

I do as he says, noting that his nails are pointier than the apothecary's sharpest knife. The large table is made from a single slab of dark oak, and I cannot help admire its smoothness. The stone floors beneath it gleam with firelight from carefully arranged sconces on the walls. All around me are plush couches and colorful lounge chairs and unique pieces of art. I certainly cannot fault him for his taste in decorating. Judging by what I can see, he is in no need of free labor. I force myself to look away from all the beauty around me and stare him full in the face. He is not exactly ugly. Rather, his features do not seem to go together well. Like he reached into a costume bag and pulled out the nearest items and stuck them on.

"No one has ever brought me flowers before," he says, his voice a low rumble.

"Perhaps more people would," I snap, "if you did not dress up like a beast and threaten people's lives."

"Dress *up*?"

"Forgive my rudeness, for I do not mean to insult you in your own home, er, *castle*, but this is a pretty poor costume. The wig is much too long, the nails are obviously stuck on with some kind of glue, and the fur, well, the fur simply looks ridiculous, all blotchy like that. And part of it is green."

I hear what sounds like muffled laughter behind me, but when I spin around I see no one. Papa had said the beast lived alone, so it must be the storm picking up again. I continue. "I have seen a man nearly your height before, but no one could be as wide as you. Clearly you have pillows under your clothes. And your nose! It must be made out of wood and poorly worked into shape. Why you would go to these lengths simply to frighten an old man into sending you his daughter as a servant I cannot imagine."

The beast stares at me, then squares his shoulders. "'Tis no costume, I assure you."

I know I should hold my tongue, but his lies are simply too much to bear. "You frightened my father nearly to his grave with your lies, and now you shower me with them as well? Shame on you."

His eyes fill with water. Could he be about to . . . cry? He blinks rapidly and looks around the room as though looking for some support in the shadows. Then he says, "Please, come see for yourself. I will not hurt you." He steps closer and bends down. His hair is within arm's reach now. "Pull," he instructs.

I hesitate, then my anger rises up again. I grab a handful of the coarse hair and give a soft tug. Then a harder one. Then a full-out yank.

"Ouch," he says, backing away.

I stare in surprise. Not a single hair came out in my hand. The beast leans over the back of the couch and neatly slashes a pillow with just one fingernail. I swear I hear a gasp from across the room, but we are still alone. He quickly turns the pillow over and pats it once, almost like he's apologizing to it.

"All real," he says, wagging his fingers in the air. "Trust me, I would not have them if I had a choice. They make even the simplest chore quite difficult. Forget trying to wash my face or even lace up my boots. I have run out of ointment for my gashes."

I back up until I bump against the side of a large chair. My mind is a whirl. Could he possibly be telling the truth? Is he half a man and half an animal, or a talking animal? Or a mixture of many different animals? If such a thing is possible, then are all the other things possible, too? Was Veronica right to believe in unseen forces after all? And *trust him*? How am I supposed to trust such a creature as this?

"Do you need to lie down, Beauty?" he asks, with a note of genuine concern. "I am indeed a beast, but I will not hurt you. Someone once told me my bark is worse than my bite."

I study him from across the room. He is large, but I am fast. I could probably run out the door and be gone before he could lumber after me. But as he awaits my answer with an expression both hopeful and hopeless, I realize I cannot run away. I am not a quitter and I made a promise. "Were you . . . were you born this way?"

He shakes his head, then pushes the hair from his eyes again with a bit of annoyance. He should just tie it back. "I was the victim of a curse. But more than that I cannot say."

"So magic is real, then?" I ask, holding my breath.

He nods. "It would appear so."

I sink down into the chair. "Witches and goblins and fairies? Princesses that sleep a hundred years?"

"I cannot speak to all of those," he says. "Only to the witch."

"Was she . . . horrible?"

He grimaces with the memory, then says, "Not at first."

I feel a tiny door in my heart open up for the beast. Yes, he frightened Papa and basically kidnapped me, but something truly terrible has befallen him. Unless perhaps he did something truly terrible first! "Why did the witch curse you?" I ask, narrowing my eyes at him. "A punishment for an evil deed? Did you cheat or lie or rob an old woman of her last penny?"

"What? No! Why would you think that?"

Now it is my turn to shrug. "In the stories, witches do not simply go around cursing people. The person usually does something to bring it upon himself."

He begins to pace, his huge feet thumping against the floor. "Well, your stories must be wrong, then, for I did nothing to bring it upon myself." Then he pauses. "Or nothing that I know of, anyway."

"You do not sound certain of that."

He scowls. "Can we talk about something else, please?"

For some reason that makes me laugh. "What do you have in mind, the weather? It is early for a winter squall, is it not? Is that what you prefer we speak of?"

Another chuckle behind me, but again, it belongs to no one. Perhaps all this talk of magic and curses is muddling my thoughts and making me hear things. "I think I would like to lie down after all."

He nods. "I shall show you to your room."

I half expect Clarissa to be right, that my room would be the dungeon below the ground. But the beast leads me to a room upstairs, where a window seat overlooks the back lawn and gardens. The gardens are nearly upstaged by the pinkness of the room itself. Pink flowers, pink canopy over pink blanket, pink pillows, even a pink ceramic bathtub. And frilly! So much lace everywhere. Out of politeness, I suppress a shudder. Clarissa would think she died and went to Heaven.

"Are you in need of anything?" the beast asks, hanging back in the hallway.

I shake my head. A glance around the room reveals that my belongings have been not only brought up to the room but unpacked. The comb that Clarissa snuck into my bag rests on the dresser next to a washing basin and a towel. I suppose if I am to believe in witches and beasts, I may as well believe that my belongings unpacked themselves.

"I shall leave you, then, to recover from your journey. And, um, everything else."

The silence when the door closes is complete. I untie my boots and lie down on the softest bed I have ever felt. It must be made from a cloud! I stare up at the pink canopy and pull Veronica's necklace out from under my collar. The stone warms my hands and makes me miss everyone that much more. No doubt they are worried about me, and I wish I could tell them I am not locked in a dungeon. Unless dungeons come in pink. By now they are surely in a comfortable home back in town. That thought brings me a bit of comfort.

The sound of a church bell startles me. The bell chimes a few more times until I realize it is not a church bell at all, but a clock signaling a new hour. I never knew anyone who could afford a real clock. But, of course, the beast must be wealthy beyond measure. I wonder how he came to possess this castle. Even though he seemed sincere before, I far from trust him.

The last rest stop I had was hours ago, and my bladder is becoming harder to ignore. I wait a little longer, staring out at what truly is a magnificent garden, until I can wait no more. Halfway down the hall, I realize I forgot to put my boots back on.

I creep as quietly as possible toward the door at the end of the hall, which I figure is most likely to be the one I need. But when I open it, instead of finding the dung chute, I am greeted with a narrow stairwell and a sign with the words *Enter at Your Own Risk*. I suppose it makes sense in a house this large to separate the dung chute from the living quarters. I begin to climb. The door at the other end is open a crack, so I push it the rest of the way, expecting to find the toilet.

Instead, I find a young boy. Singing. And dancing. With a green monkey. In what looks like a laboratory, even larger and better stocked than the apothecary shop.

I blink, but the boy and the monkey are still there, whirling around a boiling cauldron.

I should clarify that only the boy is singing. The monkey remains silent.

I am fairly certain now that madness has overcome me.

CHAPTER FORTY-TWO

↤ Beast ↦

"I like her!" Father says, slapping me heartily on the back. "She is quite the spitfire."

I sit down on the couch, which groans under my weight. A handful of soggy flowers are deposited on my lap.

"No one has ever given *me* flowers!" Alexander teases. "So very romantic. I apologize for laughing, but her tugging on your hair is one memory I shall *never* forget."

"Nor I," I reply.

"Are you all right, Riley?" Mother asks, putting her hand on my shoulder. "She is quite a girl, is she not? Alexander chose well."

Before I can answer her, Alexander says, "Not exactly the beauty I had expected." Followed closely by, "Ouch! Mother! Must you keep pinching me? I am practically an adult!"

"Then you must behave like one, Alexander. She is a lovely girl."

Alexander mutters something under his breath.

"I am not certain how I feel," I admit.

"I believe you are blushing," Father says, sitting down next to me.

"I am not!" I exclaim, as though he is accusing me of stealing the last plum pie. I put my hands to my ample cheeks. They do feel warm. "What does that mean?"

"It means you like her," Father says. "And why would you not? She is truly quite extraordinary. Taken away from all she has known to live with a beast, and she did not run away in fright."

"Not yet," I admit. "But she is hiding in her room. She may never come out."

"Let her adjust," Mother says. "It might take a few weeks."

"I don't have much more than that left."

"I know," Mother says. "But we must try to be patient."

I admit, my heart has never stirred like this before. Like Father said, she is indeed a spitfire. Bold and strong, and the melted snowflakes made her hair glitter in the most interesting way. I shake my head to clear it. Why am I noticing her hair? I am not supposed to fall in love with her, only she with me. Right?

"Prince Riley! Prince Alexander! Your Majesties!" Freddy shouts, pounding down the stairs. "Come quick! You need to see this!"

I jump up from the couch, smacking my head on the ceiling in the process. Rubbing my head, I ask, "What is the matter? Is Beauty all right? Did she jump to freedom from her second-story window?" I could not blame her if she had.

He shakes his head. "Nothing like that. Come!"

So we follow after him, looking like one very odd parade — one skinny page, one huge beast, and three invisible members of the royal family. Freddy leads us upstairs to my laboratory, of all places. "You didn't blow anything up, did you?" I ask as we climb. "We just got that wall fixed."

"I did not," he replies, and gestures for me to enter first. I step into the doorway while my invisible family squeezes around me. The first thing I see is Godfrey, standing by the window looking a bit embarrassed. And is that a . . . *monkey* sitting on a stool by the counter?

Freddy tugs on my sleeve and points to the center of the room. I force myself to turn away from the monkey (who seems to be partly green) to find Beauty standing beside the boiling cauldron, stirring it with one of my glass rods.

"Oh, hello," Beauty says. "I hope you don't mind my interruption."

As I stare, she adds two more ingredients to the mixture. A splash of vinegar and a pinch of some yellow powder, which I do not even recognize. "No," I finally say. "Of course not."

"Good," she says, dipping a ladle into the cauldron. She pours the mixture into a small beaker, not spilling a drop. Then she heads to the sink where she dips the beaker into a pot of water, no doubt to cool it off. I watch her lower it with fascination. How is it this girl knows her way around a laboratory? What is she doing? Making a slow poison, perhaps? I instinctively clamp my mouth shut.

She walks over to me, holds out the beaker, and says, "Here. This should rid you of the green on your fur. My sister had a similar problem. I mean, not with fur. Obviously."

I take it, ashamed that I suspected her of anything underhanded. "Truly?"

She nods.

"Thank you," I say, lifting the murky orange liquid to my lips.

"Wait!" she says, reaching up. "You do not *drink* it. You rub it on."

"Oh," I say, then begin to laugh. "That is good, for it does not look too appetizing."

"Here," she says, taking it from me. "Let me help you."

She leads me over to the sink, and orders me to hold my arm over it. She pours the liquid on the offending greenness, and rubs it in. She runs cool water over it, then scrubs some more. After a few minutes, the green color runs off into the sink.

"There," she says, patting it dry with a rag. "Now you look like a normal beast again."

Every time Beauty pats my arm, my heart beats a little faster. "I can do that," I tell her, snatching the rag perhaps a bit too quickly. She takes a step back.

"Wait, I am sorry. No one, well, no one outside this room, has shown me any kindness in a long time."

She nods. "Freddy here does seem to like you. And Godfrey. The monkey did not give his opinion."

I turn to Freddy. "Would you care to explain the monkey?"

He shakes his head. "Not really. Merely an experiment gone amiss."

"And is Godfrey's hair slightly . . . green?"

"I shall tend to them," Beauty says, heading back to the pot for more of her secret mixture. I watch as she patiently de-greens both the monkey and Godfrey. Mother takes this time to whisper in my ear, "I know you cannot see, but I am dabbing my eyes with my skirt."

I roll my eyes. But I would be lying if I didn't have a tear or two in my own. This girl brings out my tender side. I didn't even know I had one.

CHAPTER FORTY-THREE

⌒ Beauty ⌒

Godfrey leads me down to breakfast, and I am so tired I nearly trip every other step. When I met his friends (and the green monkey), the anger I felt toward the beast started to slip away. By the time I had de-greened him, it was gone entirely. In its place was curiosity and sympathy.

We had stayed up until very nearly sunrise. I told him about what I learned at the apothecary shop, and he told me of his experiments in the laboratory. We spoke of a mutual love of books and reading. He told me he can tell the exact date by studying the stars. I told him of our fire, and of losing everything we owned. Perhaps I should not have shared so much, but he is easy to talk to. He reminds me of Handsome, in that way. I cannot imagine what Handsome would think of all this, of me being here, of me choosing to come in Papa's place. He would likely march down here and demand my return. Not that I know where *here* is, exactly.

As forthcoming as he was with everything else, the beast shied away from anything personal — he spoke nothing of his life before the curse, nothing about how he befriended Freddy or Godfrey. The two of them were similarly tight-lipped when first I had stumbled across them in the lab.

I have yet to figure out what I'm actually doing here. The beast clearly does not seem to want me as a servant, since he has been the one to ask after *my* needs, not the reverse.

Perhaps he simply wants a friend. I truly do not know. All night he kept asking me if he was boring me, and I kept assuring him he was not. He is actually the most interesting person I have ever met. I have never stared up at the stars before, nor questioned the milky cloud that spans the heavens. But for him it is an unending source of mystery and fascination. Under all that fur he has a very big heart. I choose to ignore the fact that he could slice a regular-size person in half with one swipe of his claws.

Also, he makes me forget about my own appearance, and for that alone, I am grateful.

"Are you all right, miss?" Godfrey asks.

I nearly stumble again as I drag my thoughts back to the present staircase. "Yes, thank you, I am just tired."

"Did you not sleep well? I can get you a new mattress by tonight."

"No truly, 'tis fine. I was up late." I feel my cheeks begin to heat as I add, "Talking with the beast, I mean."

"He is quite special," Godfrey says, not looking directly at me. "Is he not?"

I nod, although I know he cannot see me. Before the beast, the only male other than Papa who I had befriended was Handsome. And Handsome did not make me feel like this after less than a day. A pang of guilt strikes me as I realize I have not yet thought of Papa or Clarissa this morning.

The beast awaits me in the dining room. He looks a little tired around the eyes, but otherwise he is quite well groomed. A green ribbon holds his hair back from his face. His cheeks are smooth, and while wide, they frame his face nicely. He catches me looking at him and smiles. I quickly focus on the gold plate before me.

The food is so excellent and plentiful that I manage to eat enough food for three people before the beast offers to take me on a tour of the castle. The first stop is the library. I cannot help but stare. Although I have only the monastery library to compare it to, this is beyond anything I have imagined. Thick velvet rugs and oak-paneled walls, glorious oil paintings on the walls between shelves. And the books! Rows and rows of them. Plain and ornate, ancient and new. Every shelf has a few gaps where the books Papa now owns once rested. To my utter surprise, I find myself feeling guilty that he took them away from this place, which is so clearly their home. And then, of course, I feel guilty for feeling guilty!

"What do you think?" he finally asks.

"Your library is truly magnificent." I squint at an object on the floor by his foot. "Is that a dead leech?"

He quickly scoops up the bug, pushes open the window, and tosses it out. "What dead leech? Imagine, a beast like myself, the king of the castle, with a dead leech on the library floor."

I pretend to curtsy. "Again, my humblest apologies. It was so clearly a piece of dust."

"You are forgiven," he says. "But I shall be keeping my eye on you."

I blush, and so does he. "Come," he says, hurrying from the room and the awkward moment. "There is much more to see."

The next few hours pass quickly. Although the snow-storm has passed, the air outside is cold. Still, we walk through the castle gardens, where fresh vegetables, herbs, and fruits have managed to escape the frost. They surely should have been harvested by now, but with only a young boy, an old man, and a beast (whose age I cannot even guess) to tend them, I am not surprised that they remain in the ground. The flower garden, however, is in full bloom and well cared for.

As we walk, I tell him of finding the map inside the book. I do not go into detail, for it is Veronica's story, not mine.

"We must return to the library!" he exclaims when I am done. "Maybe one of our books has a secret map hidden within!"

I laugh. "Trust me. I have taken apart many a book, and no other ones will contain such a secret. Your books are far too precious to destroy." I tell him how the book was not the only thing we "borrowed." When I mention how Handsome and I took the two robes from the monks, he stiffens a bit, and I fear I have offended him. "Do not worry," I say quickly. "Veronica returned them, only a little worse for wear."

He does not reply at first, then says, "Handsome must be very . . . handsome."

I turn to him in surprise. Is that a hint of jealousy I hear in his voice? I laugh. "He does not think so. But beauty is in the eye of the beholder, right?" Then I feel my cheeks grow hot. "I mean, I know I am not beautiful, and my name . . . well, you are the first person not to laugh or cough or otherwise react negatively when you heard it."

He examines me so carefully I have to look away.

"Have you *seen* me lately?" he asks. "Who am I to judge another's appearance?" He looks down, then back up at me again. "I am sorry that you were treated that way in the past. But, Beauty, you must know. You are quite beautiful." He looks down again and I am glad, for I do not think I could meet his eyes. No one has ever spoken to me like this. It feels . . . odd. And it makes me feel grown-up. And a little giggly, which is embarrassing.

"And I do not mean beautiful only in comparison to me," he adds. "Although it does help that you are not made out of various animal parts."

I laugh, grateful to have an excuse to do so. "Thank you, I think."

I swear I hear a woman sighing behind us, but, of course, no one is there. I follow him across the garden path toward the kitchen, looking back over my shoulder. As we step inside, I ask, "Do you ever get the feeling your house is haunted by invisible ghosts?"

"All the time," he says, quickly locking the door behind him and leaning against it. "All the time."

CHAPTER FORTY-FOUR

↤ Beast ↦

"You never brush your fur for *us*," Alexander teases when I walk into the dining room for supper. "And you are wearing the new shoes Mother had made for you."

"Do not tease your brother," Father says. "He looks very dapper."

"Any comments from you, Mother?" I ask, assuming I have the pleasure of her company, too.

"We did not appreciate being locked outside this morning," she says icily.

"You should not have been following me. Or sighing loudly. Beauty can hear you."

"Perhaps we were overly bold. Well, you will be pleased to know, then, that you and Beauty shall be dining alone tonight, so you will not have to worry about us interfering."

"Alone? Without Godfrey or Freddy, either?"

"That is correct. You should go on a proper date."

"But, Mother, what if I make a mess of it?"

She pats me on the arm. "You will do fine. Just be yourself."

"Or someone else entirely!" Alexander says. "Did I not tell you to refrain from boring her with tales of alchemy? And a tour of the library? What could be more boring?"

"She did not seem to find it so," I argue.

"She was probably just being polite."

I wave my arm toward the door. "If you are leaving, now would be a good time." Silence. "Alexander, I can still smell you. You truly must bathe more."

Father chuckles.

"I do not know what you find so funny, dear husband," Mother says as she brushes past me. "You have not trimmed that beard in weeks! A small rodent may have taken up residence there and we would not even know it."

They continue to argue over the proper level of personal hygiene for invisible persons — a conversation they never seem to agree on — until their voices fade away. I take a few deep breaths, willing myself not to say anything dumb when Beauty arrives. We had spent the afternoon digging for worms so I could reenact some of my experiments for her. Maybe Alexander was right, and she had only been pretending to be interested in such things.

The clock in the great hall chimes to mark the hour, and before it finishes the sixth chime, Beauty walks into the dining room. She is wearing a pink dress, white shoes, and the red rose I gave her tucked behind one ear. When she sees me, she stops and puts her hands on her hips. "All of my clothes have mysteriously disappeared. In their place hang ten dresses, all pinker than the next, all miraculously my size. Have you any explanation?"

This has Mother's handiwork written all over it. "Um, laundry day?"

"I feel ridiculous," she says.

"You look . . . lovely." I hurry to pull out her chair. She stumbles a bit getting into it.

We both nibble our roast lamb and mutton, offering only harmless comments about how well prepared it is. Meat will soon be scarce as winter closes in. I hope Beauty is too distracted by the food to notice how messy an eater I am. Indeed, she is polite enough to look away when food falls back onto my plate. I give up on the spiced carrot soup after three spoonfuls, most of which wind up on my chin.

I look up to see a tear sliding down Beauty's face. She tries to hide it by wiping it away as she dabs her mouth with her napkin.

"Are you all right?" I ask.

She sniffs and wipes another tear away. "Today is my sister's birthday. I had forgotten."

I do what Alexander told me, and make sure she knows I am interested in her life. "How old is she now?"

"Sixteen. She always thought she would be married by now."

"Why is she not? I heard she was quite charming."

She stops sniffling and looks up in surprise. "You did? How?"

I put my hand over my mouth. Where is that invisible brother when I truly need him? I almost let it slip that she is not here purely coincidentally. "I mean, I suspect she is charming since, well, you are wonderful to have around, and since you are sisters . . . it stands to reason."

I do not know if she accepts my bumbling explanation, because she just starts crying again. "You must miss her a lot."

She nods. "Our birthdays are so close. We've always celebrated them together."

I push back my chair and stand up. I do not even realize I am doing it until I find myself leaning over the table. In my deepest, firmest, beastliest voice I say, "You should go home, then. I do not have the right to keep you here against your will. You should be with your family."

"But I —"

"You do not belong here. I am a beast, remember? I have eaten entire families! Now go!"

For the first time, I see something like fear in her eyes, and anger, which I have not seen since our first meeting. And then she is up and running.

CHAPTER FORTY-FIVE

⤳ Beauty ⤶

It does not take me long to pack my bag, considering all of my clothes are missing except a few undergarments, my cloak, and the boots I arrived in. I angrily throw Clarissa's comb and the book I brought from home into the bag and cinch it up. If he does not want me here, I shan't stay another moment. I upheld my end of the agreement by coming at all. I need not have shown him any kindness, just because he showed it to me. I am the prisoner, after all. Well, I *was* the prisoner. Now I am just a girl who feels all tangled up inside.

I sling my bag over my shoulder and bound down the stairs. I do not pass the beast on my way to the front door, for which I am grateful. I do not think I could pull off my storming-off-in-a-huff exit if I begin to cry again.

"You should not be out here, miss," the guard tells me when I push the door open and step outside into the cold. The setting sun is nearly as pink as my dress, but I do not stop to appreciate it.

"I would like a carriage, please. The beast is sending me home."

The guard does not wait around to hear any more. He simply says, "Wait inside and I shall find a coachman." I watch as he rounds the corner of the castle toward the stables. I do not want to wait inside and risk seeing the beast again, so I huddle against the doorway. The wind howls, and

I shiver. I think I feel worse than when I left home! I reach inside my cloak and pull out Veronica's necklace. The last rays of sun glint off of it, and I find myself holding it up to my eye to see the light shoot off in all directions, bathing the front lawn in gold.

A rustling in the bushes beside the door draws my attention. I lean over, and at first all I see are some hedges bent at odd angles. And then suddenly a shape appears, seemingly out of the air. A boy! A boy hunched in the bushes, crying, and not even trying to hide it! He is older than me by a year or two, dressed in what looks like his pajamas although it is not yet fully dark. I feel another shiver and I hunch back against the door again. As I move, he vanishes!

"What happened?" I call out, looking around wildly. "Where did you go? Who are you?"

"You . . . you could see me?" the now-invisible boy asks. A rustling follows. "Beauty?"

His voice sounds like he is getting closer. I back up against the hard door, glad for its solidity. "How do you know my name?"

"Do not be afraid," the voice says.

"That is easy for you to say. You are not the one seeing ghosts!"

"I am not a ghost," he says, his voice coming at me from the left now.

"Then show yourself."

"I cannot," he says. Then he begins to weep again. "Please do not leave. None of this is Riley's fault. I am the one who spoke to the witch. It is my fault he is the beast, and then I let him believe it was something *he* did. What kind of brother am I?"

I turn in the direction of the voice, beginning to feel dizzy. "The beast is named Riley? He has a brother?"

A gasp, followed by silence. Then more weeping. "Now I have truly ruined everything! You were not supposed to know his identity until you fell in love! I warned him not to talk about all those boring things and chase you away, and now you will never love him and he will remain the beast and I shall remain invisible, forever!"

Now I am the one stunned to silence. His words run around one another as I try to make sense of them. The beast is really a boy named Riley. This boy in pajamas is Riley's brother. And he has ruined something? I was supposed to fall in *love*? "I need to sit down," I announce to the empty air.

An invisible hand on my elbow leads me to a stone bench by the door. I think the boy sits beside me, but I am not certain.

"I am sorry," the voice says, sounding truly miserable. "I should not have laid that upon your feet. It is I who ruined this, not you."

We sit in miserable silence for a moment. Then I ask, "What exactly did the witch say when she cursed your brother?"

"She said the girl couldn't know who he really was until she fell in love with him. And then the curse would break when she kissed him. And now you know who he is and there are only a few days left before the deadline. All is lost."

"You have ruined nothing," I whisper, so softly I am not even certain the words came out. Handsome said I would know my future when I found it, and I have. The beast — or Riley as he is called — he is my future.

CHAPTER FORTY-SIX

✦ Beast ✦

I know not how long I have huddled here in the dark. The root cellar was never a very inviting place. Damp, dank, and windowless, it is perfect for storing wine and vegetables, but I would much rather be sulking and miserable up in my bedchambers. I am hiding from the others, though, who have no doubt figured out by now that Beauty has left and that I chased her away. This is the last place in the castle I could think of where I could be alone.

I feel a ghastly ache inside me, and I know there is more to it than the anguish of realizing I shall remain a beast forever, the property of an evil witch. I have only read about it in books, but if I had to guess, I think the pain is heartbreak. I also fear I am coming down with a cold. I feel a strange chill, like an insistent buzzing inside my head unlike anything I have felt before. I wrap my arms tighter around myself, but it does not help.

A wine bottle crashes to the floor a few rows away from where I am crouched. I look over and see a lantern making its way toward me. "Go away, Freddy," I call out. "Nothing you could say would make me feel better."

"Perhaps you will want to hear what *I* have to say, then." The lantern draws closer and Beauty steps into view. I nearly fall backward in surprise. Her dress is covered in purple stains.

"I owe you a bottle of wine," she says. "I hope it was not too valuable."

"What . . . what are you doing here?"

She smiles and in her eyes I see no anger, no fear. "I have come to kiss you."

My jaw falls open. If I were not already sitting on the ground, I would surely have fallen to it in surprise. As much as I want the kiss, I cannot take it. I lower my head. "But I have behaved like the beast I am. You deserve much better than me."

She shakes her head. "A real beast would never feel that way. And you are not a beast. You are a boy trying to save his family. And then you tried to save mine by sending me away."

"But . . . how did you know all that?"

"I know you are Prince Riley. I know your family is invisible and that they care about you very much."

My eyes widen as her words sink in. "Then all is lost."

She shakes her head. "Not lost." She reaches out and lays her hand in my glove, where it looks so tiny but feels so nice. She squeezes, tight. Suddenly, I understand what she means. She loved me *before* she learned my identity! I meet her eyes, dazed.

Before I have a chance to think one more thought, to apologize in one more way, she moves toward me. All my experiments, all my knowledge about nature and the sky and music and worms, none of it has prepared me for how it feels to have someone you love about to kiss you for the first time. I close my eyes.

"Wait, stop!" a voice cries out. My eyes fly open. Another lantern rushes toward us, this time with Freddy at the other end.

I turn to glare at him, hoping to scare him away with the force of it. But he only comes closer. He better have a good reason for ruining my first kiss.

"I am sorry," Freddy says, out of breath. "But you must listen."

"Can't this wait?" I ask through gritted teeth. "We were in the midst of something important."

He shakes his head. "I'm truly sorry, but you want to vanquish the witch, right?"

"Of course I do."

"If Beauty kisses you now, the curse will break, but you'll lose all the beast's advantages — the speed, the strength. I do not think Prince Riley would fare as well. No offense intended, of course."

Beauty takes a step backward. "He has a point."

With each step she takes away from me, I feel a tiny stab in my heart. What I truly want to say is, "Can't someone else vanquish the witch and we can get on with the kissing?" But as I look from one to the other, I see that response is not the correct one. And yet . . . with the original plan I get to be kissed — the one thing I thought for certain would never happen to me, either as the beast or as Riley.

"Come," Freddy says, waving us forward. "Everyone is waiting for us in the fireside room."

"Can you believe it!" Alexander says as we surface, eyes blinking in the brightness. "All you needed to do to get a date was to turn into a beast!"

Beauty laughs and squeezes my hand again. I would be annoyed at his comment, but I am too busy smiling. My upper lip hurts from where the nose/beak is digging into it, but I care not a bit. Mother and Father embrace both of us, talking over each other in their pleasure at the turn of events. Godfrey and Freddy hang back, beaming.

We gather around the couches, where after a lot of shushing and interrupting, I learn about how Beauty and Alexander met outside. When they are done, I ask Alexander, "You have no idea what you did in order for her to see you? Did you feel any different for that moment?"

"I did nothing," he insists. "One moment she was looking at me, claiming to see me. The next she gasped like she had seen a ghost, and I became invisible to her once more."

Beauty suddenly jumps up from the couch. "My necklace! I was looking through it when first I saw him!" She reaches under her collar and pulls out a pink stone on a leather string. She holds it up to her face and turns toward Alexander's voice. She laughs with delight. "You have changed since I saw you last!"

"Just in case it happened again," Alexander says, "I thought I best change from my nightclothes!"

She walks slowly toward the hearth, still looking through the stone. "Your Majesty," she says, and gives a low curtsy.

Mother gasps. "You can see me? But I must look a fright!"

"Not at all," Beauty insists. "You look quite lovely."

"She always does," Father says.

Beauty turns toward the sound of his voice, blushes, and lowers the stone. "Perhaps I should wait for you to put on a robe."

"Honestly, Silas," Mother scolds. "How many times did I tell you?"

I watch all this with utter fascination. Somehow, even though I am living proof that magic is real, I never would have believed a stone could reveal what is hidden to the eye.

"Riley," Mother says. "Please do not think me uncaring or selfish, but what if you did not try to vanquish the witch, and just ended this now?"

I glance hopefully at Beauty, who has taken her seat beside me. She looks unsure. Then she shakes her head. "I have seen people go to great lengths to protect the people they love. A dangerous witch is on the loose. How can we sit by and do nothing?"

"You speak the truth, of course," I tell her, "but we don't know the first thing about the witch, or how to bring her down."

"We have a book about witches," Freddy adds, "but it is written in symbols we do not understand."

"May I see it?" she asks. Freddy jumps up to fetch it from upstairs. That buzzing I felt in the cellar returns as we wait. It is not a good feeling. My stomach clenches. Beauty must have felt me shiver through my glove. "Are you all right?" she asks.

I squeeze her hand, careful to be gentle. I don't want to worry her, so I say, "I'm merely excited."

She tilts her head at me suspiciously, but does not press further. When Freddy comes back with the book, Beauty holds her crystal rock up to the pages. And there, over and over again, are the same words: *You must find a witch's weakness to drain her power. That is the only way.*

"That is one powerful necklace," Mother says in a hushed tone. "Where did you get it?"

Beauty tells her the story about Veronica and their quest to find the stone.

"But how did the girl's mother come to possess it?" she asks.

Beauty shakes her head. "I do not know. Veronica never knew that part of the story."

"Sorry to change the subject," Alexander says, "but how are we supposed to find the witch's weakness? She seemed pretty unstoppable."

"We will have to observe her," Father says. "That is what we do if the kingdom is threatened. We watch our enemies, and we learn. There is strength in numbers, and you have all of us."

Freddy nods in agreement. "We will have to find where the witch lives, and spy on her."

"But how will we find her?" Mother asks. "We have no idea where she lives."

"We will not have to find her," I tell them calmly. "We simply have to wait. The witch said I would be drawn to her."

"Is it happening yet?" Alexander says. "There is only a few more days to go."

I shake my head.

"Let us all get some sleep," Mother says decisively. "This has been a big day!"

I watch as Beauty's hair is pushed aside by my mother's invisible hands and a lipstick mark in the shape of a kiss appears on her cheek. Beauty puts her hand up to it, obviously pleased. I remember how she grew up motherless, and my love for her grows even more.

I have just blown out the candle by my bedside when I hear a knock on the door. "It is me," Beauty announces.

I bang my knee and stub my toe but make it to the door in record time. I open it an inch. "Is everything all right? Do you need anything?"

She shakes her head. "You felt it. Earlier. You felt something, did you not?"

I hesitate for only a second before nodding.

"Why did you hide it?"

"You heard them. Everyone wants to help me. But it is too dangerous. All I feel is a little buzzing, a sort of tugging. But not enough to guide me anywhere. I do not want them making plans."

"But when it is time to go, you shall tell me, right?"

I do not answer.

"Riley! I am just as big a part of this as you. You need me there. What if she tries to take you before the time is up? I need to be there to kiss you!"

She is right, of course. But the thought of putting her within reach of the witch is a terrible one.

"Plus, I am an experienced quester," she says proudly.

I smile. "I do not think that is a word."

She laughs. "Perhaps not. But I do know how to survive on my own, and I have a feeling you did not get out much on your own in your previous life."

I cannot argue with her logic. "All right. I promise to tell you."

"Thank you," she says. "Good night, then."

"Wait." I open the door a bit more. There's a question I've wanted to ask her all day. "What did you see when you looked at me with your necklace?"

"I have not turned it upon you," she replies.

"Why not?"

She shrugs. "I already know what is inside you." She hurries off down the hall and I stand there with what is no doubt a very silly grin on my face.

"You should really put a cork on the end of that thing

you call a nose," she calls back in a loud whisper. "It would be a lot more comfortable!"

That night I have the dream again. I am running, panting, through a dense wood. As before, I have a companion by my side. But before in the dream, I never knew where I was running to, or running from. But when I awake, panting, and it is still not yet dawn, I know the answer. I know exactly where I am heading, and exactly who will be waiting on the other end. I shudder and climb out of bed.

CHAPTER FORTY-SEVEN

∽ Beauty ∾

The beast — I mean, *Riley* — walks into the dining room for breakfast with a wine cork on the end of his nose. I laugh so hard that juice flies from my mouth. I hurry to wipe it up. Now that I have discovered I am dining with the royal family, I am trying to be more ladylike. I did not even grumble this morning about having to wear a dress. I suspect the queen was the one who took all my old clothes, but I do not want to insult her by asking, or seem ungrateful for the new ones.

"Just when I didn't think you could look any stranger," Alexander says, "you prove me wrong."

Riley tries to eat with the cork on but makes more of a mess than usual. Usually, I would look away so as not to embarrass him. Now it doesn't seem to matter as much.

In the late afternoon, I sit down to write a letter to Papa and Clarissa telling them everything and requesting their secrecy. In case danger befalls us on the trip, I want them to know I am happy now, and that the beast is not evil at all, quite the opposite. Once the letter has left the castle — in the hands of a trusted messenger — I feel like a huge weight has been lifted.

That night after dinner, Riley walks me back to my room. "The pull is getting stronger," he whispers. "We should leave tonight after dark."

"So soon?"

He nods. "The buzzing in my head is getting stronger every moment. My body keeps trying to lead me out the door."

Now that the time is upon us, I don't want to leave.

"Are you all right?" he asks, bending down to peer into my face.

I nod. How can I tell him his castle feels like home to me now? All that is missing are Papa and Clarissa. "I am just nervous, that's all."

"Me, too," he says, and begins stroking my hair absent-mindedly. I close my eyes. I am reminded of the gentle way Clarissa used to brush my hair.

This feels very different.

A moment later he pulls his hand away. "Forgive me!" he says. "I did not mean to be so forward. I don't know what came over me. I've never, um, felt this way about anyone."

I smile up at him. "Me neither."

His cheeks redden. "What about Handsome?"

I shake my head. "My sister wanted me to like him in that way, but to me he was always a friend."

"That is a relief," he says.

We stand together for another moment just enjoying each other's company until he clears his throat and says, "Well, then, I will see you in a few hours. Meet me in the kitchen after sundown."

"Okay." I open my door. Sitting on the end of my bed is a small but sturdy case, packed full, with my traveling cloak and boots beside it. I turn back to Riley and point it out. "I have a feeling Godfrey is one step ahead of you."

Riley grins. "He always is."

*   *   *

I am the first to arrive at the kitchen, and I set my bag at my feet. The smells from dinner linger in the room, along with the warmth from the embers in the bottom of the oven. Outside the thick windows, the wind is picking up again. I do not relish braving the outdoors. But I trust Riley completely and am excited to be on a quest again. He arrives a moment later, looking back over his shoulder.

"Did you check the room?" he whispers. "I trust Godfrey to keep our secret, but the castle is unusually quiet."

I slip the crystal out from under my thick traveling clothes, and look around the room. "Your mother is sitting on a stool beside the counter, your father is sitting on *top* of the counter, and Alexander is glaring at me from the floor beside the sink."

Riley swings open the door to the pantry to reveal Freddy and Godfrey and a large pile of trunks. Freddy waves happily. Godfrey shrugs guiltily.

"Well!" Riley says in his deepest beast-voice. "Looks like our leave-taking has gotten a bit more complicated."

"We are coming with you," Alexander declares.

"You are not," Riley says. "Only Beauty and I are going. This is too dangerous for anyone else."

"But we could be useful," the queen argues. "Being invisible has its advantages."

"I doubt you would be invisible to the witch," Riley says, which is probably true.

The group continues to argue about it until Riley stamps his huge boot upon the floor. "No one else is coming," he growls. "We will be passing through very dense forest. Winter is fully upon us and time is fleeting. I know you want to help, but you would be more of a burden."

I am glad Riley cannot see their hurt expressions. I can tell he feels bad having to be so direct, but it is necessary.

"Make certain the witch does not see you watching her," the king warns. "Or we will likely have another beast in the castle."

I try not to react at his words, but I feel a chill nonetheless.

"And promise you will break the curse before you run out of time," the queen adds. "Whether or not you have succeeded in defeating the witch."

"Fine," Riley says, rolling his eyes dramatically. "I promise to let Beauty kiss me."

Alexander laughs, and then the others do, too. I join in, but in truth, I am nervous at the thought of the kiss. Usually, a girl's first kiss isn't a matter of life or death.

The queen hands me a bag of provisions. "Do not forget to eat and rest. You must keep up your strength."

The king hands me another bag. "These are carrots for Mortimer. The old boy loves his carrots."

"Mortimer?" I ask, holding the bag out in front of me.

"But he is your finest steed, Father," Riley says, answering my question. "I cannot promise that he . . . that we . . ."

"I know, son," the king replies. "I know. But Mortimer is reliable and strong, and what better time to put those qualities to use than now?"

Riley nods and takes the carrots from me. The queen strokes my cheek, so lightly, so gently. I do not recall my own mother stroking my cheek, although I am sure she did, at least once. Now I know what I have been missing. A knot forms in my throat, and I am glad when Alexander ushers us out the door. I follow Riley to the stables. "Mortimer is in the last stall on the left," he whispers, stepping back into the shadows. "I will wait here in case a groomsman is still inside."

I race over to the last stall to find the largest black horse I have ever laid eyes upon. His saddle is gleaming, his reins braided gold threads. He does not even snort when I approach, only tosses his head as I lead him out of the stable. A part of me is disappointed that I will not be running, but I see the sense in riding since we have no idea how far we will have to travel. Mortimer's footrests dangle by my ears. However will I climb up?

Riley reappears and I have my answer. He places his hands on my hips and lifts me onto the horse's back as though I weigh no more than the bag of carrots. I wish he could ride behind me, but, of course, the horse could never bear his weight. Riley ties our bags to the horse, and leads us to the edge of the castle grounds, careful to stay in the shadows. Apparently, the village folk know of the beast, but few have seen him. Riley would like to keep it that way.

Once safely into the woods, we take off at a sprint. Riley easily keeps pace with the horse. In fact, I think the horse is slowing him down.

We run through the crisp night air as the stars shine bright above us. The moon is half full, and provides plenty of light to guide us. We duck around the outskirts of Riley's kingdom, and then stick to the sides of a narrow road. It is long past curfew now, and we do not expect to run into any travelers. Still, better to keep out of sight as much as possible. People can be unpredictable when they are scared. And while I am used to Riley's appearance, he would indeed cause quite a fright to strangers.

After a few hours, we find an empty barn a good distance away from other buildings. We gulp from our canteens and feed Mortimer his carrots. Then we both fall asleep the moment we rest our heads.

Breakfast consists of the bread, cheese, and dried meat sticks that Riley's mother gave us. I smile when I discover the solid gold silverware in the sack. We hardly need something so fancy, but I suppose when you are royalty all of your silverware is fancy.

"The tug toward the witch is almost unbearable now," Riley admits, pacing the length of the barn. "To be honest, I am beginning to feel frightened."

"We will be very careful. We will not get caught."

"My fear lies elsewhere." He stops beside me, but looks down. "I am afraid that as I get closer, I will not be able to stop. What if I run right to her?"

I put my hand in his. "I shall stop you." We both know that chances are my meager strength would not be able to overcome the witch's pull. Still, it makes me feel better to say it, and him to hear it.

"I wish we had a better plan," he says. "One that we know will succeed."

"Me, too, but until we know what the witch's weakness is, we won't know what to do about it."

Neither of us is willing to say what we're really thinking — that she may not *have* a weakness.

We do not talk much as Riley leads us on a race across the countryside. His pace never falters, and he never seems to tire. He has donned a cloak that covers him head to toe. Whenever we cannot avoid coming close to another person, he hunches over to appear shorter. Since everyone else is bundled and hunched against the cold, he does not receive more than a second glance.

By the next day, the passage has become so difficult that I fear Mortimer will get hurt if we keep up this pace. Rock ridges and wide streams block our way, and Riley plunges ahead. By sundown, my whole body aches from holding on to Mortimer so tightly. "Riley," I call ahead to him. "We need to rest."

"I'm sorry, I cannot stop," he says, slowing his pace only slightly so I can catch up. Ahead of us is what looks like a huge dark wall that I cannot see around. As we approach, the wall reveals itself to be a mass of twisted branches and leaves that stretch as far east and west as I can see.

"We will have to leave the horse here," Riley announces. I hesitate, but Riley reaches up for me. I give Mortimer a final pat and the last carrot and then let Riley lift me off. My legs wobble as my boots hit the ground. Unable to support my weight, I fall to my knees.

"Climb on my back," he says, kneeling down and bending over.

I do not argue. With my arms tight around his neck, Riley tears through the thick brush with his arms held in front of him. Still, the branches whip our faces and scratch our arms. The speed is thrilling. We fly through the forest now, and I realize how much Riley had been slowing his pace for me, even though time could have run out on him. My heart grows even fuller.

In the near-total darkness, Riley jumps over fallen logs, ducks under low branches. I yell when I see danger, and he obeys. We are a good team. After hours of this, I am both exhausted and wide awake. "We are almost there," he says with certainty. And a moment later, we emerge from the dense woods. Without the tree cover, the dark is a bit less total. Riley skids to a halt and I climb down, my legs so shaky from gripping that I do not try to walk. I lean against him and look around. Objects slowly reveal themselves as my eyes adjust. The moon first, then some stars. Then a vast openness on three sides. An openness that leads to . . . the sea! I turn frantically from side to side as more and more of our surroundings become visible. There is no denying it. I grab Riley by the arm. "I have been here before!"

CHAPTER FORTY-EIGHT

⤙ Beast ⤚

"But I do not understand," I say, relieved that for the moment at least, the almost unbearable buzzing in my head has now ceased. "We are in the middle of nowhere, and that forest was nearly impassable. How could you have gotten through it?"

Beauty points at a distant shoreline. "We came from across the sea, from that port over there." She whirls around. "And that's where I found Veronica's crystal! Right there in that dried-up brook!"

I shake my head in disbelief, although after the last few months, nothing should surprise me. "Why would we wind up here, amidst these ruins?"

Beauty lifts the crystal from her neck. It seems to glow with its own light. In a strained voice she asks, "Do you think the crystal led us back here, and it wasn't the pull of the witch at all?"

I consider her question. If that is true, we might be nowhere near the witch and may as well give up. If we figured correctly, sundown tonight will bring the witch's deadline with it. Then I remember something. "The buzzing inside my head has ceased completely. That must mean we are in the right place." I turn in a circle. "But how could we be? Nothing lives in this barren land, let alone a witch."

Neither of us speaks for a moment. We both just stare at the desolate landscape. Then Beauty says, "Think about it, Riley. If you were a witch, you would want to keep people far away from your hiding place, right?"

"Being a beast isn't bad enough? Now I'm a witch, too?" I can't help trying to make her smile. The corners of her mouth twitch and I wish I could be the one to kiss *her*, rather than the other way around.

"I'm serious," she says, punching me lightly on the arm. "What if she enchanted this place to try to make people leave?"

Before I can answer, Beauty lifts her stone and peers through it. She gasps, yanks the necklace over her head, and tosses it to me. "Look!" I hold it up and watch in amazement as the ruins of the old buildings disappear. Gone are the crumbling stairs, the moss-covered columns, the dust and mud. In its place is a huge, gleaming estate, surrounded by trees and fountains and babbling brooks and animals roaming free. Although it is not yet dawn, the sun shines as bright as noontime. I lower the stone. Instantly, the dark and ruins return. I hold it back up, and the white marble building reappears, brilliant in the sunlight. I see no people anywhere on the flower-lined paths that wind through the estate. I reach out for Beauty's hand. "She is in there, I know it. I can't say how, but I do."

"Then let us do what we came for, before someone sees us."

I hold the stone up again and seek out the best way to get inside. "There is a path on the left side, well hidden by the lemon trees. We can enter there and stay close to the hedges. We can duck behind them if we see anyone." I put the necklace back over her head. "You should keep this, in case I . . . well, just in case."

Beauty nods, squeezing my hand, and we creep forward. Keeping the stone in front of her eye, she leads us to the right spot. "All right," she says, stopping. "One more step and we shall be inside."

I hold my breath, not sure what to expect. Some sort of alarm to sound, perhaps. Instead, we find ourselves in the bright sunlight, on the stone-covered path, the ruins nowhere to be seen. We no longer need the stone to see!

"The enchantment must be on the outside only," Beauty whispers. "The witch knew no one would get close if they saw only ruins."

We leave our heavy cloaks behind a large rock and creep forward as quietly as possible. We pass no one. I cannot see any of the animals I had spotted before, either. Only small, well-kept farmhouses, bright green lawns, ponds and fountains. Mother would love this place. I am about to share that thought with Beauty when she suddenly stops and shrinks back into the trees. I quickly follow. Only seconds later, a beautiful young woman appears in front of one of the farmhouses, much too close to us for comfort. Her long, curly hair nearly reaches her waist. A large black-and-white spotted cat trails behind her. The woman bends down and begins petting the cat until it purrs. I want to warn the lovely woman that a witch is near, but I dare not risk being seen.

As we watch from the trees, a mud-splattered pig crosses the lawn and chooses that moment to shake its rear end. Mud flies onto the lady's skirts, and she rears back and kicks the pig halfway across the lawn. It whimpers and runs directly toward us! We shrink back even farther. The woman swoops up the cat and heads down the road, fortunately in the opposite direction of our hiding spot.

The instant the woman is out of sight, Beauty reaches out and hugs the squirming pig, trying to comfort it. "I think that beautiful woman is the witch!" she gasps as the pig continues to wiggle. Beauty only tightens her hold.

She is right, of course. I should have known by the fact that the tingling has now returned. Not nearly as power-fully but just as insistent. The time is near. "I need to follow her."

"*We* need to follow her," she corrects me, bending her head toward the pig, murmuring kindnesses. The pig visi-bly relaxes. I cannot help but smile. Beauty has the same effect on me.

She nuzzles the pig once more, then gives it a kiss on the top of its head. If I live a hundred years, I shall never forget what happens next. The pig stops moving completely. Then in a blur of movement and color, it falls from her lap and starts . . . changing! Beauty jumps up and we grab hold of each other, transfixed by the scene before us. The pig's limbs have become arms and legs. A second later, a man in peasant garb lies twitching and panting on the ground. He is shoeless and hatless, and in serious need of a shave.

We both hold our breath while the man catches his. Then his eyes fix on me. "Ye gads!" he exclaims, looking me up and down. "The witch must have really hated *you*!"

CHAPTER FORTY-NINE

∼⊃ Beauty ⊂∼

"Are you all right?" I ask, kneeling beside the pig-turned-man. He is still staring up at Riley, shaking his head back and forth.

"Enough already," Riley says, rolling his eyes. "I get it, I'm huge and hideous. But she made *you* into a pig, and that's not anything to brag about."

I turn to Riley. "Did you know the witch had cursed others?"

"I had suspected," he admits. "But I did not want to frighten you further by telling you."

"You can tell me anything," I say, a bit hurt.

"I'm sorry," he says, stepping to my side. "I will keep things from you no longer."

"Thank you," I tell him, reaching out my hand for his.

"Hello?" the man asks, leaning on a lemon tree for support as he stands. "Can we focus on the larger issue here?"

"Sorry," I say, my cheeks warming.

"Sorry," Riley mutters, squeezing my hand before letting it fall.

"All right, then. First of all, my name is Mumford. I am much indebted to you, young lady, for the kiss. I had long given up on anyone breaking the curse."

"No offense," I reply, "but the witch said the girl has to love you before she kisses you. While you were cute as the pig, I would hardly call what I felt for you love. More like sympathy and gentle affection. Perhaps something else ended your curse?"

The man shakes his head. "The witch lied. 'Tis only the kiss that matters." He nudges Riley. "But all the better if she loves you first, right, old boy?"

"But . . . we . . . I . . . but . . ." Riley stammers as he takes in the man's words. "You mean all this time a girl had only to *kiss* me and the spell would have been broken?"

Mumford nods. "Not as easy as it sounds when you're a pig."

Riley's expression of shock at this new knowledge is almost comical. With his hair all wild from the run through the woods, and his cheeks flushed, he looks like a young child's drawing of a monster.

"Most people who saw me tried to turn me into their supper," Mumford explains. "I was much too far from my home to find safety there, so I wasted most of my months of freedom running from meat cleavers. And then my time was up. Like you, I was pulled back to the witch by an invisible force. I have been here ever since. Five or six years, I think. I have lost track of time. It is never dark. It is never winter. The only voice is hers. Once you are her property, your speech is stolen as well." He stretches, smiling as he flexes his fingers. "Ah, movable thumbs. How delightful!"

Riley, wide-eyed, has now begun muttering angrily to himself and pulling at his hair. "Just a kiss!" he repeats over and over. "Just one little kiss!"

I allow him his tantrum in private and turn to Mumford. "But what is this place? What goes on here?"

"This is the witch's compound," he says, stating the obvious. "She leaves it only to collect another victim."

"But why does she bother?" I ask. "Judging by the kick she gave you, she does not seem to like having you here."

"Oh, she hates us, to be certain. But she needs us within her walls. She draws her power from ours."

"Our *power*?" Riley asks. "What power?"

"All of her victims have something she lacks. Some special skill or gift. With some it is strength, or brilliance, or perfect eyesight. Others are especially brave, or are skilled in battle, or can play the violin to make you weep."

"I don't understand," Riley says, clenching his fists, his anger clearly not spent. "How did turning *me* into the beast help her?"

"When she transforms someone, she absorbs whatever their gift is, leaving them unable to outshine her in any way. That is what feeds her magic and keeps her young. She has already outlived her rightful years by many a dozen."

Riley frowns. "Then she made a mistake by transforming me. My brother, Alexander, possesses all the talent in our family."

The man shakes his head. "The witch does not make mistakes."

Suddenly, I feel the rise of anger, too. I am angry that Riley suffered these last few months for nothing. Angry at the witch's lie about love. Angry that my own family suffered because of it, too. "The witch will never have Riley as her latest 'pet.' I shall kiss him before that happens!"

He smiles gently, unable to hide his amusement. "Then what are you waiting for?"

I lift my chin high and cross my arms. "I can't yet. We have to vanquish the witch first so she cannot curse anyone else."

Mumford laughs, then stops when we do not share in his

merriment. "Oh! You were serious! Forgive me, but the witch is very powerful. She will squash you like a bug. Or, more likely, turn you into one. I was attempting to thwart her when she captured me. Do you have a plan?"

To my surprise, Riley says, "Yes. I plan to surrender."

"Sorry?" I ask. I hope I've heard him wrong.

But Mumford only nods thoughtfully. "Keep talking."

Riley begins to pace. The ground beneath us quakes a bit with each heavy footfall. I glance around, hoping the witch isn't close enough to feel it. All I see are a few ducks and a llama eyeing us warily from a nearby lawn.

"I will approach her in surrender, as she commanded," Riley explains to me. "She will see I was unable to break the spell, so I am now her property. I shall keep her distracted while you . . . well . . . while you kiss a lot of animals. When the witch's powers are weakened enough, I shall escape her sight, you shall, um, kiss *me*, and turn me back while there is still time."

Mumford, while delighting in doing deep knee bends and lunges, has been listening carefully. He cracks his knuckles and says, "I will help you by gathering the witch's creatures to the pastures at the far end of the compound. The smells usually keep the witch far away. And when the transformations are complete, I shall dispense of the witch." He cracks his knuckles again, then grabs a lemon from the branch above his head.

I mull over their words for a moment. I do not like the idea of Riley being alone with the witch. "But, Riley, what if she bewitches you in some way? Robs you of your speech, or makes you forget who you are?"

He kneels down beside me and takes my hands in his gloved ones. "Then you shall remind me."

I stare into his eyes, nearly level with mine, and find strength there.

"You must promise me," he continues, "that you will not get caught. If you see her approaching, use Veronica's stone to find your way out. Do not come back for me. It will be too late, and I could not bear it if my fate were to befall you as well."

Tears fill my eyes.

"Promise me," he repeats.

I force myself to nod, although I am not at all sure I mean it.

He smiles and pushes a strand of my hair away from my face. The gesture is so sweet that I begin to cry all over again. Without a thought, he hugs me close. Even through all the fur, I can feel his heart beating. I have never been held by anyone other than Papa. I do not want it to stop.

Mumford clears his throat. "Hate to break this up, but we really must get moving. The witch will shortly be heading this way."

I had nearly forgotten we had an audience. Reluctantly, Riley and I release each other. "Be careful," I whisper. "Now that I have found you, I do not want to lose you."

"Nor I," he says. We lean toward each other as though going in for one last hug. His face only inches from mine, I am overcome with emotion. Without any thought whatsoever, I lean forward and kiss him so quickly that it almost might not have happened.

But it did! We stare at each other in horror.

Mumford shakes his head. "Young love. What can you do?"

CHAPTER FIFTY

↢ Beast ↣

I can feel the echo of the kiss as we stare at each other. It was as soft as a moth's wing, and as quick as a hummingbird, but I can still feel its effects all the way down to my tingling toes. We hold our breath. Maybe it wasn't enough to break the spell? Maybe we can still follow through with our plan?

But Beauty knows the truth before I do. She steps back and shakes her head. "I'm so sorry."

Seconds later, a shudder rips through my entire body and, still kneeling, I fall face-first to the ground. Where months ago there was stretching, now there is shrinking. My limbs rearrange themselves, my hair yanks itself back into my head, and my fur disappears, leaving my skin bare and raw. I press my lips firmly together to keep from screaming. Everything is dark! I am blind! Then my eyes open. I hadn't realized I was squeezing them shut.

The first person I see is Mumford, bowing low before me. "At your service, Your Highness," he says, reaching to help me stand.

"How do you . . ." But I need only to look down at myself to know the answer. I am wearing my traveling clothes. My cloak has the royal emblem embroidered on the front.

Dizzy from the transformation, I let him take my elbow and help me to my feet. It takes a second to realize when I have reached my full height, for it seems so close to the ground. I cannot help running my hands over my arms and face. Gone are the muscles and the broad shoulders and the strong arms. But so is the thick hair, the fur, the hawk nose. I pinch my nose. I cannot believe it was ever this small!

I feel a light touch on my arm and know that when I turn around, Beauty will be standing there. What will she think of me? Will she be disappointed? I turn slowly to face her.

Her eyes scan my face, void of any expression other than curiosity and wonder. Finally, she says, "You are shorter than I expected!" and then grins.

I laugh and hold out my hand. She takes it.

"A much better fit," she says.

"Indeed." This is the first time we have held hands without my gloves on, and I feel suddenly shy. My cheeks grow warm and I have no long hair to cover them.

"I have ruined our plan," she says. "I am truly sorry about the kiss."

"I'm not," I reply truthfully. It feels great to smile without the hook of my nose digging into my lip.

She squeezes my hand and I no longer care if she sees me blushing. I am human again! And a girl likes me! It is hard to think of the witch.

Mumford hurriedly shakes two lemons from a branch over his head. He tosses one to each of us, only mine lands on the ground due to me not really being aware yet of where my arms begin and end. "Let us be on our way," he instructs. "We will have to cut through the pasture, so there will be no trees nor buildings to hide behind. Stay low to the ground." He tilts his head at Beauty and says, "Due to this one being so free with the kisses, we shall come up with a new plan as we go."

"Hey," I say, defending my lady, "had she been less free with them, you would still be rolling in mud, eating worms and tree bark or whatever pigs like to snack on."

He laughs and slaps me on the back. "You speak the truth, Your Highness!" He takes off at a sprint, having apparently recovered his balance already. He begins to whistle a low tune, almost like a hum. Every animal in sight stops its grazing and follows him.

We hurry to catch up, me stumbling every few steps. When your feet are suddenly half the size they've been for months, walking is an entirely new experience. Mumford keeps turning in circles as he goes, searching the property for the witch. I feel very exposed in this pasture, with nothing but low grass surrounding us on all sides. Beauty and I stick close together. More than once she has to catch me before I hit the ground. "So much for my plan to save the day as the beast," I whisper as she steadies me once again.

"Were it not for the beast, we never would have made it here in the first place," she points out.

The animals are beginning to surround us on all sides. They sneak glances but move steadily forward toward the large barn in the distance. "That may be, but without your stone, we never would have seen it for what it was. I would have been at the mercy of the witch. And she would have shown me none, for certain. Did your friend ever mention a connection between the stone and a witch?"

Beauty shakes her head. "She never knew where her mother was headed when she left home, or even how she came by the stone in the first place."

Mumford stops beside a large red barn and motions for all of us to gather around him. I cannot help but steal glances at the animals. I am fairly certain all of them were once human, but I cannot bear to think on it. At least I still had the body of a human (well, mostly). There is nothing human about any of these poor creatures, except the expressions in their eyes. Sadness, fear, frustration, and now, a bit of hope. "I must not let them down," I whisper fervently. If Beauty hears me, she does not comment.

Mumford leads the crowd a few more feet until we are hidden from view behind the barn, and then steps onto a bale of hay to address the crowd. "Attention please, everyone. I am Mumford, formerly known as The Witch's Pig."

At this, the crowd stomps, crows, snorts, bleats, barks, and flaps.

"Shh," he says. "We must move fast." He gestures for me to stand beside him. "This is, er, I do not actually know your name?"

"I am Prince Riley from one of the seven kingdoms due south from here." I stand up straight like Mother always taught us when addressing the townsfolk. My voice still sounds strange to me, like a boy's voice. Which, of course, it is. I admit, there were elements of being the beast that I will actually miss — the deep voice being one of them. I clear my throat, and try to sound older. "This is my friend Beauty. She kissed me and broke the witch's curse. She will do the same for you."

More barking and all-around happy animal noises erupt. Mumford holds up a hand and they quickly settle down. I continue. "When everyone has transformed back to their former selves, the witch's power will be gone. At least we hope so." I do not want to admit that we have thought no further than that. We will need to keep her from starting all over again. But first things first.

Beauty joins me in front of the crowd. I notice for the first time that her arms and cheeks are scratched from the branches during our run. She never even complained.

"Hello, everyone," she says. "I would like to ask the women to stand to the left, and the men to the right."

A flurry of fur and feathers later, they are sorted into two nearly even groups. I cannot figure out Beauty's intent. She turns to me and Mumford and says, "Pucker up, boys, you have some kissing to do, too."

Mumford looks from one group to the next, and then lets out a big belly laugh. "Of course! The girl is right!" He positions himself in front of a fluffy white poodle, and points next to him at a particularly large brown sheep. The poodle wags her tail happily as she looks up at Mumford. My sheep eyes me warily. I do not blame her. I have never kissed an animal in my life, since Mother does not allow pets in the house. I may have kissed one of the royal horses when I was three, but that is the extent of it.

"Let us begin!" Beauty says. She races over to the first in her group, and kisses an owl right on the top of his head. Without waiting to see what happens, she moves on to a frog, and then a turtle. Mumford has already kissed his poodle and has moved on to a three-toed sloth. He elbows me. "Get to the kissing!"

Out of the corner of my eye, I can see the animals Beauty kissed are falling to the ground, transforming in a tangle of limbs. I quickly turn back to my sheep and kiss her lightly on the ear. It felt like kissing my blanket at home. Not that I have actually done that, of course.

Without looking back, I move quickly down the line. An antelope, a cat, three rabbits, and a hedgehog. Judging from the muffled shouts and weeping and shuffling going on behind me, I surmise my kisses are doing their job. I am about to kiss a parrot when I catch Beauty's eye. She smiles at me over the head of a donkey and winks.

I smile and kiss my parrot square on the beak. I'm about to move on to the next animal when I realize Mumford and I have no more animals in our group. Working together has allowed us to move more quickly than Beauty, who still has a handful to attend to. I consider asking some of the newly transformed women to help, but they are all still very disoriented and most are having trouble even sitting up without help. In hindsight, Mumford recovered very quickly following his own transformation. I wonder what his special gift is. Strength maybe, or bravery. Beauty has just finished kissing a mule, and is bending down toward a large gray buffalo.

"Wait a moment," I say, hurrying to join her. When the buffalo sees me, he shuffles backward until his hind legs are up against the wall of the barn. I squint at him. The shiny almost-silver-colored coat, the horns so low they scrape the ground. "I have seen you before," I tell him. "You were with the witch the day I was cursed." He only lowers his head further, his horns digging small ditches in the soft ground.

"Do not be afraid," Beauty says, approaching him cautiously. She rests her palm on his back, but he bristles and shies away from her hand.

"I am loathe to rush you, m'lady," Mumford says, joining us. "But we must finish our task and get everyone to safety."

We both glance back at the twenty-five or so fully human people huddled together. Old and young (though none as young as I), they are talking excitedly, their eyes alternately frightened, cautious, and gleeful.

Beauty turns away and quickly kisses the cowering buffalo. Soon he is a tall, thin man, huddled in a ball. He pulls his silver cloak tight around himself and refuses to look at us.

Beauty bends down beside him. "Sir? Are you all right? You are amongst friends here."

He shakes his head. "I failed the royal family. I tried to warn them, but I could not."

She looks up at me, surprised, then back down at him. "You look familiar to me. Have we ever met?"

He glances up at her and shakes his head.

"I do know you, though," she murmurs. "Wait! You are the man at the mill. The one who can tell if someone is telling a fib!"

He nods, wincing. "That is I. All the witch does is tell fibs. And I could do nothing to stop it."

Beauty leans close to me and whispers, "When I saw him last, he was confident and strong. Now he is a broken man."

I kneel down. In my most princely voice, I say, "Sir, you are not to blame. You tried to warn us as best you could, and in return you were struck by the witch. I am certain when all of this is over, our kingdom would be lucky to have a man such as yourself working with us."

He meets my gaze. "Truly?"

I nod.

He pushes himself into a sitting position. "Thank you, Your Highness. I shall pull myself together."

Satisfied that he won't have a problem on his hands, Mumford helps the man the rest of the way up, and brings him over to the other group. "Run as fast as you can," he instructs everyone. "Hide in the cellar of the slop house.

The witch never goes there. I shall come for you when it is safe." Before they turn to go, they lob oaths of loyalty and words of gratitude to me and Beauty, then take off, running and stumbling and helping each other up. They disappear around the side of the barn. I do not see where they go from there.

Just as I'm about to ask Mumford where we can find the witch, a black cat with white spots rushes up to us. It is the same one the witch was petting so lovingly earlier. "Oh, no, we missed one!" Beauty says, kneeling down and puckering her lips.

Mumford yells, "Stop! Don't go near that cat!" but it is too late. The cat has sprung up, hissing and spitting and adding to the scratches on Beauty's soft cheeks.

"Ouch!" she cries out, trying to fend off the cat with her elbows. I run up and grab the cat from behind, holding it as far out in front of me as my arms (which seem short and stubby to me now) can reach. It squirms free and dashes away.

"That is not good," Mumford says, holding his hand to his face. "If he is here, the witch is not far behind. I had hoped to have the element of surprise on our side."

"Who is he?" Beauty asks, dabbing at her face with her sleeve. "Or should I say, who *was* he?"

"I do not know," Mumford replies. "But he and the witch are very attached to each other. She turned him long ago. I think he was not a good person to begin with."

"If she likes him so much, why doesn't she turn him back to human?" I ask. "Surely she can break her own curse."

"'Tis a good question. I think she likes having him as her eyes and ears amongst the other animals."

The words are no sooner out of his mouth than the cat reappears, followed only two steps behind by a withered old

woman, bent nearly in half. Her eyes, full of hate, are
directed entirely at me.

"*You!*" She spits at my feet. A gross glob of green goo
slides between blades of grass, barely missing my boots.
"*You* have done this to me! How dare you?"

I motion for Beauty to get behind me, but instead she
stands beside me and takes my hand. "*We* have done this to
you," she corrects the witch. "We did it because no one else
should have to suffer like Riley did. Or any of the others you
took away from families who loved them. How dare *you*, is
the question." She juts out her chin in defiance. It trembles
a little, but does not waver.

I turn to Beauty in amazement. I knew she was brave —
she'd have to be to agree to live with a beast and then to
come here with me — but I did not know she was capable
of *this*.

The witch waves her hand at Beauty, dismissing her like
one would a pesky fly. "I still have enough power left for one
more transformation," she hisses at me. "I turned you into a
beast once. I shall do it again."

Out of the corner of my eye, I see Mumford sneak up on
the cat and grab him. "I do not think you will," I reply calmly.

"And why is that?" she asks.

I step to the side and point at Mumford. "Because we
have your cat."

If I thought her eyes were filled with hate before, now
they are furious. "You will not hurt one hair on that cat's
head," she says, emphasizing every word.

"No," I admit. "But Beauty just might kiss him."

The witch gasps.

"You will lose your prized companion, and the last bit of
your power, all at once."

"I would take the boy at his word," Mumford says. "I've seen the girl in action."

Beauty rolls her eyes at us. "You two did your fair share of kissing, too, as I recall."

"Give me the cat!" the witch bellows. Then she rears back and lunges for him.

In response, Mumford quickly tosses the cat over the witch's head to me as though I actually have a chance of catching him without getting sliced to shreds. He lands beside me on all fours, springs back on his hind legs, and bares his sharp teeth. Meanwhile, the witch has landed squarely in Mumford's now-empty arms, and he grabs her tight. Seeing this, the cat begins to screech in protest.

"You are not using your magic to free yourself," Beauty says to the squirming witch. "That must mean you are saving what little you have left. If you do indeed have enough for one more transformation, then we shall give you a choice. You can use it on one of us, but we will just break the curse the moment after, and you will have no power left at all. You will wind up locked in the dungeon of Prince Riley's castle."

I shudder. "I can tell you from experience that it's not very comfortable down there."

"Or," Beauty continues, "you can turn yourself into an animal and live out the last of your days in the wild."

Once again ignoring Beauty, the witch turns her fierce gaze on me. "I tried to kill you once," she hisses. "Would have saved me a lot of trouble, too. But all you did was blow a hole in the wall with the ingredients I sent you. Hard to believe you're supposed to become such a great scientist." She snarls. "What place would magic have in the world if men could control nature themselves?"

My eyes widen. "*You* sent me that box? I'm going to be a great *scientist*?" I cannot believe this! Me, who cannot even keep a *worm* alive! "*That's* why you turned me into a beast?"

"How wonderful!" Beauty exclaims, shaking my shoulder. "I knew she didn't make a mistake choosing you. You *do* have a special gift! Imagine what you will contribute to the world!"

As she shakes my shoulder, her necklace sways a bit and the sunlight glints off of the pink surface. For the first time, the witch snaps her full attention to Beauty. She narrows her eyes at the necklace with such focus that I fear she will burn a hole through Beauty's chest. When Beauty realizes what the witch is looking at, she takes a few steps backward and clutches the stone.

"Where did you get that?" the witch asks, struggling to free herself of Mumford's grasp. "That is mine!"

"I do not think so," Beauty says. "It belongs to my friend. And I intend to give it back."

The witch shakes her head. "Wrong! It belongs to *me*! It belonged to a young woman who I transformed into an ant a few years ago. Once she became my possession, so did the stone."

"Mumford," I ask, "is there an ant here that used to be a person? I thought the cat is the last?"

Mumford shakes his head. "The ant ran away a few years ago with a grasshopper. The pull on them was not strong enough to keep them here. After that, the witch turned people into larger animals."

The witch spits again, and Beauty and I back up farther. "They stole my stone. Where did you find it?"

Beauty does not reply. She is no doubt thinking the same thing I am — the young woman who became an ant must have been Veronica's mother. She could still be alive out there somewhere!

"Where she found it is none of your business," I tell the witch. "You have only a moment left to decide what will become of the rest of your life. Life in our prison, or the life of an animal."

The cat, who I had nearly forgotten about, dashes over and winds himself around the witch's legs, purring. With a final hateful glare at all of us, the witch begins to dissolve! Mumford grunts as his arms suddenly fall empty to his sides. At his feet, a new cat lays curled on the ground in front of the black-and-white-spotted one. This new one is gray, with a black spot over where its heart should be. The witch-turned-cat stretches, then springs up. The two touch noses, then turn and stroll away, heads and tails held high. The second they disappear from sight, so does the barn, the pasture, the lemon trees in the distance, and the bright sun.

I shiver in the midday fog but am glad to see the ruins again, the thick forest, the wide sea. I breathe in a deep breath. It feels clean. Mumford sits down on a rock, dazed. He must not have seen the witch's illusion of the ruins before. I scratch my head — is THIS the illusion, or was the other? I suppose it matters not.

Beauty runs over to the dried-up brook she had pointed out when we first arrived. I follow and find her crawling on her hands and knees at the edge.

I clear my throat. "Beauty, I . . . *ouch*!" I reach down to slap at my ankle. A grasshopper jumps up and down in the grass. "I think that thing just bit me!"

Beauty laughs and holds out her hand. The grasshopper jumps up on it. "I believe it is you who led me to the crystal." The grasshopper jumps excitedly in her palm.

"Um, Riley?" Beauty asks, as sweetly as can be.

I remember something Alexander told me during one of his *How to Get a Girl to Like Me* lessons. Basically it was: *"Do what they ask even if you really don't want to or it's really icky."*

And that is how I wind up kissing my first — and thankfully last — grasshopper.

We stand back as she transforms into a white-haired woman. "Finally!" she exclaims, stretching her arms out wide. "I've been waiting for that kiss for years!"

Beauty peers at the woman. "Are you . . . Veronica's mother? The first to escape the witch?"

The woman shakes her head. "Katerina escaped first, but I was only moments behind. After us, the witch stopped making insects. Far too easy for us to slip through the cracks! I have stayed here to guard the stone. Katerina always knew her daughter would come in search of her one day."

"Then what happened to her?" Beauty asks. "To Katerina?"

The old woman shakes her head. "I was already the witch's prisoner when Katerina first set out from her home to find out the origin of her stone. The witch captured her in the woods far from here, took the stone, and turned Katerina into an ant. As an ant, she was small enough to slip into the witch's drawer and strong enough to drag out the stone. When we realized we were able to get out of the compound, we hid the stone in the brook, where water still flowed and hid it from view. Then Katerina set off for home. It has been many years now, and, of course, an ant cannot travel very fast. I am sorry to say, I doubt she still lives. In the compound we are well cared for, for the witch needs us healthy. Out here in the wild, we face the same challenges as any animal would."

"Thank you for guarding the stone so well," Beauty says. "Veronica is very grateful to have it, and without it, today could not have happened."

The old woman beams and then walks off to join the others, now streaming from the compound. Mumford heads over to us.

"I am going to start some signal fires. The fishermen on shore will be too curious not to send out a boat. Once they find us, I shall ensure everyone reaches land safely."

I tilt my head at him. "You are more than a simple peasant, are you not, dear Mumford?"

He smiles. "I suppose I am. But my story is long, and we have much work to do."

"I shall help you. I have one thing to do first, though." I reach out for Beauty's hand, relishing the way it feels in mine. I doubt I shall ever wear gloves again, even in the coldest of winter.

Mumford winks and hurries away.

Our second kiss, while it doesn't transform me from beast to boy, is just as sweet as the first.

CHAPTER FIFTY-ONE

∽ Beauty ∾

The castle grounds glow with the full bloom of spring. The queen has outdone herself in preparation for the wedding. Maypole streamers whirl in the breeze while kids from all over the kingdom duck underneath, laughing with delight. Tables dot the lawn, draped with the finest silk cloth in every color of the rainbow. Familiar faces stand in groups, sipping wine and nibbling treats off of solid silver plates. I cannot help but be filled with joy as I take it all in.

The band members tune their instruments as the carriage I had been waiting for pulls up alongside the great lawn. Clarissa comes bounding out of it, even before the horse has come to a full stop.

"You look so beautiful!" she says, admiring my long dress and my hair tied up with ribbons. "You have truly grown into your name!" I feel a bit like a child playing dress-up, but today it feels right.

Even though Clarissa and I have seen each other a few times since Riley was de-beasted, we are always thrilled to see each other again. Both of us have changed so much since our house burned down, and soon she and Papa will be moving to one of the guest houses on the castle grounds. I will keep my pink room, although the queen promised to tone down the color a bit.

"Is he here yet?" Clarissa asks, bouncing on her toes.

I nod. "He is inside with his family."

She shakes her head and points toward the rose garden. "I believe he has escaped!"

I turn around, and sure enough, the groom is bounding toward us. "You are not supposed to be out here," Clarissa teases.

"I know," Handsome says, looking over his shoulder. "But the queen is making me too nervous. Why did I agree to this again? My father says if I laugh during the ceremony, it will be spoken about for years!"

"You are doing this because Riley's mother wanted an excuse to throw a big party at the castle," I remind him. "And because your lovely bride agreed and because you love her."

"Right!" he says. "Keep reminding me of that if I laugh when I am supposed to be saying a vow."

"Suzy would forgive you," I assure him, straightening his jacket. "You have a wonderful laugh."

"And so do you," Riley says, coming up behind me and taking my hand in his. Even though more than two months have passed since the curse was broken, holding his hand without a huge glove between us still feels wonderful. I turn to smile at him as Clarissa rolls her eyes at my show of affection. She takes much pleasure in reminding me that it was I who did not believe in love. Alexander ducks away from a group of his friends to join us. He is never far away when Clarissa visits. It is comical to watch how hard he tries to impress her. There would not likely be a better-looking couple in all the seven kingdoms if he were to win her heart, but she is not making it easy for him.

Young Freddy joins our little group, tugging at the tight collar of his fancy shirt. "King Rubin's carriage is approaching. Will you come with me?" I allow him to drag me over to the path where the royal coach is pulling up. I know he is excited to show the king how much he has grown up since living at his castle as a young boy.

King Rubin's coach is flanked on all sides by knights in full dress. This must purely be for ceremonial reasons, since there is little threat of attack these days. The knight on the largest horse gets off and opens the door of the carriage. While a small crowd has gathered to watch the royal couple descend the carriage stairs, my attention is focused on the knight.

"Mumford!" I cry out, not caring that it is improper for a girl my age to shout over the heads of a king and queen. Yet I cannot help it. I run to his side. " 'Tis wonderful to see you! But what are you doing here?"

He laughs and hugs me hello. This overly friendly greeting causes a few of the onlookers to sniff disapprovingly, but Mumford does not seem to care, either. "How could I miss the social event of the season?"

Riley had suspected there was more to Mumford than met the eye. I should have known from his bravery and quick thinking that he was a knight. I laugh and hug him again. It is only when I pull away that I notice Freddy has grown deathly white.

I reach for the boy's arm, afraid he is about to faint. Perhaps the crowd is too much for him. "Are you all right, Freddy?"

He shows no reaction to my words, only continues to stare straight ahead, straight at Mumford. Mumford returns the boy's gaze, then gasps and falls to his knees. "Son? Is it truly you?"

"Father?" Freddy whispers, his lips still mostly frozen. "You live?"

I stare back and forth between them. What wonderful fortune is this! One of the other knights takes over the duty of escorting the royal couple onto the lawn.

"Oh, Freddy!" Mumford scoops Freddy into his arms and swings him around and around until Freddy says, "Stop, I may toss my lunch!" They both laugh, and Mumford sets him back down onto the grass.

"How you've grown these six years!"

Freddy stares up at his father again. "But, Father, where have you been?"

Mumford glances at me. I lay my hand gently on Freddy's shoulder. "Remember I told you about the man who helped Riley and me at the witch's compound?"

He nods.

"That was your father. Only we didn't know it, of course."

Freddy's eyes widen even further. "You were . . . a pig?"

His father nods solemnly. "I missed you every day."

Freddy starts to laugh. And cry. Then Mumford joins in.

"Well," I say, grinning and lifting my long skirts from the ground. "I see you two have a lot of catching up to do!" I do not think they even notice as I make my way back to the garden, trying not to trip in these unnecessarily tall-heeled shoes. I can see Veronica by the dessert table, holding up her stone and examining each ant that approaches the small cakes. When we were leaving the witch's compound it had occurred to me that the stone would reveal the true identity of the animals. That cat that the witch ran off with? A fat old man with three hairs on his shiny head. No wonder he had wanted to remain a cat! Now that Veronica knows the truth about what happened to her mother, she spends a lot of her time crawling on the ground.

Veronica grins when she sees me, and lets the necklace fall back against her pretty green dress. I have wanted to ask her something ever since I learned of the stone's power. This is as good a time as any. I pull her aside, out of earshot of the crowd now gathering around the sweets. "May I ask you something?"

"Of course," Veronica says, reaching around me to stuff a small almond cake in her mouth.

"Do you remember when you lent me your necklace, before my journey to the castle?"

She swallows and nods.

"Your expression changed when you looked through it as you placed it over my head. I have been curious . . . what did you see?"

She leans close to whisper in my ear. "I saw a princess."

I blush in response to her words. A few months ago I'd have said a princess was the last thing I ever thought I'd be.

"And there is your beast," Veronica says, nudging me and pointing to Riley. "I mean, your prince."

Riley walks toward us, a long-stemmed red rose held out before him. Veronica slips away as he approaches.

"This is long overdue," he says, handing me the rose.

I chuckle. "If my father hadn't picked that first rose, we never would have met."

"Well," he says, drawing out the word and staring a little off to the right. "That may not be entirely true."

I lower the flower and look over it at him. "What do you mean?"

"Um, it's a long story," he says, still avoiding my eyes, "and includes some questionable actions on my family's part. But it will have to wait, for we have a wedding to attend."

Before I can argue, he grabs my hand and pulls me toward where the crowd is indeed gathering for the ceremony. I almost fall flat on my face when a heel gets caught between two cobblestones. If I'm going to be a princess, I'm definitely not going to be the type of princess to wear high-heeled shoes and pink dresses with white ribbons in my hair. I'm going to be the type of princess who helps her prince measure the life span of worms and who's not afraid to get dirt under her fingernails. After all, my husband's going to be a great scientist. Someone's got to keep him from blowing himself up along the way. Might as well be me.

Riley stops short, bends to kiss an ant, and shakes his head. "Not this time."

I smile. Yup. Might as well be me.